CITIZEN ORLOV

CITIZEN ORLOV

JONATHAN PAYNE

CamCat
Books

CamCat Publishing, LLC
Fort Collins, Colorado 80524
camcatpublishing.com

This is a work of fiction. Names, characters, places, and incidents are either products of the author's imagination or are used fictitiously.

Hardcover ISBN 9780744309010
Paperback ISBN 9780744309058
Large-Print Paperback ISBN 9780744309072
eBook ISBN 9780744309096
Audiobook ISBN 9780744309119

Library of Congress Control Number: 2022946461

Book and cover design by Maryann Appel
Artwork by Grandfailure, LesyaD

5   3   1   2   4

FOR SONYA

PART ONE

An Account

of the

Attempted Assassination

of His Majesty,

The King

CHAPTER ONE

In which our hero meets a new and unexpected challenge

On a frigid winter's morning in a mountainous region of central Europe, Citizen Orlov, a simple fishmonger, is taking a shortcut along the dank alley behind the Ministries of Security and Intelligence when a telephone begins to ring. He thinks nothing of it and continues on his daily constitutional, his heavy boots crunching the snow between the cobbles.

The ringing continues, becoming louder with each step. A window at the back of the ministry buildings is open, just a little. The ringing telephone sits on a table next to the open window. Orlov stops, troubled by this unusual scene: there is no reason for a window to be open on such a cold day. Since this is the Ministry of either Security or Intelligence, could an open window be a security breach of some kind?

Orlov is tempted to walk away. After all, this telephone call is none of his business. On the other hand, he is an upright and patriotic citizen who would not want to see national security compromised simply because no one was available to answer a telephone call. He is on the verge of stepping toward the open window when he hears footsteps ahead. A tight group of four soldiers is marching into the alley, rifles on shoulders. He freezes for a second, leans against the wall, and quickly lights a cigarette. By the time the soldiers reach him, Orlov is dragging on the cigarette and working hard to appear nonchalant. The soldiers are palace guardsmen, but the red insignia on their uniforms indicates they are part of the elite unit that protects the Crown Prince, the king's ambitious eldest son. Orlov nods politely, but the soldiers ignore him and march on at speed.

The telephone is still ringing. Someone very much wants an answer. Orlov stubs his cigarette on the wall and approaches the open window. The telephone is loud in his right ear. Peering through the gap, he sees a small, gloomy storeroom with neatly appointed shelves full of stationery.

Finally, he can stand it no longer. He reaches through the window, picks up the receiver, and pulls it on its long and winding cable out through the window to his ear.

"Hello?" says Orlov, looking up and down the alley to check he is still alone.

"Thank God. Where have you been?" says an agitated voice, distant and crackly. Orlov is unsure what to say. The voice continues. "Kosek. Right now."

"I'm sorry?" says Orlov.

"Kosek. Agent Kosek."

Orlov peers into the storeroom again. "There's no one here," he says.

"Well, fetch him then. And hurry, for God's sake. It's important."

Orlov is sorely tempted to end the call and walk away, but the voice is so angry that he dare not.

"One minute," he says, and lays the receiver on the table. He opens the window wider and, with some considerable effort, pulls himself headfirst into the storeroom, where he tumbles onto the floor. Picking himself up, he slaps the dust from his overcoat, opens the storeroom door, and peers along the hallway; all is dark and quiet.

With some trepidation, Orlov returns to the telephone. "Hello?" he says.

"Kosek?"

"No, sorry. I'll have to take a message."

The caller is still agitated. "Well, focus on what I'm about to say. It's life and death."

Orlov's hands are shaking. "Hold on," he says, "I'll fetch some paper."

Before he can put the receiver down, the caller explodes with anger. "Are you a simpleton? Do not write this down. Remember it."

"Yes, sir. Sorry," says Orlov. "I'll remember it."

"Are you ready?"

"Yes, sir."

"Here it is. We could not—repeat not—install it in room six. Don't ask why, it's a long story."

The man is about to continue, but Orlov interrupts him. "Should I include that in the message: 'it's a long story'?"

"Mother of God," shouts the man. "Why do they always give me the village idiot? No. Forget that part. I'll start again."

"Ready," says Orlov.

This time the man speaks slower and more deliberately, as if to a child. "We could not—repeat not—install it in room six. You need to get room seven. It's hidden above the wardrobe. Push the lever up, not down. Repeat that back to me."

Orlov is now shaking all over, and he grimaces as he forces himself to focus. He repeats the message slowly but correctly.

"Whatever else you do, get that message to Kosek, in person. No one else. Lives depend on it. Understood?"

"Understood," says Orlov, and the line goes dead.

Orlov returns the receiver to the telephone and searches for something to write on. He remembers the message now, but for how long? He has no idea who Agent Kosek is, or where. Now that the caller has gone, the only sensible course of action is to make a note. He will destroy the note, once he has found Kosek. On the table he finds a pile of index cards. He writes the message verbatim on a card, folds it once, and tucks it inside his pocketbook.

Standing in the dark storeroom, Orlov wonders how to set about finding Agent Kosek. He considers climbing back into the alley, going around to the front entrance, and presenting himself as a visitor, if he could work out which ministry he is inside. But it's still early and it might take hours to be seen. Worse than that, there is a possibility he would be turned away. He imagines a surly security guard pretending to check the personnel directory, only to turn to him and say, "There's no one of that name here." Perhaps agents never use their real names. Is Kosek a real name or a pseudonym? Orlov decides the better approach is to use the one advantage currently available to him: he is inside the building.

He lowers the sash window to its original position and steps into the hallway, closing the storeroom door behind him. All remains dark and quiet. The hallway runs long and straight in both directions, punctuated only by anonymous doors. He sees nothing to suggest one direction is more promising than the other. Orlov turns right and tiptoes sheepishly along the hallway, now conscious of his boots as they squeak on the polished wooden floors. He walks on and on, eventually meeting a door that opens onto an identical dark corridor.

As he continues, Orlov becomes increasingly conscious that he is not supposed to be here. He imagines an angry bureaucrat bursting out from one of the many office doors to castigate him and march him off to be interrogated. However, he has walked the length of a train and still he has seen no one.

Finally, Orlov sees the warm glow of lamplight seeping around the edge of another dividing door up ahead. He is both relieved and apprehensive. He approaches the door cautiously and puts his ear to it. It sounds like a veritable hive of industry. He takes a deep breath and opens the door onto a scene of frenetic activity. Banks of desks are staffed by serious men, mostly young, in formal suits, both pinstripe and plain; the few women are also young and dressed formally. Some are engaged in animated conversations; some are leaning back in chairs, smoking; others are deep into reading piles of papers. A white-haired woman is distributing china cups full of tea from a wheeled trolley. At the far end of this long room, someone is setting out chairs in front of a blackboard. Above this activity, the warm fug of cigarette smoke is illuminated by high wall lamps. Orlov hesitates, but is soon approached at high speed by a short, rotund man in a three-piece suit. He has a clipboard and a flamboyant manner.

"You're late," says the man, gesticulating. "Quickly. Overcoats over there."

"No, no. You see," Orlov says, "I'm not really here."

The man slaps him on the back, taking his coat as they walk. "You seem real to me," he laughs.

Orlov protests. "I have a message for Agent Kosek."

The man rolls his eyes. "Do not trouble yourself regarding Agent Kosek. He is late for everything. He will be here in due course."

He directs Orlov to take a seat at the back of the impromptu classroom, which is by now filling up with eager, young employees. Orlov is suddenly conscious of his age and appearance; his balding head and rough clothes stand out in this group of young, formally dressed professionals. He also feels anxious about being in this room on false pretenses. However, he need only wait until Agent Kosek appears; he will then deliver the message, make his excuses, and leave. He could still make it to the Grand Plaza in time for the market to open.

The flamboyant man, now standing in front of the blackboard, bangs his clipboard down onto a desk to bring the room to order. "Citizens," he says, "I would appreciate your attention." The room falls silent, and he continues. "I am Citizen Molnar, and I will be your instructor today."

Orlov turns to his neighbor, an earnest young man who is writing the instructor's name in a pristine leather notebook. "I'm not supposed to be here," says Orlov. The young man places a finger on his lips. Orlov smiles at him and returns his attention to Molnar, who is writing on the blackboard. Molnar proceeds to talk to the group for some time, but Orlov struggles to follow his meaning.

The instructor repeatedly refers to the group as *recruits*, which adds to Orlov's sense of being in the wrong place. He becomes hot under the collar when Molnar invites every recruit to introduce themselves. One by one the impressive young recruits stand and detail their university degrees and their training with the military or the police. When Orlov's turn comes, he stands and says, "Citizen Orlov. Fishmonger." He is surprised when a ripple of laughter runs through the group.

Orlov is about to sit down again when Molnar intervenes. "Is there anything else you'd like to tell us, citizen?"

Orlov says, "I have a message for Agent Kosek."

"Yes," says Molnar, gesturing for Orlov to sit down, "the agent will be here soon, I'm quite sure."

Orlov's hopes pick up some time later when Molnar says he wants to introduce a guest speaker. Orlov reaches inside his pocketbook to check that the message is still there. But Molnar is interrupted by a colleague whispering in his ear.

"My apologies," says Molnar. "It seems Agent Kosek has been called away on urgent business. However, I'm delighted to say that his colleague, Agent Zelle, is joining us to give you some insight into the day-to-day life of an agent. Agent Zelle."

Orlov is disappointed at the change of plan, but perhaps this colleague will be able to introduce him to Kosek. Taking her place in front of the blackboard is the most beautiful woman Orlov has ever seen. She is young and curvaceous but with a stern, serious expression. Her dark curls tumble over pearls and a flowing gown. Several of the male recruits shift uneasily in their chairs; someone coughs. Agent Zelle seems far too exotic for this stuffy, bureaucratic setting. She speaks with a soft foreign accent that Orlov does not recognize.

"Good morning, citizens," says Zelle, scanning the group slowly. "I have been asked to share with you something of what you can expect, if you are chosen to work as an agent for the ministry. I can tell you that it is a great honor, but there will also be hardship and danger."

She paces up and down in front of the blackboard, telling them stories of her life in the field. Orlov is entranced; these real-life tales sound like the adventure books he used to read as a boy. There are secret packages, safe houses, and midnight rendezvous in dangerous locations. There are car chases and shootouts, poisonings and defused bombs. It is so engrossing that, for a while, Orlov forgets that he has no business here aside from finding Kosek.

As he focuses on Zelle's lilting voice, Orlov is struck by a thought that has never before occurred to him in more than twenty years of fishmongering. Perhaps he is cut out for something more challenging, even thrilling. Perhaps, even at his age, he is capable of taking a position in a ministry such as this one where, instead of standing all day in the cold selling fish, his days would be full of adventure, danger, and even romance. Zelle's stories fill his head with possibilities. But perhaps this is foolish. After all, he and Citizen Vanev have a good business and a monopoly situation, since theirs is the only fish stall in the Grand Plaza. What's more, Vanev has always been loyal to him, and he has always tried to be loyal in return. Orlov tries to banish these silly ideas from his mind.

When Agent Zelle finishes, spontaneous applause fills the room. The agent seems surprised, almost embarrassed, and gives a slight curtsy in acknowledgement. She turns to talk to Molnar as the class breaks up and the recruits begin to mingle. Orlov sets off in the direction of Zelle, but several recruits are in his way, now forming into small groups, discussing what they have just heard. Orlov attempts to get past, saying "Excuse me. Sorry. May I . . ." but by the time he reaches the blackboard, Agent Zelle has gone.

"Is everything all right, citizen?" asks Molnar, seeing Orlov's distress.

"I really need to see Kosek," says Orlov. "It's very important. I have a message for him."

"I'm sure he'll be here, before induction is completed," says Molnar. "He always likes to meet the new recruits."

"That is what I was trying to explain," says Orlov. He gestures in the direction of the window through which he climbed. He is about to explain his entry to the building, but thinks better of it. "I'm not supposed to be here."

Molnar eyes him with a puzzled expression. "I assure you, citizen," he says, "that we rarely make mistakes." He brandishes his clipboard, showing Orlov a sheet of heavy, watermarked paper with a list of neatly typewritten names. Molnar runs his finger down the list ostentatiously, stopping in the middle of the page. "Here we are," he says. "Orlov."

CHAPTER TWO

In which our hero sets out on a journey

The next morning, Citizen Orlov forgoes his daily constitutional and sets out early for the Grand Plaza. In consideration of his new situation, he wears the dark suit he last wore at his father's funeral. It appears that the waistband has shrunk since those days, but Orlov finds that he can tuck it under his belly by wearing the trousers a little lower. This unattractive arrangement is hidden by his heavy overcoat, since it is another frigid day.

As he walks to the market, Orlov's head is full of possibilities. He understands that very few recruits are chosen to be agents. Most of the positions in the ministry are mundane and menial—clerks, copyists, mailroom operatives, and the like. And he should remember that no one has offered him anything so far. He needs to focus on delivering the telephone message. Already a day has gone by, and he has failed to find Agent Kosek. If he can find Kosek today and successfully deliver the message, perhaps that will stand him in good stead when the ministry comes to decide on the allocation of positions. Not wanting to incur the considerable wrath of his employer,

Orlov determines to tell Vanev only about his short-term task, for now. He will keep the possibility of a position at the ministry to himself, until it is confirmed.

Orlov is disappointed, but not surprised, to see that Citizen Vanev has arrived at the market stall before him. Vanev—an obese, unshaven man who perpetually wears the same fish-stained overalls—is busy setting out the wooden display boxes. In a vain attempt to lessen the inevitable anger of his employer, Orlov rushes up to the stall, grabs a bag of ice, and begins to fill a display box.

"So, he's not dead after all," says Vanev.

"My apologies, citizen," says Orlov.

"What happened yesterday?" asks Vanev. "I was slaving away over cold fish all day without so much as a cigarette break."

"I have a job," says Orlov.

"Exactly," says Vanev, slamming a box full of ice into position. "And it's traditional to do your job, if you expect to get paid for it."

"No," says Orlov, "for the government."

Vanev stops in his tracks. "Doing what?"

"I'm not sure, exactly," says Orlov, "but it's very important."

"Which ministry?" asks Vanev.

Orlov hesitates. "Security. Or perhaps Intelligence."

Vanev continues. "So, you don't know what the job is or who you're working for, but you're going abandon me anyway. Sounds like an excellent plan."

"I won't be gone forever," says Orlov. "There's just one task I need to complete. It's life and death. As soon as that's done, I'll be back."

"And how long will this take?" asks Vanev.

"I just have to find someone and deliver a message. That's all."

"I need you to be here on Saturday," says Vanev, reaching over to spread a dozen haddock across the ice. "I have some political business to attend to."

"The People's Front," says Orlov.

"The People's Front," repeats Vanev. "One day, you will join us."

"I don't care for politics," says Orlov.

"I don't care for tyranny," says Vanev.

"How can you be sure a republic would be an improvement?" asks Orlov.

"How can *you* be sure you or your mother will not end up disappeared, or worse?" asks Vanev.

"Let us leave my mother out of this," says Orlov, a little more sharply than he had intended.

"I mean no offense," says Vanev. "I am merely concerned for your wellbeing, as well as my own."

"I understand," says Orlov. "But I do not share your conviction that a revolution is in the best interests of our great nation."

Vanev sighs. "It is the least terrible option available to us."

Since versions of this exchange have played out between them many times, Orlov knows it is futile. He is anxious not to be late for his appointment at the ministry.

"Do not fear, citizen," says Orlov, turning to go. "I shall return." He trudges away across the snow-covered square, pausing while a tram trundles past slowly before he continues down the hill and across the bridge into the government sector.

Orlov arrives at the foot of the stone steps that lead up to the grand front doors of the Ministries of Security, on his left, and Intelligence, on his right. He felt sure, while walking here, that he would know which door to approach, but now he is singularly lacking in enlightenment. He thinks back to the remarks made yesterday by Citizen Molnar and Agent Zelle; they had plenty to say about security, but then again, they also talked about intelligence. It could be either. He imagines being interrogated by skeptical security guards in the lobby of either or both buildings. Finding this a distinctly unattractive proposition, Orlov walks around to the back of the buildings, where the dark, narrow alley is familiar and comforting compared with the formal front entrances. He finds the rear entrance through which he and the young recruits exited the previous afternoon, but the door is closed and a surly security guard leans against it, smoking a cigarette. Orlov nods politely and keeps walking, feeling the guard's eyes following him all the way up the alley and around the corner.

Once he is out of sight, Orlov leans against the wall at the end of the Ministry of Security and enjoys a cigarette of his own. He takes a couple of peeks around the corner, but the security guard is still there. He is just about to build up the courage to try one of the front entrances when he hears voices. A gaggle of besuited men is approaching at high speed, led by Citizen Molnar. Orlov stubs his cigarette on the wall and steps forward to attract their attention. Perhaps he can follow them into the building. But Molnar speaks first.

"Ah, the very man," says Molnar, holding out a hand so that one of his aides can pass an envelope to him. He hands the envelope to Orlov. "We need you on the next train to Kufzig," he says. "Your ticket is in here. Check into Pension Residenz. Kosek will meet you there."

Orlov is stunned and for a while is unable to speak. Eventually he says, "I'm not going to be working in the mailroom?"

Molnar looks surprised, and his aides laugh. "We know talent when we see it," says Molnar. "We need you in the field."

"And Kosek will be there?" asks Orlov.

"Yes, he's expecting you," says Molnar.

"What will I be doing?" asks Orlov.

"Kosek will explain your task," says Molnar and begins to walk away.

Orlov calls after him. "How will I recognize him?"

"He will find you," Molnar replies over his shoulder.

Orlov cannot believe his good fortune. He grins involuntarily while watching Molnar and his aides disappear around the corner. Agent Zelle's stories of espionage and danger flash through his head.

He is both elated and nervous. Could he really be about to leave fish-mongering behind for the life of an agent? He opens the envelope and finds a first-class ticket to Kufzig, leaving in less than an hour. It is a small town in the mountains about two hours south of the capital. Orlov has visited it only once before, as a child. He has never before travelled in the first-class carriage of a train. He considers returning to the market to explain this change of plan to Vanev, but it is a shorter walk to the railway station. He will find Kosek, deliver the message and, all being well, return in time to cover the stall on Saturday.

◂━━━━━▸

ORLOV STEPS OUT onto the platform at Kufzig and pauses to admire the view while fastening his overcoat against the thin, freezing air. The picturesque little town is surrounded by rugged, snow-capped mountains. Well-dressed travelers rush past him, lifting suitcases down from the train. Others run to board before the train continues its journey south. When the train pulls away, Orlov is still in the middle of the platform, admiring the view, and finds himself engulfed by a cloud of steam. By the time the steam has dispersed, all the other passengers have gone on their way, and Orlov is left alone on the platform with a guard, a haggard old man who limps toward his hut as though in a hurry to get out of the cold.

Orlov waves at the guard and walks toward him. "Excuse me," he says. "I'm looking for Pension Residenz."

The guard stops at the door to the hut. "Residenz, you say?"

"Yes," says Orlov. "It was recommended." He is about to say who gave the recommendation, but thinks better of it. "Is it a good place to stay? Reasonable?"

"Oh, yes," says the guard. "Quite good. And quite reasonable. Only . . ." He pauses.

"Only?" asks Orlov.

"Some people mistake it for Penzion Rezidence," says the guard. "It's an easy mistake to make." He heads inside the hut.

Orlov leans into the doorway. "I'm sorry," he says. "There's another pension called Rezidence? Here in Kufzig?"

"Oh yes, sir," says the guard. "It causes all sorts of confusion."

"I imagine it would," says Orlov.

"That's why I always like to check," says the guard.

"I'm quite sure it's Pension Residenz that was recommended," says Orlov, confidently.

"Straight down the hill, sir," says the guard, "a short walk along Feldgasse—that's our beautiful main street—and you can't miss it."

Orlov thanks the guard and sets out down the hill, admiring the view of the town beneath him. He was confident that Molnar had said *Residenz*, but the farther he walks, the more he wonders if he had misheard *Rezidence*. He would like to call Molnar on the telephone to confirm this but, even if he could find a telephone, he has no idea how to reach the ministry. Only now he realizes that he missed an opportunity this morning to ask Molnar which ministry he works for. Perhaps it would have been embarrassing to admit that he didn't know, but the embarrassment would have been over in a second, and then he would have been quite sure. As it stands, he will have to live with the uncertainty a little longer. He determines to ask Agent Kosek this evening, as soon as they meet. He hopes Kosek is a kind person, the sort of person who will not be cruel about this simple misunderstanding.

In any case, Orlov is bringing with him an important message, and he is therefore confident of striking up a good rapport with the agent. He will deliver the message, complete whatever task Kosek has in store for him, and return home without delay. Given Citizen Vanev's mood this morning, he does not want to be away from the market any longer than absolutely necessary.

At the foot of the hill, Orlov sees the sign for Feldgasse and follows it into the heart of the town. The scene in front of him stirs memories of his childhood visit to Kufzig: a quaint main street with a steepled church at one end and, at the other, a square with an ornate fountain. Between these two landmarks, the busy thoroughfare is full of restaurants, bakeries, and street cafés. Half way along Feldgasse, equidistant between the church and the square, sits Pension Residenz. Like many of the pensions in this part of the world, it is a tall, elegant townhouse that was once the home of a wealthy family but has long since been converted into a boarding house, with guest rooms spanning four floors. A faded picture of Beethoven at his piano decorates the sign that hangs above the door.

Now that he has seen the sign clearly showing Pension Residenz, Orlov is feeling more confident that this is the right place. He steps into the cramped reception area and, since no one is at the desk, he rings the bell, which elicits no immediate response. While waiting, Orlov peruses the newspaper rack and sees an interesting headline: "Kufzig Prepares for Royal Visit." He considers removing the newspaper from the rack in order to read the article but, before he does so, a curious little woman in thick spectacles appears from the back office and stares at him sideways, as though her peripheral vision is better than her ability to see straight ahead.

"How may I help you?" she says.

"I'd like a room, please," says Orlov.

"You know the king is visiting?" says the woman.

"I just saw it in the newspaper," says Orlov.

"Full up," she says. "Quite full. A lot of people want to see His Majesty. Those people booked in advance. On account of our excellent views along Feldgasse. Those with a balcony can see all the way down to the fountain."

Orlov is nonplussed. "I was supposed to stay here. I have to meet someone." She shrugs and Orlov continues. "Could you tell me if," he is about to say *agent* but corrects himself just in time, "Citizen Kosek checked in yet?"

"Can't say," she says. "Against the rules."

"But he is booked to stay here?"

"Against the rules."

"May I leave a message?"

She shakes her head. Then, to Orlov's surprise, she says, "Go to the Bierkeller later." She points along the road in the direction of the square. "Every man in town will be there tonight."

"Why?" asks Orlov.

"Trust me," she says.

"Is there anywhere else to stay nearby?" says Orlov.

The woman looks at him and for a while seems to be weighing something up. "She might have a room. Across the street." She pulls a face, as though making this recommendation is distasteful. "She's always slow to fill up. On account of the inferior views."

Orlov turns to look out through the front door and across the street. "There's another boarding house opposite?"

"Directly across the street," says the woman.

"That wouldn't be Penzion Rezidence, would it?" asks Orlov.

The woman raises her eyebrows, as though he has used inappropriate language at the dinner table. "If you say so," she says and disappears into the back office.

Orlov heads outside and crosses the street, where he finds an almost identical townhouse. Hanging above the door, under the words Penzion Rezidence, is a sign with a faded picture of Gustav Mahler waving his conductor's baton. Orlov steps inside to a similar reception area.

This time, he does not need to ring the bell because someone is at the desk. She looks much like the proprietor opposite, except that her spectacles are not so thick.

"Good day, sir. May I help you?" she says.

Orlov sounds a little more desperate than intended. "Do you have a room?"

The woman looks down at the ledger on the desk. "How many nights?"

"Just tonight, please," says Orlov. "I'm meeting a colleague this evening. Returning home tomorrow, I hope."

"You're not planning to stay for the royal visit, sir?" she asks.

"No, this is strictly business," says Orlov, and he enjoys how that sounds—much more impressive than fishmongering.

"Room three is the only one available," says the woman. "It doesn't have much of a view, but if you're not staying for the king, I dare say you won't mind that."

She fetches the key while Orlov signs the ledger. Room three is a drab affair on the second floor with a restricted view of the street and a shared bathroom in the hall. Since Orlov has no luggage to un-pack, he decides to go out again. He takes a stroll around the town, but it is too cold for a prolonged walk. He eats an early dinner of sausages and cabbage at the least expensive restaurant on Feldgasse and then makes his way to the Bierkeller. It is mostly empty when he arrives, and he drinks two beers alone at the bar before the place be-gins to fill up. It is a literal cellar and a typical pub in most respects, with the addition of a small stage, complete with lights and curtains.

Orlov watches all the newcomers closely, wondering which one is Kosek. By the time he is on to his third beer, Orlov is becoming agitated that Kosek has not made himself known. He does not like the sense of being powerless.

He wants to take control of the situation.

At the other end of the bar, a serious, middle-aged man has been drinking alone for some time. He is well dressed and appears to be surveying the busy cellar with eagle eyes. Orlov might be just a simple fishmonger, but he has good intuition. He picks up his beer, walks slowly toward the man, and leans against the bar next to him.

He takes a sip of beer and smiles at the man, to ensure he has been noticed. The man looks uneasy; he half-smiles back.

"Good evening," says Orlov.

"Evening," says the man.

"Are you, by any chance, Citizen Kosek?"

"Leave me alone," says the man. "I'm just here for the show." He nods toward the stage, where the lights are going up and a weasely little man with a shaggy moustache calls the room to order.

"Ladies and gentlemen, your attention please," he says in the shrill tones of a carnival barker as oriental music begins to emanate from a tinny loudspeaker. "We are very proud to announce, by popular demand, for one night only, the return of the one, the only, Mata Hari."

To Orlov's surprise, the whole cellar erupts in applause. Some men bang their beer glasses on the tables as others stamp their feet. The cacophony dies down as the music swells. From behind the curtain emerges an exotic, barefoot dancer, dressed in nothing aside from carefully placed jewels and flowing veils. She gyrates into the center of the stage to begin her act. Only when she arrives in the full glow of the spotlights does Orlov sense that this dancer is familiar. In fact, he saw her only yesterday. It is Agent Zelle.

CHAPTER THREE

In which our hero finds himself in mortal danger

O rlov experiences a complicated mixture of emotions. He is confused about why Agent Zelle is in Kufzig, not to mention why she is performing as an exotic dancer under an assumed name. On the other hand, perhaps she can introduce him to Kosek. He is enchanted by her performance, to say the least—a reaction shared by all the other men in the Bierkeller, judging by the enthusiastic reception. He is embarrassed about seeing a ministry colleague in such circumstances and wearing almost no clothing at all. He hopes he will not be required to interact with the agent on a professional level because, after this evening, he is unsure that he could look her in the eye without further embarrassment.

The dance routine continues for an excruciatingly long time. It consists mostly of vigorous gyrations of the hips combined with the judicious waving of two veils every time Zelle risks exposing too much bare flesh. Orlov hides behind his beer glass, his gaze alternating between the stage and the room. He continues to scan the bar and the tables for Agent Kosek, but he has lost enthusiasm for guesswork. Eventually, the spotlights dim, the music dies down, and Zelle disappears behind the stage. The patrons clap, cheer, and stamp their feet in an attempt to entice the dancer back onto the stage, but the show is over.

Once the raucous applause subsides, most of the patrons head to the bar. Orlov downs his beer and makes his way through the crowd toward the stage. He slips behind the curtain and finds a dim backstage room in which the weaselly master of ceremonies is counting out crowns into the open palms of Zelle, who remains almost naked.

Without pausing to think, Orlov blurts out, "Agent Zelle. I need to speak to you."

Zelle freezes, her face a picture of controlled anger. The master of ceremonies looks at Orlov and back at Zelle, confused. Zelle stares into Orlov's eyes so forcefully that he is momentarily paralyzed.

"I fear you have mistaken me for someone else, citizen," says Zelle to Orlov. "Please wait for a moment so we may discuss your confusion in private."

Orlov is mortified. He nods and watches as the master of ceremonies finishes counting out the money and then, with another glance at Orlov, returns to the bar. As soon as they are alone, Zelle approaches Orlov, puts her face an inch from his, and grasps his shirt collar with both hands so tightly that he wants to cough. Her cologne is strong. It is a very strange experience to be physically threatened at close quarters by an almost naked woman. Orlov is rarely aroused and rarely petrified, but now he is both at the same time.

She speaks to him with such contempt that she is almost spitting. "Who are you?"

Orlov is breathing so fast that he can barely make any words. He feels his heart pumping against the shirt that Zelle is pulling tight against his chest. "Orlov. Citizen Orlov. I was sent by Molnar. I need to see Kosek."

She exhales and loosens her grip slightly. "Orlov?"

"Yes."

Zelle shakes her head while maintaining fierce eye contact. "He said he was going to send an idiot. I did not think he meant it literally."

"Sorry," says Orlov. "Do you know where Kosek is?"

She lets go of him and turns to take her dressing gown off a hook on the wall. "We can't talk here," she says. "Do you know where the fountain is?"

"Yes."

"Go there alone. It needs to be late. Three in the morning. Wait for me there."

She wraps the gown around her shoulders and slips out through the stage door.

⟵——⟶

BACK AT PENZION Rezidence, Orlov lies awake on his bed, getting up every few minutes to check the clocktower at the entrance to the square, which he can see well enough to tell the time only if he opens the window and leans out. His pocket watch runs slow, and he wants to be sure not to be late. Since Zelle is probably staying across the road at Pension Residenz, like Kosek, she will have a good view of the clocktower.

Orlov is tired and ashamed. His first interaction with a colleague in the field was most certainly not ideal. He hopes the late-night meeting with Zelle will allow him to redeem himself and show her he could be a useful asset. He will listen carefully to her instructions and do his best to complete the tasks she sets for him. Perhaps then she will introduce him to Kosek and report back to Molnar about his excellent work.

When the clock reaches five minutes before three, Orlov fastens his overcoat and tiptoes out into a dark, deserted Feldgasse.

Although the street is gloomy, high lamps in the square cast the fountain in an eerie, orange glow. He is pleased to arrive first in the square; he does not want to keep Agent Zelle waiting. He sits on the edge of the fountain, listening to the water bubbling behind him and enjoying the view along the picturesque street to the church, which is lit in a similar eerie light. He watches his breath in the wintry air. At two minutes after three, there is no sign of Zelle. He takes a slow walk around the fountain and sits back in the same spot.

Without warning, a sharp crack rings out to Orlov's left, and a chunk of the stone plinth flies off into the water. He jumps up, looking around. His left arm feels hot. A wave of nausea arrives out of nowhere. Another crack against the fountain. He is dizzy. Orlov tries to run to the other side of the fountain. Somewhere en route, he falls. His head hits the cobbles.

CHAPTER FOUR

In which our hero returns to the fray

Orlov wakes in a bright room. It hurts to open his eyes. The sun is streaming in through thin curtains. Someone nearby is talking, but he cannot separate the words from one another. A young woman leans over and touches his forehead.

"Someone's shooting at me," says Orlov.

He tries to sit up, but a wave of deep muscular pain radiates out from his left arm.

He groans and lies back again.

"Not anymore," says the nurse.

"What time is it?" asks Orlov.

"One o'clock in the afternoon," says the nurse.

This time Orlov sits up. "I need to leave. I have urgent business."

The nurse leans over him again, smiling. "You are going nowhere, citizen," she says. "You hit your head hard. And the police captain wants to speak to you. I promised to call him as soon as you woke up."

"What about my arm?" asks Orlov.

"You were lucky," says the nurse. "The bullet paused to say hello, but kept moving."

"Yes, I'm the luckiest man alive," says Orlov.

He sits still for a while, watching the nurse attend to other patients along the narrow wardroom. When she returns, he says, "I hope I'm allowed to visit the water closet."

"There's a pan under the bed," says the nurse.

"I can walk," says Orlov.

"I'll give you a hand along the corridor," says the nurse.

"No, thank you," says Orlov. "I'll be fine on my own."

He takes his time climbing out of the bed, until the nurse has left the ward. He hears her placing a telephone call to the police station. He takes his clothes from a hook on the wall and treads warily into the corridor, feeling light-headed. Almost immediately, another nurse confronts him.

"You may use your curtain to get dressed, citizen," she says.

Orlov grimaces at the idea. "I'd prefer to use the gentlemen's room," he says.

The nurse indicates the route along the corridor. Orlov trudges off in the direction of the lavatory with his clothes over his arm. He hopes the nurse did not notice that he is carrying his overcoat as well as his suit. Hearing something behind him, he turns to find the nurse following him.

"Don't mind me," she says. "Just making sure you are doing well."

Orlov stops at the door of the gentlemen's room. "I'm sure I'll be all right," he says, stepping inside.

In the distance, the first nurse is ending her call to the police station. Orlov closes the door, hangs his clothing on a hook, and looks back into the corridor through the crack between wall and door. The second nurse is waiting in the corridor, wearing a broad grin directed at no one in particular. Orlov dresses quickly, easing his shirt and jacket gingerly over his bandaged arm. Seeing that the nurse has not moved, he searches for an alternative exit. The lavatory room has only high, narrow windows, but an adjoining door opens into a shower room, with a large, frosted window. Orlov is testing whether this window opens when the nurse raps hard on the door.

"Is everything all right, citizen?" she calls.

Orlov rushes back into the lavatory room and says, "Yes, thank you. Two minutes, please."

Orlov returns to the shower room, pushes the window open wide, and looks down onto a flat roof below. It is a long way down. He fastens up all the buttons on his overcoat, clambers onto the window ledge, and drops onto the graveled roof, rolling quickly onto his side in an attempt to limit the shock to his shins. Nevertheless, his ankles instantly complain at the impact, and it takes all his powers of self-control to avoid screaming an expletive into the cold afternoon air. He stands up, knocks the gravel from his overcoat and hobbles along the flat roof. At the end of the wing, he finds a rusty iron fire escape that takes him down into the hospital grounds.

Orlov walks unsteadily through the grounds, out of the main gates of the hospital, and into the street. He turns right but soon realizes he is lost. Being lost makes his head throb. He asks a stranger for directions, and eventually he recognizes the railway station up ahead, engulfed in the steam of a newly arrived train. By the time he reaches the station entrance, he is mingling with arriving passengers and notices a familiar face.

"Citizen Vanev," he calls.

Vanev is wearing a suit rather than fishy overalls and walking with a group of similarly well-dressed people, some of whom carry furled banners on wooden poles.

"Well, well, my absent employee," says Vanev, eyeing Orlov's head bandage. "What happened to you?"

"Nothing. An accident," says Orlov.

"It looks like more than nothing to me, citizen," says Vanev.

Orlov, having no idea who shot him or why, prefers to change the subject. "What brings you to Kufzig?"

"The People's Front," says Vanev. "We're here to let his so-called majesty know it's time for a republic. Since he rarely shows his face in public, we decided to have a day out."

"I see," says Orlov, always reluctant to engage in his colleague's political banter.

"And what of you, citizen?" asks Vanev. "I dare say you're en route to our glorious capital to man the stall tomorrow?"

"Not yet," says Orlov. "I have just one small matter to attend to, and then I'll be on the next train. You have my word."

Feldgasse is bustling with people. Bunting in red, gold, and green is being hung between streetlamps. Street sweepers are ushering pedestrians out of their way in order to ensure everything is pristine for the arrival of the king.

"Where are you staying?" asks Orlov.

"Penzion Rezidence," says Vanev. "I believe we have booked every room."

"I stayed there last night," says Orlov. "Part of the night, at least."

When they reach Penzion Rezidence, Orlov excuses himself and walks across the road to Pension Residenz. The strange bespectacled woman is at the reception desk. She stares at Orlov's head bandage with curiosity.

"May I assist you, citizen?" she says.

"Is Citizen Zelle here?" he asks. "Has Citizen Kosek checked in yet?"

"Against the rules," she says.

Orlov's head begins to throb again. "It's a matter of national security."

"You can wait in the parlor, if you must," she says, waving her arm. Apparently, this is a reference to the chaise longue under the window, next to the newspaper rack.

Orlov dutifully sits on the chaise longue and reads a newspaper for a long time. He watches guests check in and out. Occasionally, he spots a man who might potentially be Agent Kosek, but those checking in always give other names. Toward the end of the afternoon, as twilight sets in and the crowds are growing outside, Agent Zelle steps in off the street. She is about to march straight to the staircase when she catches Orlov in the corner of her eye and turns to him. By the expression on her face, she was not expecting to see him today.

"Citizen," she says, in a pitch higher than normal. "What a pleasant surprise. Have you been in an accident?"

Orlov dashes over to Zelle and speaks furtively, with his back to the proprietor. "We need to talk," he says. "In private."

The slightest of smiles dances at the corners of Zelle's mouth. "Are you inviting yourself up to my room, citizen?"

Orlov's face flushes. "No, citizen. Of course not. I would never . . ."

"I am joking, citizen," says Zelle. "You are welcome to visit my room. It is the only place we can talk privately."

Orlov breathes a sigh of relief and follows Zelle up to the third floor. She opens room four and invites him inside. It is a small room with only a bed and a single chair, but also an en suite bathroom and a balcony.

They stand awkwardly by the balcony door to talk.

"Someone shot me last night," says Orlov, indicating his left arm.

"I heard the shots," says Zelle. "By the time I arrived, the police were sending people away. I didn't realize it was you."

Orlov is unsure how the police could have arrived before Zelle, who can easily see the fountain from her balcony, but decides not to pursue this. "Has Agent Kosek arrived yet?" he asks. "It's now two days since I received a message for him, and I still don't have my instructions. Perhaps you can tell me what to do."

"Kosek will be here soon," says Zelle. "He will have instructions for both of us."

Orlov is delighted with this answer, which appears to put them on the same level of seniority. He touches her arm. "I see. Thank you."

"My apologies," says Zelle, "but would you mind stepping into the bathroom for a moment? I'd like to change my clothes."

Orlov feels embarrassed again. "No, no, citizen," he says. "I'll leave you in peace."

"No need," says Zelle. "I'd prefer that you stay. In case Kosek arrives. Please." She gestures toward the bathroom.

"Of course," says Orlov and steps through the bathroom door.

He is about to turn to close the door behind him when Zelle pushes him hard, face first, into the wall. She pins him against the wall with her knee in his lower back while grabbing both his hands and tying them together behind him with something that stings his wrists. He tries to shout something, but she says "Quiet" in his ear and pushes him into the bath. He slumps heavily, knocking his head against the taps. He groans. Before he is able to complain, she ties a scarf across his mouth, then ties his feet together with a short rope. Orlov makes a couple of feeble attempts to raise himself up, but slides back down into the bath. Zelle produces a handgun from the bathroom cabinet and pushes the barrel into his cheek.

"Don't move," she says, "or I will shoot you. And this time I won't miss."

CHAPTER FIVE

In which our hero learns the nature of his task

The brief struggle with Zelle has aggravated Orlov's injuries; his head is throbbing again and his left arm twitches with sharp waves of pain. He makes several attempts to raise himself out of the bath, but slides back again immediately. Zelle has locked the bathroom door and, as far as Orlov can tell, she is no longer in the bedroom. Through the high bathroom window, he can see that the sun has set, and he can hear the crowds growing. In the distance, the sound of military drums suggests the marching band of the palace guard has begun to pave the way for the arrival of the king.

Despite what the cheerful nurse said to him at the hospital, Orlov does not feel lucky. All he has attempted to do for the past two days is to perform his civic duties for the good of king and country. He has no idea why he deserves to be shot at or tied up. He wonders if it is a test. Perhaps they do this to all new recruits, to test their mettle. Perhaps Kosek is not his instructor but rather his examiner, watching from afar and assessing his performance. Perhaps Zelle's job is to train the new recruits and to assist Kosek in separating the wheat from the chaff. It seems an elaborate examination process, to be sure, but it's not impossible. He remembers all sorts of dirty tricks during his military training, many years ago: being woken in the middle of the night to go for a run, and so on. Is it possible that these strange circumstances are his new employer's version of the same sort of test? He wonders if Zelle expects him to break out of his current predicament.

Orlov has been working on his binds for some time, with no success, when he hears the bedroom door being unlocked. Zelle bursts into the bathroom. Her usual calm demeanor has disappeared, replaced by a sense of urgency, almost panic. She breaths heavily and speaks quickly.

"I'm going to remove the gag," she says, standing over him. "If you shout or scream, I will shoot you. Understand?"

Orlov nods and Zelle removes the gag.

"What about the ropes?" whispers Orlov.

"Not yet," says Zelle. "Be quiet and listen carefully."

"I will," says Orlov.

"I never wanted a third man," says Zelle, "but Molnar insists on complying with tedious ministry policies. And now Kosek is late, and the king is about to arrive at any moment. So, now I'm in charge and you're the second man. Until Kosek arrives, in which case you immediately return to being the third man. Is that clear?"

"Not exactly," says Orlov.

"Now I'm going to explain your task," says Zelle. "Remember every detail. Then you're going to repeat it back to me. If you get it exactly right, I'll untie you. If you get it wrong, I'll shoot you. Understood?"

Orlov has no wish to aggravate Agent Zelle any further, but there seems to be a flaw in this approach. "If you shoot me, you'll be the first man and the only man."

Zelle slaps his face. "We don't have time for quips," she says. "Now listen."

"Sorry," says Orlov.

Zelle continues, now with the clipped delivery of a weary military officer. "This is room four. Immediately above us is room six. Kosek is booked into room six. You will go up there—break in if you have to—and find a device that has been hidden there by our technicians. It's a lever. It should be above the wardrobe or somewhere nearby. You will open the door to the balcony and watch carefully for the arrival of the king. When he is exactly level with the pension— not before and not after—you will stamp hard on the floor three times. That will be my signal. Immediately after your third stamp, you will push the lever. Is that clear?"

"Will you not be able to see the king?" asks Orlov.

Zelle exhales impatiently. "Yes, I'll be watching the king, too. But I need your signal so that I know exactly when you're going to pull the lever."

"What will you be doing?" asks Orlov.

"I will be on my balcony, waiting for your signal, trying to blend in, with a specially modified weapon hidden in the lining of my jacket." Orlov does not follow this and is about to ask another question, but Zelle stops him. "No time. Now repeat your task back to me, step by step."

Orlov focuses hard and slowly repeats his instructions.

"Close enough," Zelle says, unties him, and holds out her arms to help him up. He takes both her hands and allows her to pull him over the lip of the bath. As he plants his feet on the bathroom floor, their bodies come together for a few seconds before parting again. Even when stressed and sweaty, she is beautiful and fragrant. Orlov is momentarily aroused again, just as he was at the Bierkeller, but this seems inappropriate given the urgency of the moment, and he puts it out of his mind.

Zelle steps away from him and continues to speak in a business-like manner.

"You must return here quickly, to confirm that you have access to room six and you have located the lever."

"I will," says Orlov.

He asks for permission to use Zelle's lavatory. He adjusts the bandages on his head and arm in the bathroom mirror. By the time he emerges into the bedroom, Zelle is sitting on her bed with her suitcase open. It is full of parts of an elaborate rifle that she is piecing together like a deadly jigsaw. Orlov looks out across Zelle's balcony to see crowds lining the far side of Feldgasse. Among them are Vanev and his various companions, standing in front of Penzion Rezidence, proudly holding banners confirming their allegiance to the People's Front.

With his hand on the doorknob of room four, Orlov is about to step out into the hallway, but stops for a few seconds to watch Zelle's intricate reassembly operation.

"What are you going to do with that?" asks Orlov.

Without looking up, Zelle says, "I'm going to shoot the king, of course."

CHAPTER SIX

In which our hero has a revelation

rlov hovers in Zelle's doorway, unsure how to make sense of what he has just heard. A sour feeling emanates from the pit of his stomach.

"Why are you still here?" says Zelle, agitated, but still looking down at her rifle components.

"I thought we were protecting the king," says Orlov, in a voice that emerges unexpectedly mournful and pathetic.

Now Zelle looks up at him. "We're not all loyalists, you know."

Orlov is confused. "Aren't we?"

"I'm a zealot," says Zelle. "So is Kosek. And now, so are you."

Orlov is unsure what this means, but is reluctant to admit it. "What happens when I pull the lever?" he asks.

Zelle is becoming agitated. "You're going to create some fireworks."

Orlov's gut tells him something is very wrong. "I don't believe I'm the right person for this," he says.

A brief pause hangs in the air, and Orlov hopes that he might be dismissed. However, Zelle puts the rifle down, picks up her handgun from the bedside table, and points it at his head. "Perform your task exactly, and do it now, or I'll shoot you," she says. "When this is over, the ministry will give you an award."

Orlov lumbers up to the top floor, confused and anxious and still wondering whether this is part of his training. He pauses at the top of the staircase, holds on to the banister, and tries to clear his mind. He wants to believe that he is on the right side and doing the right thing. He also wants to impress his new employer; a whole new future full of excitement and intrigue could depend on it. He has no idea, however, what a zealot is, and no idea how anyone working for a government ministry could contemplate harming the king. He takes in some deep breaths and hopes this confusing predicament proves to be nothing more than a test.

Perhaps the test is that he's supposed to realize Zelle's instructions are dangerously unpatriotic and intervene to stop her. On the other hand, he most certainly does not want to be shot at or tied up again. He has so many possibilities to consider and so little time to think.

The pressure makes Orlov feel nauseated.

As expected, the door to room six is locked. He rattles it hard, to no avail. He steps back and lunges into the door with his shoulder, once, twice. The door to room six remains resolutely closed, but the door to room seven opens and a distinguished, white-haired gentleman steps out in a pristine, formal suit.

"Is everything all right?" he asks.

"I'm having trouble with my door," says Orlov.

"Then I suggest you seek help downstairs," says the man. "We are enjoying a bottle of wine on our balcony and waiting for the arrival of the king. We would prefer to do so in peace."

"Yes, of course," says Orlov. "My apologies. I'll ask downstairs."

After the man returns into room seven, Orlov makes a couple of silent attempts to force the handle of the door to room six, with no success. He lumbers down the stairs and ponders his options. He could ask Zelle to break through the door, but she is busy and in any case she would consider him a failure for having been incapable of completing such a simple task. He could attempt to check in as Kosek, but the strange woman at the desk would recognize him from yesterday. By the time he arrives in the reception area, Orlov has decided on an alternative plan, and immediately walks out into a bustling, festive Feldgasse. The streetlamps are blazing and reflecting from the bunting, which swings in a stiff evening breeze. The pavement is full of well-wishers waiting to greet the king. There is a heavy police presence. Orlov marches briskly across the road and heads for the huddle of People's Front supporters. He finds Citizen Vanev holding a banner that reads Patriotic Citizens for a Republic.

Orlov leans in to Vanev and whispers in his ear. "My contact is late. I need to get into his room, in Pension Residenz. I need someone to check in as him, as Citizen Kosek. I can't do it, because the proprietor knows I'm not him."

Vanev says, "What have you got yourself mixed up with?"

"Don't worry, everything is under control," says Orlov, sweating.

Vanev pauses and watches Orlov breathing heavily. "Does it have to be me?" he asks.

"You're the only other man I know here," says Orlov.

Vanev sighs and consults his pocket watch. "We'll need to be quick," he says.

They walk across Feldgasse, and Orlov breaks away to wait in the street in front of the window to Pension Residenz while Vanev marches toward the entrance. Vanev pauses and turns to Orlov.

"Citizen *Kosek*, you say?" asks Vanev.

Orlov nods and watches anxiously through the window as Vanev steps inside. No one is at the desk, so Vanev rings the bell. Eventually, the proprietor appears. Orlov sees them exchange a few words, but there appears to be a problem. Is Vanev going to back out? Orlov holds his breath, trying to concentrate on the scene through the window while being jostled by people forcing their way along the pavement, hoping for an improved position from which to see the king.

Eventually, Vanev leans across the desk to sign the ledger and the proprietor hands him a key. They exchange more words before Vanev lumbers slowly up the stairs.

Vanev is gone for a painfully long time. What can he be doing? All he needs to do is to walk up to the top floor, to make it appear that he's going to his room, and then return to the street to hand over the key. In fact, he does not need to visit room six at all, as long as he goes up the stairs long enough for the proprietor to retreat into her back office.

Orlov hates the feeling of being helpless. He wants to do something, but there is nothing to do except wait. He turns to watch the scene along Feldgasse. Some of the crowd nearby is singing a patriotic song. Across the road, outside Penzion Rezidence, the other members of the People's Front are singing a different song with gusto, trying to be heard above the throng. They wave their banners with a passion that Orlov admires, even if he does not share their politics.

Orlov returns his gaze to the reception area through the front window of Pension Residenz. His headache is returning. There is still no sign of Vanev, and the proprietor is for once loitering at the desk, at exactly the time when Orlov is willing her to retreat into the back office.

Eventually, Orlov can stand it no longer. He decides he will have to go inside to intervene, even if this causes confusion. He walks to the front door and is about to step inside when Vanev appears again, climbing down the last few stairs. Vanev glares at Orlov, who returns to his position outside the window. Vanev exchanges some pleasantries with the proprietor before emerging onto the street. He reunites with Orlov by the window and hands him the key.

"You owe me a strong drink, citizen," says Vanev. "I assume you are now returning forthwith to be at the market first thing tomorrow."

"Sorry, citizen," says Orlov, "there's just one more thing I need to do. It won't take long."

Vanev returns across the street to his comrades and Orlov peers through the window, willing the strange, bespectacled woman to leave. He could claim to be visiting his colleague, Citizen Zelle, but he prefers to avoid the proprietor, if possible. Despite the cold, he is sweating and wipes his forehead with his sleeve. He is in serious danger of incurring the wrath of Agent Zelle even more than he has already. The drums of the palace guard band are growing louder, and there's a buzz of anticipation running through the crowds. The woman moves, and for a second Orlov believes she is about to return to her office, but she steps in front of the desk and walks toward the front door. Orlov curses under his breath and turns to mingle with the crowd. He inserts himself between two onlookers and glances surreptitiously to his left to see the proprietor of Pension Residenz leaning against her front door, watching the scene outside.

Orlov is preparing mentally what he will say to the owner when he spots movement in his peripheral vision. She has moved back inside the reception area. He dashes to the window just in time to see her disappearing into the back office. He marches through the front door, keeping his eye on the reception desk, and straight up the staircase to room six. He is badly out of breath by the time he arrives. Vanev has left the room unlocked.

Room six is identical to Zelle's room below: just a bed, a chair, a wardrobe, a small bathroom, and a balcony. The wardrobe is in the corner opposite the door. Orlov rushes over there and begins to search for the lever. He opens the wardrobe, but it is empty aside from a few coat hangers. He pulls the chair over and stands on it so that he can see the top of the wardrobe; there is nothing up there besides dust. Now he is sweating more heavily and breathing hard. He looks around and under the bed, and checks the small table beside the bed. All of it produces nothing out of the ordinary.

Now beginning to panic, Orlov steps out onto the balcony. To his horror, he sees the band of the palace guard marching from the church end of Feldgasse, which means the king is not far away. He looks down onto Zelle's balcony below. She is sitting at a small table with a bottle of wine, sipping from a glass with her left hand. Her right arm is straight, lying stiffly against a railing.

Orlov turns and looks back into the room. He is seriously considering walking down to tell Zelle he has failed in his task, when a thought occurs to him. He takes out his pocketbook and unfolds the index card.

We could not—repeat not—install it in room six. You need to get room seven. It's hidden above the wardrobe. Push the lever up, not down.

CHAPTER SEVEN

In which our hero gets a surprise

Now sweating heavily and suffering from a throbbing headache, Citizen Orlov straightens his crumpled suit and head bandage before knocking on the door of room seven. He stands tall and clears his throat. The distinguished gentleman opens the door and eyes Orlov with an agitated expression.

"Yes?" he says.

"I'm very sorry to disturb you sir," says Orlov. "I'm with the Ministry of . . ." he pauses to make a quick choice between the two options, "Security. We're doing a security sweep before His Majesty arrives. It's nothing to worry about. If I could just have access to your room for a few moments, I will then leave you in peace."

The man appears skeptical. "Do you have identification, citizen?"

"Ministry of Security personnel never carry identification," says Orlov, "for security reasons."

The man sighs with exasperation and opens the door a little wider. "Please hurry," he says.

"It will be very quick," says Orlov, making a perfunctory check of the bed and the chair before going to the wardrobe. Orlov nods politely to the man's wife, who is sipping wine on the balcony. He looks quickly inside the wardrobe, then says, "Would you mind terribly if I stand on your chair to check on top?"

"If you must," says the man.

Orlov prepares himself for the moment of truth. He stands on the chair, holds on to the top of the wardrobe doors and peers over the top.

"How did you sustain your injury, citizen?" asks the man.

"It's a dangerous job," says Orlov.

There is nothing on top of the wardrobe besides dust; exactly like room six. Orlov is flabbergasted. He steps down from the chair and feels around inside the wardrobe, before stretching his arm into the gap between the wardrobe and the wall. Nothing. He climbs back onto the chair and knocks on the wall above the wardrobe, in case something is concealed up there, but finds nothing at all.

"Have you quite finished?" asks the man.

Orlov climbs down from the chair. "I'm very sorry to have disturbed you," he says. "Everything is fine here. I hope you enjoy the festivities."

Now completely stumped, Orlov returns to room six and steps out onto the balcony. The front of the parade is now nearby, and the drums are louder than ever. He peeks down below to see Zelle still sitting in position. By now, she must be furious. He must go down there and tell her something. But what?

Putting off the inevitable moment of his failure, Orlov makes another sweep of room six. This time, he searches the bathroom and under the bed, and returns to the top of the wardrobe, to no avail. As a last resort, he copies what he just did in room seven: he reaches his arm into the gap between the wardrobe and the wall, for the short distance before it will go no farther. He feels nothing, but repositions himself so that he can peer into the gap. Once his eyes begin to adjust to the darkness, he sees something affixed to the wall, in the bottom corner between the foot of the wardrobe and the wainscotting. Whatever is down there is covered by a rough cloth, like sacking. Orlov heaves the wardrobe away from the wall a few inches and then lies on the floor, reaching into the corner. He pulls the cloth away and finds not a lever but a device of some sort, with multiple colored wires and three sticks of dynamite.

Orlov jumps up and pushes the wardrobe back into its original position. He does not want to stay in room six a moment longer. Whatever is going on here, it seems the technicians working for the Ministry of Security, or Intelligence, chose not only the wrong room, but the wrong hotel.

CHAPTER EIGHT

In which our hero hatches a plan

Citizen Orlov stops at the top of the staircase on the top floor of Pension Residenz and takes deep breaths to calm himself before descending. In the short walk from room six to room four, he hatches a plan. He finds the door to room four open and walks straight to the balcony. He gives a polite wave to a pair of onlookers on the balcony of room five.

Agent Zelle hears him and turns her head, keeping her body stiffly in place. "Where the hell have you been?"

"Sorry. I had a problem getting in. Nosey neighbors upstairs," says Orlov.

"Is everything in place? You found the lever?"

"Yes, everything is ready," says Orlov.

Zelle looks along Feldgasse, where the band of the palace guard is now visible. "Good. Go quickly, citizen. And remember, stamp three times."

"You can rely on me," he says, and slips out of room four and down the stairs. In the reception area, the proprietor is once again hovering at the front door, watching the parade, which is now deafeningly loud even inside the pension. As Orlov steps past her in the doorway, he says, "Just visiting my colleague, Citizen Zelle," and marches out into Feldgasse without waiting for her reply.

Orlov pulls the bandage off his head, to limit the chances of Zelle spotting him from above, and weaves through the crowd to the front of Penzion Rezidence. He finds Vanev, who is once again standing with his comrades from the People's Front.

"I'm sorry, citizen," says Orlov. "I need your assistance again, and this time it's life and death."

"Can it wait until the king has passed by?" asks Vanev.

Orlov leans in to whisper in his ear. "If we don't act now, the king will be dead before he reaches us."

Vanev looks him in the eye. "What have you got yourself mixed up with, citizen?"

"Trust me, citizen. I need your help," says Orlov.

"Very well," says Vanev, handing his banner to a comrade.

"What room do you have?" asks Orlov.

"Seven," says Vanev. "On the top floor."

"Lead the way," says Orlov. "And hurry."

The two men, both older and heavier than they once were, attempt to rush up six flights of stairs.

On the top floor, they stop to catch their breath before Vanev unlocks the door. Room seven of Penzion Rezidence is much the same as room seven of Pension Residenz, except this room has no chair. Orlov rushes to the wardrobe and feels on top of it, but he is not tall enough to see over it.

"Citizen," he says to Vanev urgently, "help me to move your bed over here."

The two men push the bed so that the foot is near to the wardrobe. Orlov stands on the bed and holds on to the top of the wardrobe doors. In the corner immediately above the back of the wardrobe, invisible from the rest of the room, is a small, black metal box attached to the wall. In the center of the box is a lever. Orlov reaches over to check that he is able to operate the lever, but he is careful not to touch it.

"What's up there?" asks Vanev.

Orlov climbs down again. "Do you trust me, citizen?" he asks.

Vanev hesitates. "I used to. Now, I'm not so sure."

"Quickly," says Orlov. "Let's watch from the balcony."

Vanev opens the balcony door, and suddenly the sound of the military band beneath them is deafening. There is a short gap in the parade behind the band before the arrival of the palace guard, in full regalia. And behind them are the carriages conveying the king and his entourage.

"What are we looking for?" asks Vanev.

"Look over there," says Orlov, "at the pension opposite."

Agent Zelle is still in position on her third-floor balcony, but now Orlov sees a man on the balcony with her. He is tall, dark-haired, and dressed in a dark suit, although too far away for Orlov to see his face in any detail. After a short conversation with Zelle, the man leaves and appears again on the balcony above her. He is searching for something frantically, going back into the bedroom and returning to the balcony twice.

The lines of palace guard troops will reach the hotel in just a few seconds. After that, it will take only a minute for the king's carriage to draw level.

"Citizen," says Orlov. "I have a question. Answer quickly."

"Very well," says Vanev.

"If you had to commit an evil act in order to prevent an even greater evil, would you do it?"

Vanev begins to say, "What do you mean by . . ." but Orlov cuts him off.

"No time for questions. Would you do it?"

Vanev exhales heavily. "If the other evil were greater, then yes, I suppose I would do it."

"Do not move," says Orlov.

The besuited man is still standing on the balcony of room six of Pension Residenz. Orlov steps into the bedroom and onto the bed. He leans over the top of the wardrobe, grasps the lever, and pulls it up.

PART TWO

The Aftermath

of the

Attempted Assassination

of His Majesty,

The King

CHAPTER NINE

In which our hero makes a swift getaway

A dull, percussive boom echoes across Feldgasse. It is followed by a second of silence, aside from a lone drummer who is slow to notice that everyone else has stopped playing. Orlov rushes to the balcony to find Vanev sheltering in the corner. Someone is face down in the middle of the street; it looks like the tall stranger from the opposite balcony. Room six of Pension Residenz is a smoldering mess; a plume of gray dust spews out, depositing rubble into the street. The crowds scatter to avoid it. The posture of the palace guard shifts in an instant from ceremonial to operational; they quickly cordon off the pension and move the crowds away. The vibrant, deafening music has given way in seconds to an eerie silence punctuated by disparate shouts of orders and cries of anguish. The carriages of the king's entourage are turning to leave Feldgasse the way they entered. The balcony of room four appears intact, but there is no sign of Zelle.

Orlov slumps down against the wall next to Vanev, who is pale and sweating.

"What did you do?" asks Vanev, desperately.

"The lesser evil," says Orlov.

"They're going to come after us," says Vanev.

"Why?" asks Orlov.

"Because we're the People's Front," says Vanev, exasperated. "We wave banners saying Down with the King, and now the king is yards from a bomb."

Orlov looks over the balcony again at the chaos below. "We need to get out of here," he says.

"We can't just walk to the railway station," says Vanev. "It will be surrounded by police."

"Maybe so, citizen," says Orlov, "but they don't know who we are."

Vanev stares at him, nonplussed. "Trust me, citizen," says Vanev. "The authorities knew the People's Front were protesting today. And they were watching us."

A noise comes from the hallway, and Vanev goes to investigate. He returns with a gaggle of People's Front comrades, who crowd into his room, flinging their banners onto his bed. Vanev ushers them in and shuts the door. In the distance, multiple sirens are blaring.

The comrades are five men and two women, all of whom started the day dressed in their best formal outfits.

Now they are disoriented and covered in dust. There is a feverish atmosphere as the comrades whisper between themselves in urgent, angry voices.

Vanev calls them to order. "Comrades, please. We need to act quickly."

The comrades eye Orlov suspiciously. "Who's this?" asks one of the men.

"This is Citizen Orlov," says Vanev.

"Can we trust him?" asks someone else.

Vanev hesitates. "He's with me."

"That's not what I asked," says the comrade.

Vanev waves his arms as if trying to erase the frantic atmosphere. "Comrades," he says, "we don't have time for arguments. Listen. We can't stay here; they'll be sweeping the buildings. And we can't walk to the railway station."

One of the comrades speaks up. "What about Comrade Horvat's bus?"

Everyone looks at Comrade Horvat, who is huddled in the corner with his wife. He shakes his head vigorously. "Comrades, please. I really don't think . . ."

Vanev chimes in, addressing Horvat in kindly but persuasive tones. "Comrade, yourself and Madam Horvat are the only ones among our number who live in Kufzig. And you drive a bus. It makes good sense."

"We can't take you all to our house," says Horvat. "It's too dangerous."

"No, no," says Vanev. "There's no need to go to your house. We just need to take a drive out of town. Get away for a few hours, until all this dies down."

Horvat looks at his wife, who shakes her head. But other comrades begin to move, as though the plan is decided upon.

Finally, Horvat says, "Is a there a back door out of here?"

"There's a servant's entrance," says another comrade, and he leads the way out of Vanev's room, across the hall and through a service door to a cramped rear staircase.

The party of nine files out through the servant's door into a back alley. Sirens continue to blare into the frigid night air.

"Follow me," says Horvat and marches quickly from one dark alley to another, away from Feldgasse. The party follows him in single-file silence until they emerge around the side of a factory and into a wide yard that houses several passenger buses. "Wait on the street," says Horvat. "I won't be long."

The rest of the party waits on the pavement next to the gate, stamping their feet and clapping their hands to keep warm. Orlov is anxious to get away from Kufzig; he looks up and down the street searching for movement. Just as the sound of an engine starting floats over the wall from inside the yard, two policemen emerge from around the corner, marching purposefully toward Feldgasse.

One of the policemen addresses the whole party. "Good evening, citizens. What is going on here, please?"

Madam Horvat hesitates a moment before stepping forward. "Oh, officers, it was terrible. Our friends here are visiting from out of town to see His Majesty. Well, we were very close to the explosion. Just look at the dust on our clothes. And it's chaos at the railway station, so . . ."

At this moment, Horvat's bus begins to emerge from the yard. The policeman looks at the bus and back at Madam Horvat. "I'm sorry, madam, but we've been instructed to secure Feldgasse. I'll have to ask you all to present your papers, please."

Madam Horvat doesn't miss a beat. "Oh, yes, officer. Quite right. In fact, we've all just been interviewed by your colleagues on Feldgasse. Of course, they wouldn't let us leave the scene until we'd presented our papers. And now we really need to take our visitors home."

The other policeman indicates that they should keep moving. His colleague says, "Very well, please be careful." The officers continue walking, but the policeman calls back over his shoulder. "And stay away from Feldgasse."

Soon, Orlov and his eight People's Front companions are following a winding road into the mountains. The engine of Citizen Horvat's bus groans in complaint at the gradient. Orlov is relieved to be out of Kufzig. From his seat at the back of the bus, he looks down on the town, where police lights continue to flash along Feldgasse. He wonders if the body in the street was the elusive Agent Kosek. He wonders if Agent Zelle was hurt in the explosion. Perhaps she escaped unscathed and is right now scouring Feldgasse to find him.

The higher the bus climbs into the mountains, the colder the temperature and the more Orlov begins to breathe more easily.

For a while, Orlov sits with Vanev and learns that the other comrades, aside from the Horvats, are Comrade and Madam Balog, plus Comrades Sandor, Nemeth, and Weisz. All of them keep their distance from Orlov and treat him with some suspicion. Once the road levels out, Vanev stands up at the front of the bus as if to address the group. Orlov wonders what he is going say. To his surprise, Vanev clears his throat, takes a deep breath and begins to sing.

The People's Flag is deepest red,
It shrouded oft our martyred dead,
And ere their limbs grew stiff and cold,
Their hearts' blood dyed its every fold.

Orlov has never before heard Vanev sing and is most impressed. With no instruction from Vanev, all the comrades—including Comrade Horvat at the wheel—break into a lusty chorus.

Then raise the scarlet standard high.
Beneath its shade we'll live and die,
Though cowards flinch and traitors sneer,
We'll keep the red flag flying here.

Orlov recognizes the tune; it is "O Tannenbaum." It transpires that this peculiar song has many verses, and when they reach the chorus on the second and third occasion, Vanev waves at Orlov to encourage him to join in. Although not much of a singer, Orlov appreciates the gesture and does his best to sing along. Perhaps Vanev is trying to encourage his comrades to accept Orlov into their group, or perhaps this is his way of recruiting Orlov to become a member. Orlov is most grateful but, looking around the bus as the chorus of

"The Red Flag" booms out, he is not convinced that the other comrades are feeling any more warmly toward him.

It is late in the evening when Comrade Horvat maneuvers the bus off the road and into a sheltered area surrounded by tall fir trees. He parks the bus next to a wooden shelter, beside which are the remnants of a campfire. Horvat consults briefly with Vanev, who then makes an announcement.

"Comrades," says Vanev. "It is late and cold. Comrade Horvat tells me this shelter is used by mountaineers, in the warmer months. It is basic in appointment, but we can make a fire to warm ourselves. I recommend we plan to spend the night here and seek to make our way home tomorrow, once the situation has become calmer. All those in favor?"

After brief, whispered conversations between the comrades, one after the other calls out, "Aye."

Vanev addresses Orlov. "Is that plan acceptable to you, comrade?"

Orlov is taken aback. Vanev has only ever before addressed him as *citizen*. "Yes, comrade," says Orlov, self-consciously.

Orlov joins Vanev in investigating the shelter, while Comrades Nemeth and Weisz work on making a fire. The shelter is rudimentary, with nothing more than wooden benches for sleeping, but at least it offers protection from the elements. Orlov feels the need to discuss with Vanev what happened on Feldgasse. He hopes there will be the opportunity to do so privately. Of the two choices available to him, he chose the lesser evil. If he had done nothing, or even if he had waited until later to push the lever, the king might now be dead, the nation would be in crisis, and the People's Front would be in even more danger.

On the other hand, if Orlov had chosen to do nothing, he himself might be in the clear, whereas now he could be accused of killing or injuring whoever was on the balcony of room six. On top of all that is the real possibility that Zelle—who has shot him once and threatened to do so again—will be furious with him for walking away from his duties and will track him down to exact revenge. He still does not understand Zelle's plan, nor what she meant by *zealot*.

While they are still inside the shelter, Orlov says, "Citizen, there are some things we need to discuss."

"Not here," says Vanev. "Let's join the others around the fire."

By the time they emerge outside, the campfire is beginning to crackle and the comrades are huddled around it, sitting on logs. A group discussion ensues about the plan for tomorrow. Some comrades are hoping that Comrade Horvat will drive them all the way to the capital, but he resists, pointing out that the bus could be reported missing if it is away from the depot for too long. That in itself could raise suspicions related to the People's Front. It is agreed instead that, first thing in the morning, Comrade Horvat will drive the bus to another railway station, some miles north of Kufzig. From there, comrades will be able to split up and make their way home on different trains.

"All those in favor?" asks Vanev, when the time comes for a vote.

The "Ayes" ripple in a circle around the campfire.

Once the vote is over, the discussion becomes more informal and breaks into smaller groups. Orlov sees his chance for a word with Vanev.

"Citizen," he says, "I have a question."

"Very well," says Vanev.

"When she was giving me instructions, my contact at the ministry, Agent Zelle, told me she is a *zealot*."

"Really?" says Vanev, with an expression that suggests Orlov has caught his interest. "What else did she tell you?"

"That when I pushed the lever, she would shoot the king."

Vanev's eyebrows go up so high that Orlov thinks they might never come down again. "So why did you push it?"

"I pushed it early," says Orlov, "to save the king."

"Would you not have saved the king by doing nothing?" asks Vanev, gravely.

"I don't think so," says Orlov. "The agent had a rifle. She was on the balcony, waiting for him to draw level. I think she would have shot him either way."

"But you cannot know that for certain," says Vanev.

Orlov's headache is returning. "There's something else you need to know. The bomb was in the wrong boarding house."

"Where should it have been?" asks Vanev.

"At Penzion Rezidence, where you were staying. The lever was supposed to be in Pension Residenz, where the agents were staying. But they were switched. By mistake, I think."

Now Vanev's expression changes from concern to relief. "The bastards must have known the People's Front had reserved most of the rooms. No doubt they didn't care if they killed any of us in the process of framing us. But why hire you to do the deed?"

"It wasn't supposed to be me," says Orlov. "I was only the *third man*. It should have been Kosek. He was the man blown off the balcony, I think."

Vanev leans back and says, a little too loudly, "Now I'm beginning to see why you decided to detonate it."

Comrade Weisz has broken away from a conversation with Comrade Nemeth and hears Vanev's comment. He squares up to Orlov and pushes him. "So, this is the bomber," he spits, turning his anger to Vanev. "What's the matter with you? I thought there was something suspicious about this fellow. You've put us all in danger."

Vanev stands up. Comrades Nemeth and Sandor move toward Orlov threateningly. Comrade Weisz pushes Orlov again. Vanev raise his arms. "Comrades, please. Calm yourselves." He puts his considerable bulk between Orlov and the others before continuing. "Comrade Orlov is not our enemy. He was tricked by government agents. He has possibly killed one of those agents this evening, and in doing so he might have saved the life of the king."

"That's what he says, is it?" sneers Weisz. Comrade Nemeth holds Weisz back to prevent him from reaching Orlov again. On the other side of the campfire, the Horvats and the Balogs look on in horror.

"I believe him," says Vanev.

"How do we know he's not infiltrating the group?" asks Sandor. "Perhaps he's going to hand us over to these government agents."

Nemeth, still restraining Weisz, chimes in. "Yes. How do we know, comrade?"

Vanev, now red-faced, tries to regain control. "Comrades, please. There are factions within the government who want to smear us. We know that. But Comrade Orlov is not one of them. He is a fishmonger, like me, and nothing more. We gain nothing by accusing him."

Weisz is now walking away and straightening his clothes after his tussle with Nemeth. "I want him gone," he says. "Let's vote on it."

"No, no," says Vanev hurriedly. "There will be no voting on Comrade Orlov. He's doing us no harm. Let's get some sleep, and in the morning we will go our separate ways."

Orlov, feeling decidedly vulnerable, has stepped away from the campfire, keeping Vanev between himself and the rest of the group. Vanev continues to talk to his comrades, now in hushed tones, in an attempt to calm the atmosphere. Madam Balog has become tearful and is being comforted by her husband. Vanev moves the conversation on to sleeping arrangements.

The two women decide that the shelter is too crude for their liking; it is agreed they will sleep in the bus while the men take the shelter.

Orlov avoids these discussions and stays outside by the campfire until everyone else has settled into their sleeping positions. After a while, Vanev emerges from the shelter to find him.

"Don't worry, comrade," he says. "They will be more rational in the morning."

"I don't believe I'm going to be accepted as a comrade," says Orlov, before Vanev returns inside.

Orlov considers spending the night alone by the campfire, but the logs are uncomfortable, and the ground is damp. Eventually, in the early hours, he sneaks inside the shelter and, fumbling in the dark, finds a bench against a wall, away from the others. He removes his overcoat, spreads it over himself like a blanket, and attempts to sleep.

Orlov is woken by shafts of golden sunlight streaming into the shelter through the high windows and the sounds of pine branches creaking against a stiff wind. He is disoriented and cold. Sitting up to pull on his overcoat, he is the only man left in the shelter, and instantly he feels guilty for making them wait. He runs his fingers through what's left of his hair, buttons up his overcoat, and trudges outside to let the others know he is ready to leave.

Outside, it is a beautiful mountain scene; the smoldering campfire is illuminated by the early morning sun, the sky is as blue as any Orlov can remember, and the pine trees sway gracefully in the wind. There are, however, no comrades and no bus. Orlov is all alone.

CHAPTER TEN

In which our hero pushes on alone

Citizen Orlov is cold and hungry. Worse still, he has never felt more alone than in this moment. Although not a political person, he likes to think he is honest and loyal and patriotic. He does not know why Molnar recruited him or why Zelle and Kosek tried to embroil him in their schemes. All he knows is that he has responded at every turn by doing what he believed was the right thing. And what has he got in return?

Although it was dark long before they arrived here in the bus the previous evening, Orlov cannot remember seeing any sort of civilization nearby. He decides to walk on farther into the mountains in the hope of finding somewhere to buy food and hopefully someone who can help him return home, preferably not via Kufzig. The road is narrow and meandering, sometimes flat but frequently climbing higher. It is surrounded on both sides by dense fir trees. As he strides out along the edge of the road, the deep ache in Orlov's injured arm returns; he unfurls the bandage and attempts to tie it into a sling such that his injured arm remains bent against his side.

As he walks, Orlov wonders what is in store for him when he returns home. He wonders if the man on the balcony was Kosek, and if he is now dead. He wonders if Zelle has passed information about him to the police or if she has had to keep it from them in order to protect herself. He wonders if, in the absence of information from Zelle, the police could discover his involvement in the normal course of investigations, or if they will focus on implicating the People's Front. Will the police notice that, aside from his association with Vanev, he stayed at Penzion Rezidence the night before the comrades arrived?

Orlov is grateful for his heavy overcoat, but wishes he were wearing something other than his best dress shoes, which are not suited for hiking up mountains. After a couple of hours, his feet are throbbing and sore. He finds a break in the trees where a small brook runs down off the mountain.

He sits by the brook and takes off his shoes while scooping up water with his hands. The water is ice cold but delicious. He washes his face and then makes another attempt to tie the bandage into a sling for his left arm. He grimaces when the time comes to force his feet back into his shoes.

Above the brook, the road climbs a little farther before the trees begin to thin out. Then the road flattens out and suddenly Orlov has a spectacular view down into a steep valley. Although the winter sun is low in the sky, it is no longer blocked by trees, and Orlov pauses by a stone wall to warm his face. He spots sheep or goats in the lower fields and determines to head in that direction in the hope of finding a farm or even a village. Soon, he comes to a fork in the road and chooses a left turn heading down into the valley rather than following the road farther into the mountains. Part way down the valley, a thin pillar of smoke offers the hope of civilization, and Orlov follows it to an idyllic white cottage lodged into the hillside. Next to the cottage stands a wide shed, in front of which are numerous vehicles in various states of disrepair. As he nears the gate of this property at the end of a long, winding driveway, Orlov sees a man in front of the shed working on one of the vehicles. He turns into the driveway and, feeling self-conscious, tries to decide what he will say about the reason for his visit. In order to avoid fielding questions about his injury, he removes the sling from his left arm and hides it in the pocket of his overcoat.

Before Orlov reaches the house, the man (who, despite the cold weather, is working outside in only his shirtsleeves) wipes his brow on a rag and steps out from behind a tractor.

"Good morning, citizen," bellows the man.

Orlov waves. "Good morning, citizen. Please forgive me for intruding."

"Not at all," says the man. "We rarely see visitors out here, and certainly not on foot."

Orlov smiles, relieved at this friendly reception. "I'm sure you don't," he says.

By now, Orlov has reached the man, who steps forward to shake his hand. He is a ruddy fellow with glowing cheeks and a muscular frame. "Citizen Petrovich," he says.

"Citizen Orlov," says Orlov.

"Is there anything I can do to help you, citizen?" says Petrovich.

Orlov stops and leans against the tractor to catch his breath. "I'm sorry to impose on your hospitality. Unfortunately, I became separated from my party. We were due to spend the day hiking, you see. I was lucky enough to be offered a lift to the rendezvous point, but they never arrived."

"Those are not really hiking clothes, citizen," says Petrovich.

"No, indeed," says Orlov. "In fact, my wife was with the rest of the party and was due to bring the correct attire for me. Sadly, I fear that I arrived at the wrong point, and now there's no option but to return home."

Citizen Petrovich looks a little skeptical about this story, but does not say so. "Do I detect from your accent that you are from the north, Citizen Orlov?"

"That's correct," says Orlov. "And I really must return by this evening."

"Well," says Petrovich, "I'm afraid we're a long way from the railway. But, if you'd like to take a drive with me, I could take you into the village. There is a taxi service there."

"Perfect," says Orlov. "That would be most kind." He looks around to see which of the many vehicles they are taking, but Petrovich waves him into the house.

"I hope you don't need to leave right away, because my wife was about to make lunch," says Petrovich.

Orlov is so hungry that he doesn't care about the time. "That's most kind," he says and follows Petrovich into the house.

Petrovich ushers Orlov into a comfortable chair in the parlor; it is a delightful relief to rest his feet. Almost immediately after he sits down, Madam Petrovich arrives to introduce herself, carrying a tray with a teapot and china cups, which she sets on a table between them.

Orlov stands to greet her. "Thank you," he says. "It's almost as though you were expecting my visit."

Madam Petrovich smiles. "We rarely see visitors out here," she says. "Please enjoy your tea. Lunch will be ready soon." She retreats to the kitchen.

Citizen Petrovich pours the tea for both Orlov and himself before saying, "Excuse me, just for one moment." He follows his wife into the kitchen, exchanges a few words with her that Orlov can't hear, and returns moments later, sinking into his armchair.

Not being especially comfortable in social situations, Orlov attempts to make polite conversation. "What is your line of business, citizen?" he asks.

Petrovich waves a hand to the vehicles visible through the window. "Mostly, I repair things," he says. "Anyone who lives on this mountain and needs repairs to a machine or a vehicle, they bring it to me." It occurs to Orlov that this cottage is the only house he has seen for miles. "And does that produce enough work for a good living?" he asks.

"I take on contracts as well," says Petrovich, "from the government. Even from the Palace, sometimes. Mostly, that involves building work, alterations, that kind of thing."

"I see," says Orlov. "I dare say that involves some travel."

"Sometimes," says Petrovich, "but I prefer to be here in our beautiful valley."

"I imagine you do," says Orlov.

"And what's your line of business, citizen?" asks Petrovich.

"Fishmongering," says Orlov. "If you know the Grand Plaza, ours is the only fish stall for these many years."

"I know the plaza, indeed," says Petrovich, "although I don't believe I have ever visited the market there."

Madam Petrovich returns and announces that lunch is ready. They follow her into a neat dining room with three places set at a table adorned with cold meats, bread, and pickles. Orlov is relieved to eat something after an uncomfortable night and a long walk.

While passing plates, Madam Petrovich says, "When I visited the butcher this morning in the village, he said the king's visit to Kufzig was cut short, on account of a security incident of some kind. I asked what had happened exactly, but he wasn't sure."

"Really?" says Citizen Petrovich. "Terrible." He pauses to shovel a mountain of cold sausage onto his plate. "Did you hear anything about this, Citizen Orlov?"

Orlov freezes momentarily. He looks down at a plate of pickles to avoid eye contact while gathering his thoughts. "I did not," says Orlov. "I hope His Majesty is safe and well."

"Yes, yes," says Citizen Petrovich. "I'm sure we can all agree on that."

Orlov expects the conversation to move on to other matters, but Madam Petrovich continues. "One would expect His Majesty could travel safely anywhere in the kingdom to visit his subjects, would you not agree, Citizen Orlov?"

Orlov attempts to nod and eat pickled cabbage simultaneously. "One would certainly hope so," he says.

Orlov is relieved when Citizen Petrovich changes the subject. "Have you always been a fishmonger, citizen?" he asks.

Orlov is momentarily prevented from answering when Madam Petrovich stands up suddenly, excuses herself, and leaves the room. Once she has left, he says, "Oh yes, ever since national service. So, very many years now. It's a good trade."

"I dare say so," says Citizen Petrovich. "The reason I ask is that, well, I must say that your voice is familiar. But I'm quite sure we have never met before."

"I don't believe so," says Orlov.

Petrovich continues. "My contract work is mostly for the government, you see, or the Palace. And on occasion I have the need to speak to officials there on important matters, on the telephone, you understand."

"I see," says Orlov, wondering where this topic of conversation is leading.

Madam Petrovich returns, exchanges a look with her husband, and takes her seat. Citizen Petrovich continues. "I suppose, if you've been a fishmonger for years, you've never had occasion to take work at, say, the Ministry of Security, or the Ministry of Intelligence?"

Orlov stops dead with a slice of blood sausage dangling from his fork. He looks up from his plate to see that both Citizen Petrovich and Madam Petrovich are staring at him, awaiting a reply. It seems to Orlov that time has stood still. He wonders how Petrovich could have arrived at this conclusion. And only now he remembers Petrovich's voice. Could this be the man who called the telephone by the open window and left a message for Agent Kosek? The man who called Orlov the village idiot? That was rude and aggressive, but perhaps Citizen Petrovich was under a lot of pressure at the time. It was, as he said himself, a life and death situation, and perhaps that pressure contributed to the confusion that followed in terms of the work being done on the wrong room in the wrong boarding house. For half of one second, Orlov considers acknowledging that he was the person who answered the telephone and went looking for Agent Kosek. However, he is not entirely sure that Citizen Petrovich was the caller, and neither is he sure that Petrovich can be trusted. He decides, therefore, to err on the side of caution in terms of his reply.

"Oh, no," says Orlov. "I would not be qualified for government work of that kind. After all, I'm just a simple fishmonger. The village idiot, you might say." He smiles at both Petroviches before eating the blood sausage.

Citizen Petrovich pauses before replying, eyeing him carefully. "I see," he says. "I must have confused you with someone else. Someone with a similar voice."

"Indeed," says Orlov.

A sharp rap sounds on the front door of the cottage. Madam Petrovich glances at her husband and stands up. "Excuse me," she says and leaves to answer the door.

Seconds later, three police officers march purposefully into the dining room, with Madam Petrovich trailing behind. The badge on the uniform of the first policeman indicates that he is a commander, and thus probably the most senior officer in this remote mountain community. He nods to acknowledge Citizen Petrovich, as though they are known to each other, then turns to Citizen Orlov with a steely glare.

"Citizen Orlov?"

"Yes," says Orlov, horrified, but trying not to show it. He sets down his knife and fork.

The commander continues with stern, clipped efficiency. "You are hereby under arrest for the murder of one Citizen Kosek, and conspiracy to assassinate His Majesty, the King."

CHAPTER ELEVEN

In which our hero encounters the long arm of the law

Even while the commander is still speaking, the other two officers rush around the dining table; each grabs one of Orlov's arms from behind, and together they hoist him off the chair and march him to the door.

Orlov shouts out in complaint. "It was him, Petrovich," he says, nodding toward Petrovich in lieu of the use of his arms. "If you want to know who planted the bomb, it was him."

The two policemen ignore his protestations and keep marching. The commander removes his hat briefly, thanks the Petroviches for their cooperation, and follows his officers outside. They handcuff Orlov and bundle him into a police truck, the back of which is no more than a cage. The officers force Orlov to sit down on one of the hard benches, lock up the back of the cage, then take their seats in the cabin. As the truck pulls away, Orlov looks back to see Citizen and Madam Petrovich standing at their front door, watching the vehicle trundle along their driveway and out onto the road until it disappears from view.

Orlov's heart is racing so hard that he can hear the blood in his ears. He takes deep breaths to calm himself. He briefly considers remonstrating with the officers, but each of them is armed, and he is trapped in an enclosed space. In the circumstances, he decides to sit quietly. It transpires that sitting in a bouncing truck on uneven roads while your hands are handcuffed behind your back is in itself quite challenging. Orlov grips the cage with his fingers to steady himself, and he sits in that position for many miles, wondering how he got himself into this mess. What does the Ministry of Security, or the Ministry of Intelligence, have against him? What does Citizen Petrovich have against him? Why do those assigned to protect the king seem to be putting the king in danger? None of it makes any sense.

Orlov thinks back to what the commander said. The tall man in the dark suit must have been Kosek, that much seems sure. If only he had found Kosek and given him the message, none of this would be happening. Then again, the king would probably be dead and, had he been unable to prevent it, Orlov would potentially be partly complicit in his assassination. The other part of what the commander said was less clear. Orlov is familiar with the word *assassinate*, but less sure about *conspiracy*. Does this mean they think he's a member of the People's Front? He wonders if Vanev and his comrades made it home safely or if they've been arrested and charged with conspiracy, too. He considers pointing out to the commander that he is not and has never been a member of the People's Front, but he decides that it might be better to raise this with a lawyer. Assuming that he's allowed to see a lawyer. He wonders how much a lawyer costs.

By the time Orlov is worrying about his pitiful lack of savings and the potential costs of hiring a lawyer to defend himself, the truck has descended out of the mountains and joined the main road, heading north. Orlov hopes that he might be taken to a police station, at least for tonight, but fears that he will instead be taken to the notorious Prison Zhotrykaw, a miserable, forbidding place that appears to be hewn from the rock of the cliffs under which it stands. Like most upstanding citizens, Orlov has never seen the inside of Zhotrykaw, but he has heard the stories of squalid conditions, overcrowding, and arbitrary cruelty meted out by vindictive guards.

Two hours into the journey, as Orlov's hands are turning numb from gripping the cage for so long, his worst fears are realized. They reach a fork in the road and, instead of taking the right turn toward the capital, the truck swings left, back into the mountains. But these are not the beautiful, snowcapped peaks beloved of hikers in the south; here in the north, the mountains are rocky and angular, like permanent clouds darkening the landscape. As if to emphasize this effect, the truck is hit by a sudden downpour of freezing rain. Although the cabin is covered, the cage is not, and Orlov is soaked.

Soon, the cliffs close in on both sides, and an ominous building looms up ahead. The sinking feeling in Orlov's gut sinks a little further as they pass a sign reading Prison Zhotrykaw.

Orlov spends a miserable few hours, still soaking and freezing cold, locked into a dingy waiting room. The paint is peeling from the walls and there is an overwhelming stench of urine. Eventually, a surly officer arrives to process him. Orlov is required to strip in the presence of the officer and hand over all his possessions in exchange for prison overalls. While changing with his back to the officer, it occurs to Orlov that the index card with the telephone message from Petrovich is still in his pocketbook. It is the only piece of evidence he has regarding the incident on Feldgasse. He is not sure, however, whether it would be regarded as evidence by a lawyer or by a court. After all, this is just a note that he wrote to himself; does it prove anything? Since the message is all he has, Orlov decides to hang on to it. He removes the folded index card from his pocketbook and is in the process of slipping it into the pocket of his overalls when the officer's baton lands hard on his knuckles. Orlov screams and lurches backward, nursing his hand.

"Stand still," says the officer, without emotion, while searching both pockets. He takes Orlov's clothes and pocketbook away and then makes him strip again so that he can check inside the overalls. Orlov is embarrassed and sore. The blow to his left hand has made the injury to his arm flare up again, and he feels waves of dull pain radiate through his body.

Saying nothing further, the officer marches Orlov through a series of heavy, locked doors and leaves him in another dank room much like the first, except here there is another guard in a tiny office, visible through a narrow window. Orlov approaches the window.

"Prisoner Orlov," says the officer.

Orlov is unsure if this is a statement or a question. "Citizen Orlov," says Orlov.

"Prisoner Orlov," repeats the officer, writing something in a ledger.

Orlov leans in closer to the window, in an attempt to make eye contact, but the officer is still focused on what he is writing.

"There's been a terrible misunderstanding," says Orlov. "You see, I was simply following orders, from the Ministry of Intelligence. Or perhaps Security. Either way, it was the government."

The officer looks up. "Tell your story to the judge," he says, dispassionately, and waves to indicate that Orlov should approach a door in the corner.

Orlov tries to continue with his explanation, but the officer has disappeared, reappearing again as he opens the door and ushers Orlov into a long, dismal corridor, lit only by the tiniest slits of windows high up against the ceiling. As they walk, the prevailing aroma changes from urine to excrement. Orlov sees the infamous cells of Zhotrykaw for the first time: an almost endless row of heavy, metal doors, each with a thin viewing hole covered by a cage. They walk and walk until the long corridor gives way to a tighter group of cells clustered on both sides of a short corridor beyond a dividing door.

The officer marches Orlov to the far corner and unlocks the final door. Saying nothing, the officer holds the door open and looks at Orlov, who peers inside. The tiny cell comprises only a small bench, a bed pan, and a tap in the wall, from which water is dripping into a small drainage hole in the corner. Seeing the cramped, filthy space and the thick walls, Orlov panics and steps backward.

"How long will I be here?" he asks. "What about a lawyer? I need to speak to someone."

The officer pushes him inside. "Ask tomorrow."

Orlov turns and says, "Ask who?" but the door is already locked behind him.

CHAPTER TWELVE

In which our hero must have his wits about him

It is a long, uncomfortable night on a hard bench with no more than a thin blanket. Orlov is exhausted, yet he gets almost no sleep. His mind is spinning with how he could have been so foolish to end up in this mess, what has happened to the People's Front, and what he will say to a lawyer whenever he gets the chance. Having never before been arrested on any charges, let alone for charges quite so serious as these, he has no idea what happens next or how long it will take. He wonders if he will be in Zhotrykaw for a day or a week before the legal process begins—or a year. The thought of this alone is horrifying, and he sits upright on the narrow bench that now passes for his bed. He thinks of his real bed in the apartment that he used to consider small and spartan; right now, the thought of being back in that bed feels like the height of luxury.

Orlov has no idea of the time, but the feeble light seeping in through the slot in the door tells him it must be morning. He hears voices and the harsh banging of an officer rapping on cell doors with a baton. A metal tray appears through the door; it carries a pitiful bowl one-third full of something that might be porridge. There is no spoon. Was he supposed to bring his own cutlery? He eats the tasteless porridge with his hands and listens to the sounds of the prison waking up.

He hears voices everywhere now, mostly quiet mumblings interspersed with angry bursts that sound like arguments between inmates and officers, but he cannot distinguish the details. Perhaps someone does not appreciate the porridge.

Some of the voices are emanating from somewhere other than the hole in the door. Orlov takes a tour of his cell and discovers whisperings emerging from the drainage hole under the tap. He gets down on his hands and knees, trying to ignore how filthy the floor is. He puts his ear to the drainage hole and listens. Two voices are hissing frantically. They are familiar. The louder voice sounds like Comrade Horvat, the bus driver. Perhaps the People's Front has met the same fate as Orlov himself. The quieter voice might just be Citizen Vanev.

Orlov moves his mouth to the drainage hole, almost gagging at the stench.

"Psst," he says. "Vanev. Is that Citizen Vanev?"

There is a pause. The whispered voices fall silent. Then Vanev's voice says, "Orlov. Is that you?"

"Yes, it's me," hisses Orlov.

"When did you arrive here?" asks Vanev.

"Why did you leave me all alone up the mountain?" says Orlov.

Another pause. "We can't talk now," says Vanev. "They're about to collect the trays. Let's talk after that, once the guards have gone."

Orlov paces around his cell for a while. A poor substitute for his usual morning constitutional over the bridge and through the government sector, before arriving at the Grand Plaza to set up the market stall for the day. There is another flurry of banging and shouting while the guards remove the trays from doors all along the cell block.

Once he is sure the guards have moved on again, Orlov returns to the corner and puts his head down into the stinking drainage hole.

"Psst," he says. "Citizen Vanev. Your employee is calling."

After a pause, he hears Vanev's voice. "Citizen, I am sorry about yesterday. I was outvoted."

Orlov is exasperated. "Why do you have to vote on everything? I was on my own out there, in the middle of nowhere."

"In the end, it makes no difference," says Vanev. "The bus was stopped by the police even before we left the mountains."

"Are you all charged with conspiracy against the king?" asks Orlov.

"Yes," says Vanev. "And you?"

"The same," says Orlov. "And the murder of Citizen Kosek."

"Oh, dear," says Vanev, ominously.

"I need to ask you a question, citizen," whispers Orlov.

"Yes," says Vanev.

Orlov takes a pause before continuing, turning away and breathing some fresher air to stop himself from gagging. "I still don't understand what the agent said about loyalists and zealots."

"Loyalists are supporters of the king," whispers Vanev. "Zealots are supporters of the Crown Prince. I heard rumors about zealots in high places plotting against the king. I never believed it, until now."

Orlov pauses to consider this, turning to gulp fresher air, then putting his head back into the hole. "I don't see what that has to do with the People's Front."

Vanev pauses, perhaps also taking in some fresh air before answering. "The government has been trying to smear us for years," whispers Vanev. "I'll bet the ministry was planning to bomb our hotel, before the king arrived. After that, we are forever terrorists."

"But the zealots added a twist," says Orlov.

"Yes," says Vanev. "Perhaps your zealot friends who were supposed to protect the king were planning to get him out of the way, hand power to the Crown Prince, and blame the whole thing on the People's Front."

"Why bring me into it?" asks Orlov.

Another pause. "Let's say the ministry required them to take a third man," says Vanev. "Don't be offended, citizen, but perhaps they wanted an accomplice who would go along with their zealot plan, rather than someone who, shall we say, might be more likely to work out what was going on."

"'He said he was going to send an idiot,'" says Orlov.

"Pardon me?" says Vanev.

"Nothing," says Orlov. "Do you know if they let us out for exercise?"

"This is the high security wing," says Vanev. "No idea."

Orlov spends the rest of the morning pacing his cell, going over what Vanev said and pondering the arguments he will discuss with his lawyer. He might be merely a fishmonger, but he is not, in fact, an idiot. Although Orlov knows little about the law and the courts, he knows the main obstacle is that he pushed the lever. One does not need to be a lawyer to know that. He could deny it, but that might be a risky strategy.

He has a better idea.

At some point in the afternoon, Orlov is hungry again and still wondering if he will be allowed outside for fresh air before the day is over. A guard raps on the door hard with his baton, peers in through the slot, and announces that Orlov has a visitor. He marches Orlov past countless cells and into a cold room with whitewashed walls and several gnarled wooden tables, carved with the names of former prisoners. Orlov complies with the instructions to sit at a table and wait. Three other prisoners wait at other tables. Eventually, another door opens and a guard ushers in a gaggle of visitors who spread out to greet prisoners. In the middle of the room stands a thin, angular fellow with a formal suit that hangs off him on account of being too large. He waits until all the other prisoners are spoken for, then smiles weakly at Orlov and approaches his table.

The man extends his hand. "Citizen Uzelac, criminal defender," he says.

Orlov stands and shakes his hand. "Citizen Orlov, fishmonger." They sit. Uzelac opens a small notebook and turns to a blank page before taking an ink pen from his briefcase and writing the date at the top of the page. He writes the name Orlov next to the date. Then he smooths the page to ensure the book stays open at the right place.

"I understand you were charged yesterday and brought directly to Zhotrykaw." Uzelac speaks in an uninterested tone, as though reciting a shopping list, while holding his ink pen just above the page, ready to write down whatever Orlov says next.

"Yes," says Orlov.

Uzelac writes in his notebook. "And have you been mistreated in any way since you arrived in Zhotrykaw?"

"I've been imprisoned for saving the king's life. Isn't that mistreatment?" says Orlov.

Uzelac appears agitated by this and waves his hand. "We'll come to your defense in due course," he says. "Do you have any significant assets, such that you could fund your own lawyer?"

"No," says Orlov.

Uzelac writes in his notebook again, before looking up and smiling at Orlov for the first time. It is the oleaginous smile of the traveling salesman. "Very well. Once again, I am Citizen Uzelac, a very experienced criminal lawyer, and it will be my job to keep you away from the gallows and ensure these very serious charges result only in a life sentence here at Zhotrykaw."

Orlov stands up but sits down again quickly when one of the guards moves toward him. He hisses at Uzelac. "Are you making a joke, citizen?"

"I never make jokes," says Uzelac, with an expression so grave that Orlov can believe this to be true.

"I was tricked," says Orlov, still agitated. "Luckily, I realized before it was too late and took the only action available to me in order to save the life of the king."

"You saved the king's life by detonating a bomb, citizen?" asks Uzelac.

"Do you want to hear what happened or not?" says Orlov.

Uzelac leans back in his chair. "They always want to tell you a story," he says, apparently to himself.

Orlov leans across the table. "Citizen, please. Something serious is going on in the Ministry of . . ." he pauses, "one of the top ministries in the government. A plot against the king. And I stopped it. They should give me a medal, but instead I'm in here. So, you're going to get me out of here or find someone else who will."

Uzelac gathers himself, apparently offended. "So, now you have the money to fund your own lawyer?"

"No," says Orlov. "But you can listen to my story, or I'll fire you and defend myself."

Uzelac laughs. "Citizen, if you attempt to defend yourself in a court of law against charges as serious as these, I guarantee you will swing from a rope."

Orlov is exasperated. "Will you at least have the courtesy to hear my story?"

Uzelac exhales and consults his pocket watch. "Make it quick," he says.

Orlov explains the telephone call from Petrovich, the message for Kosek, the task from Molnar, the threats from Zelle, her admission about being a zealot and her intention to shoot the king, the protest by the People's Front, the late appearance of Kosek, apparently also a zealot, Orlov's realization of the mix-up between boarding houses and his decision, just a minute before the arrival of the king, to push the lever. When he has finished, he sits back in his chair and waits for the lawyer's reaction.

Uzelac checks around the room and leans into the table. "A very compelling story, citizen," he whispers, "but I cannot utter a word of it in the courtroom."

Orlov's left arm begins to throb again. "It's the truth."

"Even if every word of it were true, which I doubt," says Uzelac with his salesman's smile, "these are matters of national security."

Orlov is flummoxed. "Of course they are. Zelle was about to shoot the monarch. And I stopped her."

"Yes, yes," says Uzelac. "Let's take this Agent Zelle, for instance. If indeed the government has an agent of that name working, let's say, at the Ministry of Security, her name cannot be mentioned in court because her role is secret, but the courtroom is a public place. There are reporters from the newspapers, members of the public, and so on. Most judges will simply not permit evidence of that kind."

"But that's my defense," says Orlov.

Uzelac shakes his head in the condescending manner of a disappointed parent. "This is what you need to understand, citizen," he says. "It is *my* job to make the case for the defense, not yours. Your job is to wear your best suit and sit quietly in the dock."

Orlov exhales and sits back in his chair. "Very well. Let us hear my defense, according to the great Citizen Uzelac."

"Well, this is my current plan," says Uzelac, turning the page back to consult previous notes. "You had only recently become a member of the dangerous militant group, the People's Front . . ."

Orlov interrupts him. "The People's Front is a political party, nothing else. And I have never been a member of it."

Uzelac looks puzzled and consults his notes again. "Do you deny, citizen, that you work for a prominent member of the People's Front, that you stayed in the same hotel as they did in Kufzig, namely the

Pension Residenz, and that you were seen fraternizing with members of the group moments before the arrival of the king?"

"It was the Penzion Rezidence," says Orlov, wearily.

Uzelac consults his notes. "According to the police, it was the Pension Residenz."

"Never mind," says Orlov.

"Very well," says Uzelac. "If I may continue with the case for the defense. You had only recently become a member of the dangerous militant group, the People's Front, and you attended the event in Kufzig believing that it would be a simple protest, waving banners, shouting obscenities at the monarch, and so on." Orlov buries his face in his hands, but Uzelac continues, undeterred. "However, when you arrived at the pension, you discovered the other members of the Front had planned for the king's visit to be your induction ceremony. Hence, you were chosen to be the one who would detonate the bomb. No, I have it," he says, and makes an amendment to his notes. "That's better. You were threatened at gunpoint by the leader of the Front, one Citizen Vanev, and told that you would be shot if you did not detonate the bomb." He looks up from his notes, apparently pleased with himself. "The beauty of this, you see, is that the other members of the People's Front will certainly hang for conspiring against the monarch, but I believe a judge will sympathize with you, if we present you as the poor, new member, threatened at gunpoint by the wicked, violent leader. Makes a good story."

Every conversation in the visiting room is brought to an abrupt halt by the shrill ringing of a bell on the wall.

"Time's up," says Uzelac, smiling. He stands up and returns his notebook to his briefcase. "See you in court."

CHAPTER THIRTEEN

In which our hero takes a stand

In the darkest early hours of the next morning, Orlov is woken by a ferocious rapping on the door.

A guard peers in through the slot and shouts, "Wake up. Transfer. One minute."

Orlov leaves his bed too quickly and the room spins. He puts his head under frigid water from the tap and presents himself for inspection at the door. The guard, saying nothing, leads him at speed through the labyrinthine corridors and into the checking-in room. Someone produces Orlov's suit and shoes at the desk, and the guard orders him to put them on.

"Where am I going?" asks Orlov as he changes.

"I don't answer questions," says the guard. "I just put you in the truck."

Once Orlov has changed, the guard handcuffs him and marches him outside, where they are hit by a blast of cold night air. A prison vehicle is waiting, much like the police truck in which Orlov arrived, a cage on wheels. Orlov sits on a bench and hangs on to the cage. As on his arrival at Zhotrykaw, he is the only prisoner in the truck. In the cabin are a driver and a guard, neither of whom speaks to him. Once they have driven for perhaps half an hour, it is clear they are heading for the capital. After about an hour, they trundle into the familiar government sector, through which Orlov takes his daily constitutional, whenever he is not in custody. The city is still dark and deserted. They pass the High Court building and then circle around to a rear entrance, where the guard marches him to a reception desk and then down into the basement. The guard removes Orlov's handcuffs and hands him over to a court security officer, passing him a small bag containing Orlov's pocketbook and watch. The officer marches Orlov into a cell. Although a dank basement, the conditions here are a welcome relief compared to Zhotrykaw—a half dozen barred holding cells, only one of which is already occupied. Orlov takes a seat on the bench. Although desperately in need of more sleep, he sits and makes a plan. He cannot trust Uzelac, and he does not ever want to see the inside of Zhotrykaw again. If his plan fails, he might spend the rest of his life there. He would prefer to be dead.

Over the next hours, the other holding cells fill up with newly arrived prisoners, and the basement takes on the buzz of activity. At one point, the prisoner in the adjacent cell attempts to engage him in conversation.

"Be quiet," says Orlov, without looking at the man. "I'm thinking."

Citizen Uzelac arrives, apparently late and flustered, and stops outside Orlov's cell.

"Let me take a look at you," he says, as though inspecting his daughter's wedding dress. Orlov stands up. "Well, that will have to be sufficient," says Uzelac.

"What is going to happen today?" asks Orlov.

"Don't worry," says Uzelac. "Just sit in the dock and leave the talking to me." He beckons Orlov to step near to the bars and straightens Orlov's tie while talking. "If the judge addresses you directly, refer to him as Your Honor and answer his question politely. Is that clear?"

"Very clear," says Orlov.

Uzelac leaves and eventually two court security officers arrive to escort Orlov. They lead him up a steep staircase, stopping on the top step to remove his handcuffs, and then open a heavy wooden door. They are standing underneath the dock, and Orlov takes several more steps up into an ornate wooden box that looks out across the courtroom.

Orlov gasps and staggers forward to grab the wooden barrier to prevent himself from falling over with the shock of what he sees in front of him. The courtroom is packed to the rafters with people in their best suits and hats. There are gasps and frantic whisperings throughout the public section.

Someone at the back of the room shouts, "Traitor." The judge bangs his gavel and calls for order. On the balcony, journalists strain for a better view of the accused, scribbling frantically into notebooks and talking among themselves.

Orlov is still trying to take in the scene when Uzelac approaches the dock.

"Don't worry," says Uzelac, apparently sensing Orlov's shock. "Remember, I'll do the talking."

Orlov senses sweat forming on his brow. He feels nauseated. He wishes he could return back down the stairs to the relative tranquility of the cell in the basement. "Why is half the city here?" he hisses.

If Uzelac's smile is intended to be reassuring, it fails. "Everyone wants to know who was plotting against the king," he says.

Orlov can barely contain his anger. He answers through gritted teeth. "I was the one who saved him."

Uzelac pats him on the arm. "Yes, yes, we'll come on to that in due course," he says and returns to his seat.

The judge bangs his gavel ferociously again, and the room slowly comes to order. "Citizens and journalists," he says, "today's hearing concerns grave matters relating to the personal safety of His Majesty, the King. I will not tolerate any disruption to the proceedings. Regular attendees at the court will note that we have additional security today. Anyone unable to remain calm will be ejected from the court forthwith."

Orlov looks to the back of the public section and sees a line of palace guardsmen. The bright red insignia on their uniforms tells him these are the personal guardsmen of the Crown Prince. Why does the Crown Prince's own company need to guard the High Court?

Perhaps he is taking a personal interest in the case.

The room is finally silent, and the judge continues. "The Crown will state the charges."

A lawyer in cloak and wig approaches a lectern and shuffles his papers. He looks up briefly to acknowledge the judge and then begins to read in a pompous bellow. "Your Honor, the charges we present today relate to the first of nine defendants who, the Crown will demonstrate, plotted to assassinate His Majesty, the King. In common with the other eight defendants, this defendant, one Citizen Orlov, is an active member of the terrorist group known as the People's Front."

"No, I'm not," says Orlov, too loudly, from the dock.

The judge slams down his gavel so hard that Orlov thinks it might break. "Order," he says.

The lawyer continues. "In that regard, he is charged with conspiracy to assassinate the monarch, one of the gravest crimes in our penal code, the penalty for which is death. In addition, defendant Orlov is charged with the murder of one Citizen Kosek, and for that reason he is presented to the court before the remaining eight defendants. Citizen Kosek was a long-serving, well-respected, and senior civil servant who, until his untimely death, was employed by the Ministry of Works."

"No, he wasn't," says Orlov. The comment is directed at Citizen Uzelac, but it rings across the courtroom.

The judge slams his gavel again. "Citizen Uzelac. I strongly recommend you bring your client to order, unless you want him to be found in contempt of this court."

Uzelac stands. "My apologies, Your Honor. If I may have a moment with my client."

The judge waves his hand, and Uzelac approaches the dock.

Orlov speaks first, in an agitated whisper. "It's a lie. Kosek was not at the Ministry of Works. He was an agent."

"Citizen, please," says Uzelac. "That may or may not be true, but it is not yet my turn to speak. The Crown is speaking, and we must listen, whether we like it or not."

Orlov begins to say, "You must expose their lies," but Uzelac is already returning to his place.

The other lawyer continues. "The Crown is in possession of significant and compelling evidence to demonstrate that this defendant, Citizen Orlov, was not only an active member of the group planning this despicable crime, but that his was the hand that detonated the bomb that killed Citizen Kosek, but which was intended for His Majesty, just seconds later."

Orlov expects that to be the end of the opening speech, but instead the lawyer launches into a long monologue regarding the duties of the monarch and the importance of his personal safety as he travels the country. Orlov's attention wanders, and he scans the courtroom, watching the expressions on the faces of the public and journalists.

His gaze rests on a woman in the far corner of the public section, about as far from Orlov's position in the dock as it is possible to be. She wears a dark headscarf and large spectacles, a young woman attempting to appear older. It is too far for Orlov to see her face clearly, but he wonders if this might possibly be Agent Zelle, enjoying his fate. He watches her for a long time, trying to catch her eye, but she is resolutely focused on the lawyer's speech.

Orlov's focus on the woman in the corner is broken only when Uzelac, now standing, hisses at him in a stage whisper.

"Citizen," says Uzelac, "pay attention."

Orlov looks around to find that the judge is addressing him. "Citizen Orlov," says the judge, "you must stand, please." Orlov stands, straightens his tie, and the judge continues. "I have two questions for you before I invite Citizen Uzelac to address the court."

"Yes," says Orlov, unsteadily. He coughs and tries again. "Yes, Your Honor."

"Firstly," says the judge, "please state your name loudly and clearly so that the whole court can hear you."

"Citizen Orlov," says Orlov.

The judge continues. "Secondly, please confirm that you intend to be represented in this hearing and any subsequent trial by Citizen Uzelac, who is standing to your right. A simple *yes* will suffice."

Orlov looks at the judge, then at Uzelac, then at the woman in the headscarf. Slowly he returns his gaze to the judge, saying nothing.

"This is not intended to be a difficult question," says the judge. "I need to know that you plan to be represented by Citizen Uzelac."

Orlov says, "May I represent myself?"

Murmuring ripples across the court. The judge bangs his gavel and says, "Citizen Uzelac will approach the bench, please."

The judge and Uzelac have a short, whispered conversation that no one else can hear, then Uzelac walks over to the dock, his face red with rage.

"Citizen," says Uzelac. "This is a life and death matter. Do not send yourself to the gallows."

"Please move out of my way," says Orlov. "I need to speak to the judge." Uzelac steps back slightly, but does not return to his place. Orlov continues, now addressing the judge. "If it is permitted for me to speak for myself, Your Honor, then that is my choice. I do not intend to be represented by Citizen Uzelac."

Uzelac begins to march back to the bench, but the judge waves him away. "Very well. That is the end of the matter. Citizen Orlov will represent himself." Uzelac returns to his seat and slumps onto his desk, head in hands. The judge continues. "Citizen Orlov, how do you plead to the first charge, conspiracy to assassinate His Majesty, the King?"

"Not guilty, Your Honor," says Orlov, as loudly and clearly as he can muster.

The judge continues. "And how do you plead on the second charge, the murder of one Citizen Kosek?"

"Not guilty, Your Honor," says Orlov, again.

"Now," says the judge, "you are permitted to make a brief statement to the court to explain your plea. This is intended, in the case of a not guilty plea, to give me an indication of the nature of the defense case. I strongly recommend you reconsider your decision to dismiss your lawyer, but whatever your decision, I invite one of you to speak briefly now."

There is a murmur of anticipation around the courtroom. Orlov says, "I hope never to see Citizen Uzelac again, Your Honor." Uzelac shakes his head and begins to pack his briefcase. Orlov continues. "Your Honor, please forgive my language, but the statement by the gentleman over here . . ." He points at the other lawyer.

"Counsel for the Crown," says the judge.

"Thank you," says Orlov. "The statement by Counsel for the Crown was a pack of lies."

The courtroom explodes into gasps and comments and laughter. The judge brings down his gavel with force and calls, "Order. The defendant will be heard. Citizen, please modify your language."

"Yes, Your Honor," says Orlov. "My apologies. May I explain?"

"Briefly," says the judge.

"Well," says Orlov, "I am not a member of the People's Front. Just ask them; I am sure they will confirm it. Also, I don't see how anyone could call them terrorists. They're just a band of socialists who spend all their time singing awful songs and cannot be excused to use the water closet without voting on it." A titter of laughter emanates from the journalists on the balcony. Now Orlov is beginning to warm to his theme, and the room is hanging on his every word. "Citizen Crown over here was right about one thing: it was my hand that detonated the bomb, but it was never intended for the king. You see, Your Honor, here's the truth. I was tricked. I was taken for a fool and used, not by the People's Front. I was used by agents from the Ministry . . ." he changes tack. "By government agents who were pretending to protect the king while actually planning to assassinate him."

The public section breaks out into gasps and comments. People are shouting. Some people stand up and hurl insults at Orlov. The judge gavels them back into silence. "Citizens," he says, "I remind you that this is my courtroom, and I will decide who speaks and who is silent." Now he turns to speak to Orlov. "Bring your remarks to a conclusion, please."

Orlov continues. "Citizen Kosek was one of the agents plotting to assassinate the king. The bomb was intended to frame the People's Front. I detonated it before the king's arrival in order to foil the plan and save the king's life. It is unfortunate that Agent Kosek was standing next to the bomb when it detonated, but the plot against the king was his, not mine." Orlov pauses and casts his gaze slowly across the room. "The other agent who was working with Kosek on this terrible plot is sitting in this room right now."

This time, the room is out of control. People stand and stare around the room, looking for Kosek's accomplice. Others hurl more insults at Orlov, refusing to believe his story. The judge waves at the palace guard, who remove some of the more disruptive members of the public. Once calm has been restored, the judge addresses the public section again.

"Citizens, may I remind you that your presence here is optional," he says. "If you do not care for the defendant's comments, you may leave." He turns back to Orlov. "Citizen, my patience is wearing thin. Your conclusion, please."

As the judge is speaking, Orlov sees the woman in the headscarf slip out through the rear door. There is an ongoing murmur around the room, but it seems the judge has lost the will to contain it.

"Your Honor," says Orlov, over the noise, "when the time comes for my trial, I will explain exactly what happened and what I was told to do by agents working for the government. I will be pleased to give you the names of those agents. And when the members of the People's Front are on trial, I will gladly come back here—eight times, if necessary—to explain it all again."

Orlov sits down. The courtroom is in disarray. The journalists in the balcony stand and talk to each other. Some of them call across to Orlov, attempting to ask him questions, but he ignores them. The judge, now apparently beyond caring about the disruption, slams his gavel again and again.

"The court is adjourned," he says, still gaveling. "Adjourned. Adjourned."

CHAPTER FOURTEEN

In which our hero makes a new start

After a night of fitful sleep on an unforgiving hard bench with nothing more than a thin blanket, Citizen Orlov wakes very early. He lies for a while and thinks about his strange nightmare: his first appearance in court in his new job as a criminal lawyer took a strange turn when the presiding judge turned out to be Citizen Petrovich and the defendant was the rotting corpse of Agent Kosek. He needs to stop thinking about court proceedings for a while, until his trial starts. He swivels slowly to a sitting position and plants his feet firmly on the cold cell floor.

He is momentarily disoriented before remembering that he is no longer in Zhotrykaw but has spent the night in a holding cell in the basement of the High Court. Since there are no uniforms here, he has slept in his shirt and trousers, now badly crumpled. His jacket and tie hang from a hook on the cell door.

One of the frustrating things about being a prisoner is that no one ever tells you anything. You are moved from pillar to post like a piece of baggage without so much as a simple explanation as to what

Jonathan Payne

will happen next. Orlov is hungry and thirsty, but has no idea where his next meal is coming from, nor indeed if he will be moved back to Zhotrykaw today, or to somewhere else. Perhaps there will be more court proceedings. Perhaps a more experienced prisoner will at least know what time breakfast arrives. He stands up and peers along the line of cells.

The only light in the basement emanates from a narrow staircase leading up to the reception area. It is difficult to be certain, but it appears he is the only prisoner lucky enough to have spent the night here. He sees no one to ask about breakfast. He must wait for a guard to appear, at which point he will ask for permission to visit the water closet, since there are no bedpans.

Orlov sits on his bench for a while, waiting for a guard and wondering what the criminal justice system has in store for him next. He decides to get dressed in his jacket and tie so that he is ready to walk to the water closet as soon as the guard arrives. While putting on his jacket, he is surprised to feel something in the pockets: his pocketbook and watch—which he thought were in storage upstairs—have been returned. His watch tells him it is almost six o'clock. He checks his pocketbook and finds that everything is intact, even the index card with the message from Petrovich to Kosek.

We could not—repeat not—install it in room six.
You need to get room seven. It's hidden above the wardrobe.
Push the lever up, not down.

Orlov straightens his jacket and reaches for his tie. As he does so, the cell door swings open, just a little. Orlov steps back and looks up and down the line of cells to see if anyone is there to witness this, but he is still the only person in the basement. Perhaps overnight prisoners at the court are entitled to leave their cells to use the water closet. He puts on his tie and walks along the corridor, where he

· 96 ·

finds a cramped gentlemen's lavatory. He washes his face in the sink and straightens what remains of his hair.

Since he is now out of his cell, it will do no harm if he finds a guard and asks about breakfast. If he is not supposed to wander about the basement, they should have locked him in. He walks along the corridor to the foot of the stairs, where he finds a small guard station. The desk and chair are unoccupied.

If a guard is anywhere, he will be upstairs at the reception area, so Orlov walks up tentatively, concerned that at any moment an angry guard will scold him for wandering and order him back to his cell.

Up on the ground floor, it is also dark. The wall lamps are unlit; the only light is a wan, silvery glow from the window that overlooks the rear entrance. The ground floor smells of wood, which reminds him of the courtroom. The reception desk is deserted. Orlov wanders along the corridor, but finds only offices. When he reaches the door to the courtroom, he walks back along the corridor to the reception desk. There is no one here.

The only option remaining is to try the rear entrance. It is unlocked. The heavy wooden door swings suddenly, allowing in a sharp blast of frigid morning air.

Orlov looks around to check that he has not been seen and slips outside. He expects to find a guard outside, perhaps taking a cigarette break, but sees no one. He walks briskly to the ornate iron gate onto the street, fully expecting it be locked. It is unlocked, and with a hard push, the gate swings open and Orlov is standing in a puddle on the cobbled street.

Orlov is bemused. For a moment he thinks it might be best to ask his lawyer for advice on what is going on, but then he remembers that he dismissed Uzelac in front of the whole courtroom. For now, he will walk home and get some rest. If the authorities want to contact him, no doubt they know where he lives.

The route to his apartment takes Orlov past the Grand Plaza, just at the time the market is setting up for the day. After the few days he has had, it is a welcome relief to see the familiar sight of his fellow market traders setting out their wares, brushing puddles away from the cobbles, and huddling together over cigarettes. Consulting his pocket watch, he notes it is almost time for Citizen Vodnik to arrive with the daily fish delivery.

Since Vanev is in Zhotrykaw, it is down to Orlov to ensure the stall opens up again. He abandons the idea of going home, ducks into the storeroom for his apron, borrows a cigarette from the greengrocer, and begins to fill the display boxes with ice. Once the stall is ready for the delivery, Orlov pauses and looks out across the plaza, the grand government buildings behind it and, beyond them, the forbidding mountains.

On many a morning he has stood here cursing his bad luck at having to work outside in cold weather but, after two nights in Zhotrykaw and another in the basement of the High Court, it is a pleasure to stand here and breathe in the fresh air.

Orlov has brisk business all morning, and several regular customers want to know why the stall has been closed all week. Orlov has no idea whether he has been named in the newspapers; if so, his regular customers appear not to have noticed.

"Citizen Vanev and I had some urgent business to attend to, in the South," he explains.

Several customers express gratitude that the stall is open again, and one wants to know when Citizen Vanev will return.

"I'm afraid I don't know," says Orlov. "Unfortunately, he may have to be away for some time."

By lunchtime, the flow of customers slows to a trickle, and Orlov sits on a packing crate for a cigarette break. He is about to return to work when he sees a familiar figure lumbering across the plaza. He stays seated and waits, to ensure his eyes are not deceiving him. By the time the figure advances to the middle of the plaza, it is clear this is Citizen Vanev, dressed in the crumpled suit in which he was arrested.

He looks even more disheveled and unshaven than usual. Orlov stands up to greet him.

"Citizen," says Orlov, "what a pleasant surprise."

Vanev stops for a moment to appreciate the normality of the scene—the two fishmongers at their market stall, much like any other working day in all respects aside from their formal attire.

"A surprise to me, too," says Vanev.

"What happened?" asks Orlov.

"I don't know," says Vanev. "This morning I woke up in Zhotrykaw. They drove us here."

"And the others?" asks Orlov.

"The same," says Vanev. "What about you?"

"Yesterday I was in court. This morning, the cell door was unlocked," says Orlov. "Did you receive any explanation?"

"No," says Vanev, "although the guards in the prison truck were talking between themselves. They were unhappy about our release. Apparently, so were the police. One guard kept saying they were 'overruled by the ministry.'"

Orlov considers this. "Perhaps the ministry preferred me not to appear in court again."

Vanev fetches his apron and borrows a cigarette from the greengrocer. "What did you say?" he asks as he lights the cigarette.

"Just the truth," says Orlov.

"I imagine they weren't expecting that," says Vanev.

Toward the middle of the afternoon, the clouds break up a little, and thin shafts of sunlight reflect in the puddles. Some of the traders begin to pack up their stalls for the day. Vanev is about to retreat into the storeroom to do the same, when Orlov spots someone approaching across the plaza.

"It seems we have a late customer," he says to Vanev. "Stay with me out here for just a few minutes. Strength in numbers. I'll do the talking."

Vanev is bemused. "As you wish," he says. "Is everything all right?"

"To be honest, I'm not sure," says Orlov. "Just stand there and look menacing."

The two fishmongers stand behind the stall, side by side, and watch as a woman walks slowly toward them. Her head is almost entirely obscured by a dark headscarf and large spectacles. It is clear to Orlov that this is the woman who sat in the corner of the courtroom for most of the proceedings yesterday. He is unsure of her identity until the moment she arrives at the stall and removes her glasses in order to inspect the fish.

It is Agent Zelle.

"Good afternoon, citizens," says Zelle.

"Good afternoon," says Orlov.

"It seems the weather is improving today," says Zelle.

"Yes," says Orlov. "I was just saying to my colleague here—Citizen Vanev of the People's Front—that today is probably the best we've had in almost a week."

"I dare say that is the case," says Zelle, looking at Vanev, who must be twice her size and twice her weight. Vanev smiles at her politely but says nothing.

"May we assist you with anything, citizen?" asks Orlov.

"Yes, please," says Zelle, "I'm looking for a haddock."

Orlov feels the injuries to his head and left arm begin to complain, as though aggravated by Zelle's proximity. He attempts to ignore the pain and focuses on maintaining a calm demeanor. "In that case, you are in the right place. We have two large haddocks remaining. Take your pick."

Zelle chooses a haddock and Vanev wraps it.

"Since it's the end of the day, let's call it half a crown," says Orlov.

"You are most kind," says Zelle.

Orlov holds his breath as Zelle reaches into her handbag, and exhales again when she produces only a half crown and hands it to him. Zelle takes the wrapped fish from Vanev.

It appears she is about to leave, but instead she turns back to Orlov.

"In exchange for your generosity," she says, "perhaps I may offer a little advice."

Orlov attempts to smile, but his headache is now sharp behind his eyes. "Of course," he says.

Zelle continues. "Sometimes, when one holds secrets—secrets that may threaten the safety of others, for example—one will find that life is better for everyone if those secrets remain hidden. Would you not agree, citizen?"

Orlov considers this for a moment. "I dare say you are right about that," he says. He glances at Vanev and back to Zelle. "Perhaps you will also agree with me that those who are exercising their lawful rights—to express their political opinions, for example—should be left alone to do so in peace."

Zelle glances at Vanev, returns her gaze to Orlov, and speaks slowly. "I believe we agree on both those points. In fact, perhaps one could say that the one is dependent on the other."

She smiles, and for a moment Orlov remembers how beautiful she was onstage at the Bierkeller in Kufzig. He smiles back. "I believe one could say that, indeed."

For a second, Zelle's composure cracks slightly, and Orlov believes he can detect the beginnings of a tear in the corner of her eye. "Unfortunately, I lost a colleague recently," she says. "So, if you know of anyone who might be interested, I'm looking for a new recruit."

Orlov ponders this for a moment, unsure if it amounts to the offer of a position at the ministry. He is about to ask her to specify which ministry she works for, but thinks better of it. "I find that I am better suited to the simple lifestyle of the fishmonger," he says.

"I understand, citizen," says Zelle. "Please contact me if you change your mind."

She spins on her heels and walks away slowly across the plaza with the haddock under her arm. The two fishmongers watch in silence as she navigates the puddles among the cobbles before leaving the plaza and crossing the bridge into the government sector.

"Was that who I think it was?" says Citizen Vanev.

"Indeed, it was," says Citizen Orlov.

PART THREE

An Account

of the

Government's Novel Attempt

to Fight Terrorism

CHAPTER FIFTEEN

In which our hero receives an unexpected proposition

I t is exactly one month after Citizen Orlov's release from the cells under the High Court when he next sees Agent Zelle. It is also the first time since his release that he has managed the fish stall on his own, Citizen Vanev having been called away on pressing business regarding the People's Front. The worst of winter has given way to slightly longer days and the promise that spring is not too far away. In the middle of the morning, in a short gap between customers, Orlov enjoys a cigarette with the warmth of the sun on his face, looking out across the government sector to the glistening, snowcapped peaks beyond. The injury to his arm has finally begun to heal, and all seems right with the world once again. In fact, he is right in the middle of saying to himself that the simple life of the fishmonger is far preferable to the confused and violent world of a government agent, when he spots a familiar figure approaching across the plaza: a woman in a dark headscarf.

Orlov stubs out his cigarette on the cobbles and stands up straight behind the stall, moving one of the long, curved gutting knives closer to his right hand, but ensuring it is hidden from view behind a display box full of carp. He straightens his apron and, although feeling an unwelcome heat at the back of his neck, attempts a cordial smile as the woman arrives and removes her sunglasses.

"Good afternoon, citizen," says Orlov. "What a pleasant surprise."

"I imagine it must be," says Zelle softly, casting her gaze across the varieties of fish.

"May I assist you with anything today?" asks Orlov. "Haddock, perhaps. Or carp."

Zelle lifts her gaze up from the fish to Orlov. "No fish today," she says. "We need to talk."

Orlov catches movement in his peripheral vision and is relieved to see one of his regular customers, Madam Kristof, approaching. He nods slightly in her direction before replying to Zelle. "I'm afraid I'm a little busy at the moment."

Zelle glances at the approaching Madam Kristof and back at Orlov. "I'll wait."

Orlov serves Madam Kristof as slowly as possible, all the while keeping one eye on Zelle, who hovers conspicuously at the corner of the stall, pretending to inspect the fare with an unlikely intensity. He spots an elderly couple approaching and proceeds to wrap Madam Kristof's fish twice, to ensure the couple arrive before he has finished. Madam Kristof watches on, bemused, before going on her way.

Ignoring Zelle, Orlov turns to the newly arrived customers and greets them with exaggerated enthusiasm. "Good morning, citizen, madam," he says, clapping his hands together for warmth. "What a fine day it is. Please let me know how I may be of service to you today." They begin to examine Orlov's wares slowly. Zelle hisses at him to pay attention to her.

"Citizen," she says, beckoning him to come closer so that he can speak without being heard by his customers. "I do not have time for this. Meet me this evening, six o'clock, on the steps of the Palace."

Orlov turns his back to the elderly couple before replying in a whisper. "The last time I accepted such an invitation from you, someone shot me in the arm."

Zelle grimaces at him, as though agitated that he should raise such matters within earshot of others. "At six o'clock it will still be light and there will be plenty of people present to ensure your safety. But you must come alone." Before Orlov has time to answer, she turns on her heels and disappears across the plaza.

Orlov spends the whole afternoon wondering whether he should meet Zelle. He has no reason to trust her and every reason to consider her dangerous. On the other hand, they arrived at a truce of sorts, in which his bargaining chip is still intact: he knows about her zealot tendencies and her attempt to twist an official government operation for her own political ends. Between afternoon customers, he takes cigarette breaks while sitting on a barrel and wondering why Zelle has reappeared. Perhaps she is nervous about someone who knows so much remaining at large to tell the story whenever it takes his fancy.

Off the top of his head, he can think of two ways in which she might choose to resolve that concern: recruiting him to work for her, or getting him out of the way. On balance, providing that they remain in a safe, public place at all times, he decides it is better to hear what Zelle has to say rather than have her turning up uninvited at the market again. What's more, if he is honest with himself, he still finds Zelle very alluring and not a little mysterious.

By six o'clock, it is still a bright day, but the temperature is dropping sharply, and Orlov is concerned to see only a few people milling around the Palace. It is a grand, ornate structure surrounded by shaded cloisters, beneath which the wide stone steps sweep down to announce the beginning of the government sector. Orlov walks to the top of the steps in order to get a good view around him and waits for a few minutes, wrapping his arms around himself for warmth.

Still wrapped in a headscarf, Zelle appears from the direction of the government sector and joins him at the top of the steps.

"I always prefer it when our meetings don't begin with you shooting me," says Orlov.

Zelle ignores this remark. "Let's go for a walk," she says.

Orlov looks down the steps at a few passersby and looks around to check there are still some tourists wandering around the Palace. "I prefer to talk here," he says.

Zelle makes her own checks, apparently deciding if the tourists are far enough away to allow her to speak freely. "Very well. I'll explain quickly," she says. "Things are changing. Even in the month since your release, things have changed. Your friends in the People's Front. They are growing and becoming more organized. There is real concern at the ministry."

Orlov briefly considers asking Zelle to clarify which ministry she works for but decides this is not the time. "That has nothing to do with me," he says, attempting to be firm.

"Do you know where your colleague Citizen Vanev is right now?" asks Zelle.

"I do not."

"I'll tell you," says Zelle. "He and his comrades are in a secret meeting with representatives from the Workers' Party. Do you know what that means?"

"I have no idea," says Orlov.

Zelle pauses to allow some tourists to pass them while descending the steps. "It means a network of radicals is actively plotting against the monarchy."

"Which you would never do," says Orlov, a little more aggressively than intended.

"I'm speaking on behalf of the ministry," says Zelle. "My personal views are not relevant."

"What does this have to do with me?" asks Orlov.

"We have a task for you," says Zelle. "Assuming that you wish to remain in good standing with the government."

Orlov is unsure what to make of this and studies her face for clues. "I believe we have already arrived at a settlement acceptable to both sides."

"We had, indeed," says Zelle, "but—as I said—things are changing, becoming more serious. And now we have no choice but to put our own person on the inside."

"On the inside?" says Orlov.

"Of the People's Front," says Zelle.

"A mole?" says Orlov.

"An informant," says Zelle. "A trusted asset who can become an active member of the group and pass relevant information to us, from time to time."

Orlov senses sweat beading under his collar. He wants time to think and so attempts to divert the conversation. "How does a foreigner such as yourself happen to be in such an important role regarding national security?"

Zelle waves a hand as if to swat the question like a fly. "I found myself in some trouble during the Great War. Both sides accused me of working for the other. I made a quick exit and here we are. That is not to the point. I need to recruit a loyal, patriotic citizen to pass information to me. Nothing more. Do you have what it takes, citizen?"

"I met some highly qualified young officers the day I went to the ministry," says Orlov. "I feel sure one of them would suffice."

Zelle shakes her head and pauses to let some tourists pass them down the steps. "We tried that already. Your People's Front friends are more capable than you think. They looked into him and refused to let him join. We need an outsider."

Orlov senses that he is being maneuvered into a corner and— although his head injury has healed—the headache he associates with Zelle stabs him behind the eyes. He exhales slowly to buy himself some thinking time. "It cannot be me," he says. "They don't trust me. I was the reason they were all incarcerated in Zhotrykaw."

"And you were the reason they were all released again," says Zelle. "I think you would find a warmer reception now, if you were to return. And you could not be more of an outsider, which is exactly what we need."

Orlov feels his palms sweating and wipes them on the sleeves of his overcoat. It is clear to him that he must bring this conversation to an end before he agrees to something he will later regret. Zelle is a professional manipulator, after all. He is not going to win an argument with her. "I'm sorry," he says firmly. "I am not the right person to assist with your scheme." He begins to walk down the steps, but pauses and turns back to look at Zelle once he is a few steps below her. "I pledge not to mention this to Citizen Vanev, if you leave me alone."

Zelle says nothing until Orlov reaches the bottom step. Then she checks that no one is nearby before calling down to him, "How is your mother, citizen?"

Orlov stops, his headache suddenly ferocious. He spins, his mind racing, and looks up at her. "What did you say?"

Zelle smiles a wicked smile that Orlov has not seen since she invited him up to her room at the Pension Residenz in Kufzig, shortly before tying him up in the bath. "Your mother, citizen," repeats Zelle. "I trust she is well."

Several options run through Orlov's mind. Most likely, Zelle is simply plucking something personal out of the air to unnerve him. Has he ever even mentioned his mother to Zelle? He does not remember doing so.

On the other hand, this could be a real threat directed at his only living relative. Worse still, it could even be notice that something has already happened to her. No doubt the ministry would be more than capable of tracking his mother down, if it chose to do so. Orlov feels blood rush to his face. "Don't you dare," he says, rushing up a couple of steps, unsure what to say next.

"I hear she has a delightful cottage in Havlinik," says Zelle in a deadpan voice, as if to sound intentionally insincere. "What a beautiful part of the country that is. Were you lucky enough to grow up there, citizen?"

Orlov feels that his blood will boil. He fishes inside his overcoat to check his pocket watch, then turns away from Zelle without another word, rushing with all the speed he can muster toward the railway station.

CHAPTER SIXTEEN

In which our hero returns to his childhood home

I t is late in the evening and well past dark when Citizen Orlov steps onto the deserted platform at the tiny provincial railway station of Havlinik. A thick fog hangs over the town, as it so often does at this time of year, and Orlov sticks close to the flickering street lamps as he picks his way carefully down the station steps and along the cobbled street. It is a route he walked many times as a boy; no doubt he could find his way home in pitch darkness, if necessary, but he is not as young as he used to be, and the cobbles are slick underfoot.

Havlinik is a small town that seems to Orlov to have become suspended in time. Every time he returns—more often since the death of his father—he looks for changes, signs of modernity, but finds none. This evening, however, as he rushes past the lamplit Bierkeller on Havlinik Prospekt, his mind is racing with what might have happened to his mother. Could Zelle really be so cruel to use his elderly mother to force him into cooperating with the government's schemes?

Orlov is breathing heavily as he reaches Hugelgasse and turns up the steep hill toward his mother's humble cottage. Bursting through the wooden gate, he scans the front door for signs of a forced entry, but all appears normal. Instead of his usual polite knock at the door—which his mother prefers even though the house is never locked—he bursts into the dim hallway and scans around for anything untoward.

"Mother, it's me," calls Orlov, ducking into the kitchen, which is dark and deserted. "Hello?"

Hearing no response, he peers up the stairs, but sees no signs of life. Now sweating heavily, he picks his way toward the parlor, where the embers glowing in the hearth provide the only light.

"Mother?" says Orlov, again. He hears a muffled groan in response.

As Orlov's eyes adjust to the dark, he spots the frail figure of his mother slumped in the armchair by the fire. He rushes to her, kneels, and grasps both her shoulders.

"Mother, it's me," says Orlov.

His mother slowly stirs and opens her eyes. "Why is it dark in here?" she says.

"What happened?" asks Orlov.

"I must have fallen asleep," says Madam Orlov.

"Are you all right?"

"Just as right as usual."

Orlov stands and lights the lamp. "I was worried about you," he says.

Madam Orlov sits up straighter and rearranges her housecoat. "Would you like some tea?"

Now the parlor is filled with a warm light, and Orlov settles into the other fireside chair, opposite his mother. "Has anyone visited you recently?"

Madam Orlov considers this.

"Well, let me see. The farm boy was here. And Father Miklos drops in from time to time."

"I mean strangers. Have you had a visit from someone you don't know?"

His mother thinks again. "Oh, I was forgetting. Two lovely young men were here this morning. Or was it yesterday morning? Professional, they were. Lovely suits."

"Where were they from?"

"Would you like some tea?" asks Madam Orlov, half rising from her chair.

"In a moment," says Orlov. "First, I want to know who these two men were."

"Well, they were from the government, that much I know." Orlov stiffens in his chair and his mother continues, frowning as she struggles to remember. "And they didn't want any tea. I asked them more than once."

"They came inside the house?" asks Orlov.

"Oh, yes. The one who did all the talking—a very polite young man—he was sitting in that chair, where you are right now."

"And where was the other one?"

Madam Orlov hesitates. "I'm not sure. I think he was having a look around the house."

Orlov buries his face in his hand. "Mother, you need to be more careful. You must not let strangers into the house."

His mother's attention appears to be elsewhere. "I remember," she says. "They were from the Ministry of Welfare. Or perhaps it was Health. Do we have a Ministry of Welfare?"

"I have no idea," says Orlov.

"Well, whichever it was. The polite young man—the one who sat right there—he said they were checking in on older people, because of the unseasonably cold weather."

"It's precisely this cold every year," says Orlov.

"I'm just telling you what he said," says his mother.

"I'll make us some tea," says Orlov and slips out into the kitchen. While the tea kettle is on the stove, he checks the hallway, the front door, and the back door, looking for anything untoward, although he is unsure what he expects to find. Finding nothing unusual, he returns to the parlor with two china cups full of tea.

"Is it late?" asks Madam Orlov. "I should probably be in bed."

"Let's talk for a moment," says Orlov and settles back into his chair. "Please don't let any more strangers into the house. And lock your doors."

"The locks haven't worked for years."

"I will fix them before I leave," says Orlov, "but you must remember to lock them."

"Please don't do it now. It's late. If you start hammering now, the neighbors will complain about it for a month."

"Very well," says Orlov. "I'll do it in the morning. If I get up early, I might still be able to catch the first train."

Orlov spends a fitful, uncomfortable night in his boyhood bed. He lies awake for long periods, wondering whether Zelle has something specific in mind for his mother, or if the visit she received was simply a warning shot to frighten him into cooperating. He wonders if there is anyone—the police, for example—to whom he could report this harassment. But no harm has come to his mother, and he does not want to goad Zelle into moving to the next phase of her diabolical scheme, whatever that might entail. He determines, once he has secured the house, to warn Zelle to leave his mother alone. After all, he still has damning information about her, which to date he has shared with no one besides Vanev. If he can persuade his mother to avoid answering the door to strangers, that should be the end of the matter.

Orlov wakes very early, while his mother is still asleep, and ventures through the gloom to his father's garden shed, now unloved and untended for years. He searches around for a saw, a hammer and nails, and some lengths of wood that had once been intended as the legs of something his father never finished. Orlov returns into the house a couple of times to take measurements. By the time his mother appears downstairs to make tea, both the front door and back door are equipped with a sturdy, horizontal security bar that can be locked into place to prevent access from the outside.

"I've never needed locks all these years," says Madam Orlov.

"Make me a promise," says Orlov. "No more strangers in the house. And lock these bars in place every night before you go to bed."

His mother's expression is bemused but resigned. "I promise," she says.

CHAPTER SEVENTEEN

In which our hero demands an audience with the ministry

After an early train back to the capital, Orlov strides with purpose through a stiff drizzle into the government sector and soon stands at the foot of the sweeping steps leading up to the Ministries of Security, on his left, and Intelligence, on his right. Not for the first time, he wishes he knew more about the murky inner workings of the government, which would perhaps make this strange period in his life a little easier to navigate. He is, however, forced to rely on a mixture of instinct and guesswork. As grim government officials with overcoats and umbrellas march past him in a steady stream, Orlov takes a crown from his pocket and flicks it into the air. In the second during which the coin is aloft, he decides the words *One Crown* represent left, while the king's head means right. He looks down as he catches the coin, sees the king's head, and bears right up the steps and through the grand entrance, over which is carved in stone the words Ministry of Intelligence.

The elegant, wood-paneled entrance hall of the Ministry of Intelligence has the cool, calm air of a public library. In each corner is a statue of a well-dressed, serious man, none of whom Orlov recogniz-es. In the center of the concourse stand two identical security desks, each staffed by a man in an elaborate, maroon uniform. It occurs to Orlov that these uniforms might be more suitable for a carnival barker than for security guards at one of the great ministries of state, but then he is merely a fishmonger and not fully acquainted with such matters.

A queue of visitors has formed in front of each security desk, while dozens of ministry employees march between them toward an inner pair of wooden doors.

Orlov pauses for a moment to survey the scene. He joins the queue on the left, which is a little shorter. He watches carefully as the guard consults a huge ledger on the desk.

After a brief whispered conversation in each case—too quiet for Orlov to hear—the visitors are directed to continue through the in-ner doors.

When Orlov arrives at the front of the queue, he says, "Agent Zelle, please."

The stern, bespectacled guard eyes him skeptically. "What time is your appointment, sir?"

"I need to speak to Agent Zelle, urgently," says Orlov.

The guard removes his reading glasses slowly and waves them in the air. "This is the public area," he says. "We do not use the names of ministry personnel here."

"Then how can I tell you who I need to see?"

"You can tell me *your* name, sir, and the time of your appoint-ment."

"Citizen Orlov. No appointment," says Orlov. Since the guard makes no reply, he continues. "As a matter of urgency, I must speak to one of your agents," he leans in to whisper, "whose name begins with Z."

The guard waves toward the other security desk.

"Please present yourself at the other desk, citizen," he says, curtly, and looks up to catch the eye of the next visitor.

Orlov looks across and sees that the other queue is now even longer than before. "Why?" he says.

The guard's eye twitches uncontrollably for a second. He waits for it to stop before replying. "This desk is for those with appointments, citizen. The other desk is for those without appointments." He gestures again, this time more energetically, toward the other desk.

Orlov sighs and reluctantly joins the back of the other queue, now so long that it has almost reached the grand entrance. The queue progresses painfully slowly, and Orlov frequently strains to see what is happening at the desk. This guard is also serious and bespectacled and, like his colleague, engages visitors in whispered conversation before sending them on their way.

When his turn finally arrives, Orlov steps up to the desk. The guard is still peering down at his ledger.

Orlov attempts a professional demeanor. "Citizen Orlov. I have an urgent need to speak to"—he is about to use her name but thinks better of it—"one of your agents. A foreign lady. I'll say no more than that."

Without so much as looking up from his ledger, the guard holds out his hand. "Chit," he says, dismissively.

Orlov is unsure what to make of this. "I'm sorry?"

Now the guard looks up at him, his hand still open. "I will need to see your chit, please, citizen."

Orlov glances around him briefly, as though the definition of this word might be found hidden somewhere in the entrance hall. "I'm afraid I don't know what that is," he says.

The guard sighs. "Your chit." Orlov shrugs. The guard reaches under the desk and presents a curious, green ledger full of numbered tickets such as those that might be used for a coat check at a theater. "Like this," says the guard. "We have a system here. No exceptions."

Orlov holds out his hand. "Very well, citizen. Just give me one of those."

The guard frowns. "That is not the protocol, citizen," he says.

"So, what is the protocol, please?" says Orlov.

"Very simple," says the guard, gesturing toward the other desk. "Those with an appointment present themselves to my colleague. Those with a chit present themselves to me."

"And how does one acquire one of these green chits, according to the protocol?" asks Orlov.

The guard's expression darkens. "That, citizen, is a matter of national security."

Orlov runs both his hands through what remains of his hair. "I have an urgent need to speak to one of your agents, on a matter of national security."

"And yet you have no appointment and no chit," says the guard.

"Correct," says Orlov.

The guard gestures behind Orlov. "The exit is just there, citizen."

Saying nothing further, Orlov steps out into the gray drizzle, down the steps of the Ministry of Intelligence and up the steps of the Ministry of Security, where the entrance hall is a little less ornate and a little more secure. As soon as Orlov steps inside, before he has even had time to locate the security desk, a uniformed guard approaches him. This guard is young, tall, and built like a circus strongman.

"Good morning, sir," says the guard, towering over him. "Do you have an appointment?"

"I need to speak to Agent Zelle," says Orlov. "It's a matter of utmost urgency."

"And the time of your appointment is?"

"You don't understand," says Orlov.

"I understand that you need an appointment, sir," says the guard, wrapping his huge arm around Orlov's shoulders and directing him back into the street.

Orlov briefly considers trying to duck under the arm and making a run for the internal doors, but—given the size of the fellow—thinks better of it. "How can I get an appointment?" he asks.

The guard does not remove his arm until they are outside in the drizzle. "That is a matter for your contact at the ministry, not for me," he says, remaining in front of the door until Orlov is down the steps and back on the street.

Orlov needs a cigarette and, despite the rain, he settles himself onto an iron bench that stands in the no-man's-land beyond the Ministry of Security, before one arrives at the Ministry of Justice. He knows Vanev will be unhappy about his failure to appear at the market, and indeed he could still make it in time for the second half of the day. But he cannot allow the situation to rest until he has warned Zelle to leave his mother alone. He will have to explain to Vanev what is going on, by way of an apology, and that will also serve as a warning that the People's Front will need to be very careful for a while about any new arrivals asking to join their ranks, although Vanev is certainly astute enough to have worked this out already. The more immediate issue is that Orlov needs to work out a way to contact Zelle that does not involve waiting for her to appear at the market. He will track her down, make very clear that his mother must not be used as a pawn in her unscrupulous game, and then he will explain that—as a direct result of the unacceptable threat to his mother—he never wants to see or speak to Zelle again. Any failure on her part to live up to that and he will secure an appointment at the highest level in one of the ministries behind him, perhaps both, and explain every detail of her zealot plot against His Majesty. It might not be wise for him to mention this threat openly again now, for his own safety, but he knows this course of action remains open to him, and so does Zelle. That should be sufficient to focus her mind.

By the end of his first cigarette, the drizzle has stopped, and the sun makes a welcome but weak attempt to appear, casting pale shadows across the rain-slick pavement. Reluctant to go the market and explain this mess to Vanev just yet, Orlov lights another cigarette and, closing his eyes against the sunlight, tries to think of another way to contact Zelle. Hearing a noise to his left, he opens one eye to find that an old woman in a heavy overcoat and hat is clearing rainwater from the other end of the bench with a handkerchief. She works slowly and assiduously before sitting down with a sigh. Orlov closes his eye again and determines to finish his cigarette before moving. After all, the bench is more than long enough for two.

By now it is the middle of the morning and, although the government sector is relatively quiet, a steady flow of earnest civil servants still rushes along the pavement, their steely glares radiating the impression that significant matters of state are on their minds. Orlov stubs the remains of his second cigarette on the end of the iron bench and begins to stand up, when the old woman speaks to him.

"Leaving so soon, citizen?" she says. But it is not the voice of an old woman. It is the familiar, lilting, foreign voice of Agent Zelle.

Orlov sits back down and looks at her, amazed that he did not recognize who had been sitting next to him. "You?" is the only word he can muster.

Zelle continues. "I heard you want to speak to me."

Orlov's mind is filled with an image of his mother, sitting innocently in her armchair by the fire. Without thinking, he stands again and lurches toward Zelle, with no idea what he intends to do if he gets his hands on her. Zelle does not so much as wince; she simply watches him with a steely glare and holds up a hand to warn him against making contact.

"I suggest you do not come any closer, citizen," she says. "There might be people watching."

Orlov looks around but sees no one aside from pedestrians minding their own business. He backs away from Zelle but remains standing. "Yes, I want to speak to you."

"Well, here I am."

Orlov feels his neck and shoulders tightening. He takes a deep breath and tries to convince himself that his anger is better channeled into words rather than violence. He points threateningly at Zelle and imagines all his angst is being directed at her through his finger. But this causes him to talk too much and too fast. "I visited my mother last night. I know what you're doing. Whatever schemes you're cooking up with your zealot friends, they don't involve my mother. She is old and frail. She is also innocent. She has done nothing her whole life except raise a family and be loyal to her country. You could not find a more patriotic citizen than my mother. So, talk to me about your twisted schemes if you must, but leave my mother out of it." After he finishes speaking, Orlov continues to point directly at Zelle's face, so angry that he is shaking.

Zelle eyes him curiously, saying nothing for a while. She looks at his pointing finger, then returns her gaze to his face. When she speaks, it is slow and deliberate. "I hear you fitted some very sturdy new security devices behind the exterior doors of your mother's house. I'd say that's very resourceful of you, very resourceful indeed."

Orlov looks around in the street, as though the passersby might be able to explain how Zelle can possibly know this information. Finding no inspiration there, he turns back to her. "How do you know that?"

She speaks quietly and calmly. "It's my job to know. The security of our citizens is my utmost priority." She smiles.

Orlov feels as though his head will explode. He walks away into the gap between Security and Justice, forcing himself to take slow, deep breaths, before walking slowly back to Zelle, all the while running through options for what he will do next. He sighs heavily and tries to appeal to Zelle's sense of sympathy by speaking in a distraught, forlorn voice. "Look. Whatever else happens, my mother is not part of this. What do I have to do to make sure she is completely untouched and unharmed?"

Zelle smiles again. "An excellent question. I answered it yesterday. You must become a loyal, enthusiastic member of the People's Front, reporting to me their activities from time to time, via a system of communication I will be pleased to teach you."

Orlov sighs again and tries to smooth the stress out of his face with both his hands. "And you promise that my mother will be left alone?"

"You have my word, citizen," says Zelle, rising and offering her hand so they may shake on the deal.

Orlov recoils. "Please do not ask me to shake your hand, citizen," he says, gravely.

"No matter," says Zelle. "But do I have your agreement?"

Orlov turns in a circle, sighing heavily, before his gaze returns to Zelle's expectant face. "I cannot believe I'm about to say this," he says, "but yes. I will do it. Only for so long that my mother is safe and well. If anything happens to her—anything—you have lost my services forever."

Zelle nods to acknowledge their agreement and gestures that he should sit down again. Orlov exhales heavily to calm himself and then perches on the edge of the bench.

She checks that no one is nearby, then shuffles along the bench to be closer to Orlov before speaking again. "Do you know the butcher's shop on Grunplatz?"

"Of course," says Orlov.

Zelle continues with the clipped efficiency of a military officer issuing orders with supreme confidence that they will be obeyed. "Make sure Grunplatz is on your route to the market each morning. As you pass, check the curtain in the window above the shop. If it is open, I want to speak to you. If it closed, I do not."

"And where shall we speak?" asks Orlov.

"On any day when the curtain is open, go to the Grand Plaza at midnight. I will meet you there. I might be in disguise, for your protection. If you are not sure whether it is me, simply say, 'One used to be able to see the peak of Mount Zhotrykaw from here.' And I will reply, 'Yes, before they built the cathedral.'"

"One used to be able to see the peak of Mount Zhotrykaw from here," repeats Orlov.

"Excellent," says Zelle.

"What if I am the one who needs to speak to you?" asks Orlov.

"If you need to speak to me, leave the curtains in your apartment open when you leave in the morning. If not, leave them closed."

Orlov considers this. "So, you will be spying on my apartment building every morning?"

"Perhaps I am doing so already."

Orlov sees an opportunity to ask a question he has wanted to ask for a long time. "One more thing. Which ministry will I be working for?"

"You will not be working for the government at all," says Zelle, smiling. "You will be a loyal member of the People's Front and nothing more. However, we always reward our assets handsomely."

"Reward?" says Orlov.

"Yes," says Zelle. "If you are loyal and discreet, you can expect a significant reward."

CHAPTER EIGHTEEN

In which our hero attends his first meeting

I t is late morning by the time Orlov walks through the government sector, across the bridge and up the hill to the Grand Plaza. The sun is in his eyes, but it is nevertheless cool. As the busy market comes into view, he thinks back to how simple life was before he became involved with the government. He longs to return to his old life as soon as possible, not just for his own sake but also for the sake of his mother. How had he ever fooled himself into thinking that government business would be glamorous? He determines to do the very minimum necessary to satisfy Zelle, after which he will cut all ties with government people and their schemes.

Even from some distance across the plaza, the hefty figure of Citizen Vanev taking a cigarette break on a barrel is clearly seen. Orlov is struck by the fact that, in order to protect his mother, he will need to be less than truthful with his old friend and colleague. This realization causes sweat to ooze from his palms and forehead. He wipes both with his pocket handkerchief before arriving at the stall. Perhaps it will be interesting to join a political party for the first time.

Perhaps he might actually enjoy it. He consoles himself with the idea that, if he enjoys the experience at all, or at least finds it interesting, he will then not have lied to Vanev, he will simply have been less than fulsome in explaining his reasons.

Vanev flicks the butt of his cigarette onto the cobbles and extinguishes it with his heavy boot. "And now he appears, once the rush is over."

"I'm sorry, citizen," says Orlov. "An emergency trip to Havlinik to see my mother."

Vanev stands and straightens his fish-stained apron. "Is everything well?"

"All is well now, I believe," says Orlov.

"The railway station is that way," says Vanev, pointing, and apparently wondering why Orlov has arrived from the government sector.

Orlov had not anticipated this question and tries to think quickly. "An appointment, on behalf of my mother, at the Ministry of Welfare."

Vanev returns to the rear of the stall and begins to ration the day's remaining fish into fewer display boxes. "Do we have a Ministry of Welfare?"

Orlov picks up a surplus box and tips the ice into a nearby drain. "Perhaps it was the Ministry of Health," he says. "In any case, I believe she now has what she needs."

Vanev appears skeptical of this story but does not pursue it. Orlov briefly considers instigating a conversation about the People's Front immediately, but a customer arrives, and then another, and soon there is a steady stream of business to attend to until the middle of the afternoon. He goes through the motions of polite conversation with Vanev and with the customers, but in the back of his mind he is playing and replaying different versions of a conversation in which he expresses interest in joining the People's Front. The sweat returns to his palms not because Vanev will be displeased about his interest, but because he has often expressed a lack of interest in politics and now he needs to think of a plausible reason for changing his mind. Eventually, the flow of customers subsides and, as they often do in the middle of the afternoon, the two colleagues sit on barrels for a cigarette break, looking out across the plaza, the government sector, and the mountains beyond. Orlov senses that the time has arrived.

"I've been thinking," says Orlov, exhaling a cloud of smoke, "that perhaps it's time for me to become involved."

"Involved?" says Vanev.

"With the People's Front," says Orlov, glancing at his colleague to search for clues on his face regarding his likely reaction. Vanev raises his eyebrows, but says nothing initially, so Orlov continues. "I know you have asked me many times, but I never thought it necessary. Until now."

"Because?" says Vanev.

"Because of what happened in Kufzig. I always thought the government was trustworthy, but I was wrong."

Vanev laughs so heartily that he begins to cough and cannot continue smoking his cigarette. He stubs it out and lights a new one. "Comrade, I could have told you that many years ago. In fact, I'm sure I have said something similar on many occasions."

"I know, I know," says Orlov. "Perhaps I needed to see it for myself. But now I have seen it, and I'm ready to get involved."

"I see," says Vanev, apparently surprised.

"What do you say, citizen? Would you accept me? Would *they* accept me?"

Vanev exhales his own cloud of smoke and looks at Orlov with a serious expression. "I do believe you are serious, citizen."

"I am."

"Very well, then. We have a meeting this evening. Eight o'clock at the tavern. Of course, you cannot join us without a majority vote of the local branch. And we will need to give comrades some notice of that. But, if you come along to a meeting or two, you will be able to gauge if you want to proceed, and I will be able to gauge how the comrades feel about you."

"I will be there, comrade," says Orlov.

⟵⎯○⎯⟶

TAVERN KREMINIC STANDS at the corner of two narrow back-streets just yards from the Grand Plaza. There is sawdust on the floor and thick layers of dust on the wall lamps. Although a short walk from his apartment block, Citizen Orlov can count his previous visits on the fingers of one hand. He ducks under the low doorway just before eight o'clock. There is a roaring fire in the hearth and the heavy aromas of hops and cigars in the air. Not spotting Vanev immediately, Orlov approaches the bar and orders a tankard of ale.

"I'm looking for the . . ." he says, as his ale is poured, unsure of how he should describe the gathering he hopes to join.

The barmaid nods. "They're in the back," she says, indicating a door.

Orlov takes his ale and picks his way carefully between tables of animated patrons drinking and playing cards. During the short walk from the bar to the door of the meeting room, his head is filled with the incident that played out by the campfire on the night of the bombing: Comrade Weisz lunging at him; Comrade Nemeth holding Weisz back despite his own anger; Comrade Vanev intervening to prevent things from getting out of hand; waking early the next morning to discover they had left without him.

He hopes Zelle is right that his intervention in court—causing everyone to be released—has improved his standing with the People's Front. Boisterous conversation in the back room quickly subsides as Orlov enters.

"Good evening," says Orlov sheepishly, finding a seat.

About a dozen comrades—all men—are seated around a long banqueting table adorned only with tankards of ale. Comrades Weisz, Nemeth, and Sandor are present, as well as Vanev, and several others whom Orlov does not recognize. Weisz and Nemeth exchange whispered comments.

As if to break the awkward silence, Vanev speaks up. "Comrades, this is Comrade Orlov. Some of you know him. I invited him to join us this evening."

"He is not a comrade," says Weisz, with venom.

Vanev raises a hand. "No, indeed, not yet. But I'm pleased to say that Citizen Orlov is interested in our cause, and I think we are all agreed that we need to swell our numbers."

"Not with terrorists," says Weisz. There are murmurs around the table. Weisz and Nemeth whisper again.

"Comrades, please," says Vanev, sitting up straighter in his chair. "Let us treat visitors with decorum, please. If not for Comrade Orlov, some of us would still be in the high security wing at Zhotrykaw."

Comrade Nemeth speaks up. "If not for Comrade Orlov, we would never have been in Zhotrykaw in the first place." There are murmurs of agreement around the table.

Unsure what to say, Orlov says nothing and simply sips his ale.

"Comrades," says Vanev. "Comrade Orlov is here as my guest. We are not voting on his membership this evening. He might not decide to join. With a welcome like that, I can't imagine why he would want to." There are indistinct mumblings around the table as comrades look down into their beer. The atmosphere relaxes a little as Vanev continues. "Now, let us proceed. I move that we are quorate, and the meeting can begin. Seconded?"

"Aye," says a comrade Orlov does not know.

"Very well," says Vanev. "First item on the agenda is a report of our meeting with the Workers' Party. Comrade Sandor, please."

Comrade Sandor takes a long swig of his ale and then stands up in his place. "Comrades, if it pleases you to hear my report." Everyone except Orlov shouts "Aye" and slams his tankard down onto the table. Orlov jumps, and Sandor continues. "An excellent meeting with our comrades from the Workers' Party. Both sides agreed that our aims and values are sufficiently aligned such that a merger is agreed in principle." He pauses for enthusiastic applause around the table. "We have already made progress toward merging our manifestos. I anticipate that process will be complete in the next few days. We also have in place a draft accord covering the terms of the merger which, once signed, will create the People's Party, the largest progressive, republican movement in the history of our nation." More applause. "Once the People's Party is constituted, there will be no stopping our march for reform, including the dismantling of this corrupt government and, ultimately, our rebirth as a glorious, modern republic."

This time, the other comrades spring to their feet, cheering and raising their tankards in the air. Orlov stands, a little after the others. Unsure what to do next, he takes a swig and then follows the others in sitting down again.

"Excellent progress, excellent," says Vanev. "Soon we will need a larger venue for our meetings." He pauses for laughter around the table. "This wretched government has no idea what's coming. We must move forward as quickly as possible with the creation of the People's Party. Of course, we will be holding elections for the leadership of the new party and for all its major offices. All this must stay strictly between us until that process is complete. When our new movement is launched, this corrupt monarchy and its aristocratic cronies will soon realize their days are numbered."

Everyone stands again, ale spilling from swaying tankards as they launch unannounced into a rousing chorus of "The Red Flag."

CHAPTER NINETEEN

In which our hero passes on vital information

Early the next morning, Orlov opens his curtains wide and ties them back so there can be no doubt he needs to talk to Zelle. Despite his disgust at the ministry having brought his mother into it, he allows himself a brief stab of excitement that he is going to play the role of informant for the first time.

During a quiet moment at the market, Citizen Vanev wants to know what Orlov thought of his first meeting of the People's Front. "So, comrade, would you like to join us?" he asks.

"I do not believe Comrade Weisz will vote for my admittance," says Orlov.

"Do not trouble yourself regarding Weisz," says Vanev. "He has an angry soul. You need only a simple majority. If you become a member and show loyalty to the cause, they will accept you in time, even Weisz."

"And what of the new party?" asks Orlov. "Will you become its leader?"

Vanev dismisses this so quickly that Orlov wonders if he has hit a nerve. "No, no, no," says Vanev. "There will be a complicated election process. The Workers' Party is larger than us, so I dare say one of their people will be chosen."

It occurs to Orlov that his ability to gather useful information will be much improved if his friend and colleague wins a significant role in the new party, perhaps even leader. With intelligence coming right from the top, perhaps he would have a better chance to please Zelle and bring this strange episode to a swift conclusion. He determines to ask Zelle for advice on what he can do to promote Vanev's chances of reaching the top.

<hr />

JUST BEFORE MIDNIGHT, Orlov wraps his overcoat around himself and steps out into a cold, clear night. The almost deserted streets on the familiar walk to the Grand Plaza echo emptily with the sound of his footsteps. He is normally in bed long before this hour and finds himself yawning widely. Although scarcely anyone is out on the streets, he walks close to the buildings and stays in the shadows. This is his first official rendezvous with his government handler, and he does not wish to be seen.

At first, the Grand Plaza appears deserted, and Orlov strolls for a while near the market, watching eagerly for signs of movement. He spots a figure in dark clothes emerge from a dim doorway and stand under a streetlamp outside Hotel Melikov, popular with tourists because of its central position and—from the premier rooms—its spectacular mountain views.

Orlov hesitates for a while, unsure what to do next, waiting to see if this figure moves toward him. It does not. Since he can see no one else in the plaza, he walks slowly toward the hotel, wondering how Zelle has disguised herself for their inaugural meeting under the new arrangements. It becomes clear she is wearing a cloak with a hood and standing with her back to him. Orlov wonders whether it's necessary for her to be quite this elusive. She always seems to be testing him in one way or another. He approaches quietly from behind, clears his throat and whispers.

"One used to be able to see the peak of Mount Zhotrykaw from here," says Orlov.

She spins around, her face still shrouded under the hood. "What did you say?" Her voice sounds rough, as though hardened from years of smoking, and Orlov wonders why such amateur dramatics are necessary.

"One used to be able to see the peak of Mount Zhotrykaw from here," he repeats, slower and with more deliberate enunciation.

She lifts the hood to reveal a wrinkled, middle-aged woman in heavy makeup. "Minimum charge is three crowns," she barks. "Five if you want everything."

Orlov is flabbergasted and takes a moment to gather himself. "I don't want anything," he says, sheepishly.

The woman scowls. "Well, move on then." Her eyes dart left and right across the square. "This is my spot. Stand somewhere else."

Orlov nods, steps backward, and feels a hand on his shoulder. He spins around to find Agent Zelle standing behind him, undisguised in an overcoat and hat.

"Are you trying to conduct some business, citizen?" says Zelle with a grin.

"No, no," says Orlov, embarrassed, as the hooded woman scuttles back into the shadow of the hotel.

"Let us take a walk around the plaza," says Zelle. Once they have put some distance between themselves and Hotel Melikov, she continues. "So, citizen, you have news for me already?"

"Yes," says Orlov. "I decided to move quickly. I attended my first meeting of the People's Front last night, at Tavern Kreminic." He pauses, watching Zelle's face to see if she is impressed, but she gives nothing away. "Would you like to hear what was discussed?"

"Of course," says Zelle, deadpan.

"You were right about the Workers' Party. They are planning a merger. It's going to happen soon. They will create a new party called the People's Party and hold elections for leader and other positions. They intend that the combined party will bring down the government and eventually end the monarchy." He watches eagerly for a reaction.

"All of that is well known at the ministry," says Zelle.

Orlov is crestfallen. In an attempt to recover, he says, "Do you want my guess on who's going to be the leader of the new party?"

Zelle looks at him, nonplussed. "Volf, I expect," she says.

"Who?"

"Comrade Volf, leader of the Workers' Party," says Zelle.

"Don't you think Vanev has a chance?" asks Orlov. "That could make it easier for me to get you information straight from the top."

"Maybe," says Zelle, uninterested. "What about the military wing?"

"The what?" says Orlov.

"We believe they are secretly building a military wing, essentially a terrorist group. Most of the members may not be aware. It is headed up by a former soldier, Citizen Weisz."

"Oh, dear," says Orlov. "He is the one who's most aggressive toward me. Last evening, he called me a terrorist in front of the whole meeting."

Zelle raises her eyebrows. "In that case, you are ideally suited to join his unit." They complete a circuit of the Grand Plaza and arrive back where they started, in front of Hotel Melikov. Zelle stops under the streetlamp and rests her hands on Orlov's shoulder. "Find a way into the military wing and send me reports about their activities. Is that clear?"

Orlov starts to say, "I haven't even joined the party yet," but is interrupted by Zelle leaning in to pull up the collar of his overcoat.

She takes his face in both her gloved hands. "Time to sleep," she says. "Signal when you have something on the activities of Comrade Weisz."

Orlov is about to respond but he is distracted by a noise to his right. Two men are emerging from Hotel Melikov. They stagger down the steps, inebriated. To Orlov's horror, they are Comrades Weisz and Nemeth. Orlov begins to turn away, in an attempt to avoid being seen, but finds that the hooded woman has returned to the light of the streetlamp and almost bumps into him.

The hooded woman has chosen precisely this moment to speak to Orlov again. She reaches into her coat, produces a crown and holds it out on the palm of her hand. "Do you have change for a crown, citizen?" she says.

Before Orlov can reply, Weisz and Nemeth approach him, holding each other up in their inebriation. Weisz speaks first. "I say, comrade," he says to Nemeth. "I recognize this fellow. He's the one responsible for our incarceration in Prison Zhotrykaw." He grabs the lapel of Orlov's coat.

Nemeth looks at Orlov and then at the hooded woman, smiling. "Indeed, comrade, indeed. And it seems he's conducting some business here," he says, with mock disgust. "I'm not sure that's the sort of fellow we want in the People's Front."

"No, indeed it is not," says Weisz. "I dare say we will have to report this to our leader, one Comrade Vanev."

Orlov holds up both hands in protest. "Comrades, please, this is merely a misunderstanding," he says. "This citizen was simply asking if I had change for a crown." The hooded woman scuttles away; the comrades appear skeptical. Orlov continues. "I have no business here. I was simply taking a stroll around the square with my cousin, who is visiting from the south."

Orlov turns to introduce Zelle, but she is nowhere to be seen.

CHAPTER TWENTY

In which our hero joins a political party

Citizen Orlov attends two more meetings of the People's Front at Tavern Kreminic in the next week. He feels embarrassed about Zelle dismissing his efforts and so he determines not to signal her again until he is sure he has gleaned something valuable. At the end of his third meeting, in the same back room with sawdust on the floor and tankards of ale on the table, Vanev announces that it is time for the branch to vote on Orlov's membership. No one explains to Orlov what will happen; he feels awkward and offers to leave the room while the voting process is underway.

"No need," says Vanev. "You're entitled to see democracy in action. Enjoy your ale, comrade. It won't take long."

Orlov drags his chair next to the ornate fireplace and sits back to observe, nervously sipping his ale. There is a larger turnout than usual, about twenty people, including two women, and Orlov wonders if they have come out specifically in order to vote on his membership.

Vanev holds up his pocket watch and calls the room to order. "Comrades, we will caucus for only ten minutes, please. Ten minutes. Beginning now."

Instantly, comrades huddle in corners of the room and whisper into each other's ears. Orlov strains to hear, but he can make out nothing specific.

The whispering is quick and frantic. Huddles break up and new huddles are formed every two or three minutes. Weisz and Nemeth noticeably spend a long time together in the early stages of the caucus, but later they split up and join different huddles. Eventually, Vanev hoists his pocket watch into the air and calls out, "Secret ballot. Secret ballot. Secret ballot."

On the third instance, all the comrades except one gather near the door. A woman unknown to Orlov marches to a table in the window with a black ballot box, papers, and pencils. She takes an inordinate amount of time setting out these simple items on the table in a precise fashion.

Once she is satisfied that all is correct, she takes a seat next to the table and nods toward Vanev, who marches across the room alone, writes on a paper, and drops it into the box. Orlov watches carefully as each comrade in turn follows suit. Finally, the woman who is officiating drops her own paper into the box and then, while Vanev and the others drink their ale in silence, she empties the box onto the table and meticulously separates them into two piles. Since one pile is noticeably larger, Orlov concludes that the news is either very good or very bad.

The woman stands up and announces, "Comrade Orlov received seven *nays* and thirteen *ayes*. Seven *nays* and thirteen *ayes*. I hereby declare that Comrade Orlov is now a member of the People's Front." There is muffled applause, and the meeting breaks up into informal conversation.

Vanev walks across to shake Orlov's hand.

Orlov leans in to whisper in Vanev's ear. "Now that I'm a member," he says, "perhaps I should become more involved. I could contribute to one of your subcommittees."

"What did you have in mind?" asks Vanev.

"What are the options?"

Vanev runs through them. "We have fundraising," he says. "Communications. Manifesto. Events. And then there's security." Orlov perks up on hearing the last option. This must, he assumes, be the official name for what Zelle calls the military wing. "I wonder if security would be appropriate for me."

Vanev's grimace gives away his feelings about this idea. "It's run by Comrade Weisz," he whispers. "I think you might be wise to contribute elsewhere."

Orlov is not prepared to be discouraged so easily. "Would you object to me asking him?"

Vanev waves his hand across his chest as if beckoning Orlov forward. "Be my guest," he says.

Orlov sidles over to a small group including Weisz and Nemeth. They are in the middle of a lively conversation about the forthcoming merger with the Workers' Party. Orlov waits patiently, feeling a little out of place. He makes several attempts to catch Weisz's eye before succeeding and beckoning him for a private word by the fireplace.

"Comrade," says Orlov, "I know we have not seen eye to eye. But now I am a member, I would like to make a contribution. Comrade Vanev tells me that you are chair of the security subcommittee."

Weisz stares back dispassionately. "You know, I suppose, that I did not vote for you this evening?"

Orlov waves this away. "It was a secret ballot. What's done is done. And now I want to contribute."

"The security subcommittee has no vacancies for those whose late-night activities could compromise them," says Weisz, and walks away to rejoin his group.

ON THE OCCASION of the merger between the People's Front and the Workers' Party to create the new People's Party, Citizen Orlov is thinking about his mother. He takes the tram to Tavern Szolnok—a large ale house on the outskirts of the city preferred by the Workers' Party—and spends the whole journey staring out the window, wondering whether his mother has had any more visitations. He determines to pay her another visit, just as soon as he has made some progress that might cause Agent Zelle to be less agitated with him. He has not yet summoned her again; she would not be pleased that he has so far failed to join the military wing. Indeed, he has not spoken to her since their rendezvous was interrupted by Weisz and Nemeth in a drunken state; hopefully that incident will not increase her agitation.

Tavern Szolnok is a soulless place that specializes in heavy drinking for the working man and little else; it has none of the charm of Tavern Kreminic, but it is blessed with a large upper room where the Workers' Party conducts its business away from the prying eyes of the government. Orlov buys a tankard of ale at the bar and arrives in the upstairs meeting room just in time to hear the meeting called to order by a painfully thin man in a formal suit and an unkempt beard. The room is full of perhaps one hundred people; there is a buzz of anticipation and the mixed aromas of hops and cigarettes. Orlov scans the room in search of familiar faces; he spots Vanev near the front of the crowd.

The bearded man waves his arms to attract attention. He has the thin, hoarse voice of someone whose life has seen its share of tribulation. "Comrades. Order, please. It is time to begin the formal business of the evening. I am Comrade Volf. I will first announce the positions to be filled this evening. Comrade Vanev will then explain the procedures." Vanev emerges from the crowd to stand next to Volf, who continues. "First we will be electing the leader of the party and the deputy leader of the party. Next, we will elect chairmen for the following subcommittees: membership, fundraising, communications, events, policy, and finally, security. Comrade Vanev, please."

Vanev takes a swig of his ale before speaking. "Comrades, given that so many of us are present this evening, we will caucus for one hour, please. One hour exactly for caucusing on all the positions listed by Comrade Volf. After one hour has passed, I will call you to order, and the voting process will begin."

The room bursts into life. The process is much the same as the caucusing Orlov observed at Tavern Kreminic regarding his own membership, except much louder and livelier. Passionate debating and arm waving fill the room. Orlov decides to use the time to promote Vanev as the leader of the new party. He mingles until he finds a group discussing leadership and muscles into the conversation.

"I don't believe we have any plausible options besides Volf and Vanev," says a studious-looking woman with horn-rimmed spectacles.

Orlov jumps in. "I am concerned that Comrade Volf may win simply because more of you are from his party. But please consider Comrade Vanev; he is a loyal colleague and a strong leader. You could certainly trust him to lead with conviction."

There is a pause after Orlov has spoken. The whole group, which he takes to be members of the Workers' Party, is staring at him. The woman in spectacles speaks again. "Are you by any chance Comrade Orlov?"

Orlov is unsure what to make of this. "Yes," he says, hesitantly.

She leans across to shake his hand. "A pleasure to meet you, comrade. I am Comrade Dankova. We have all heard about your heroic acts in Kufzig."

Flabbergasted, Orlov says nothing. The other members of the group all agree and take turns in shaking his hand vigorously. "You are an inspiration to us all," says one man. "We heard you secured the release of all your comrades from Zhotrykaw," says another.

Orlov is flattered but embarrassed. He feels his face reddening. "Yes, I suppose I did."

Comrade Dankova beckons over more Workers' Party comrades from another huddle, encouraging them to shake Orlov by the hand. Soon, a stream of people unknown to Orlov are queueing to meet him. As they pass by, Dankova offers some words of explanation to each new arrival. "This is Comrade Orlov. The hero of Kufzig. Yes, the bomb in the hotel, that's right. He secured the release of several comrades from Zhotrykaw. I quite agree, a hero of our movement. Indeed, it's quite an honor." And so it goes on. Orlov grimaces when one greeter asks, "So, this is the comrade who planted the bomb?" Dankova confirms this, erroneously, and Orlov does not have the heart to correct her.

By the time the unexpected greeting line slows to a trickle and then stops, Orlov is red in the face and pauses to down the remainder of his ale.

He scours the room and concludes that he must have met more than half of the members of the Workers' Party. Most of the caucus time has already gone, however, and he has made precious little progress in promoting Vanev as the new leader.

He visits the bar downstairs to refill his tankard of ale. While waiting, he ponders what just happened. He and Vanev have scarcely talked about Kufzig or Zhotrykaw since the day of their release. None of their customers at the market have ever raised it. Neither has his mother, who seems to be blissfully unaware of what happened. And yet, among the members of the Workers' Party, soon to make up the majority of the new People's Party, he is, to his great surprise, something of a celebrity.

Orlov takes his ale back up to the meeting room and attempts to use the remaining caucus time to persuade people to vote for Vanev, but every time he encounters a member of the Workers' Party, he is met with the same fascination about Kufzig.

Comrade Vanev calls the room to order and announces the voting procedures. A separate ballot box and a separate pile of papers for each position have been placed on a long table. Members solemnly queue around the room.

Orlov takes his place in the queue, still amazed at the reaction of his new comrades but disappointed that he does not seem to have persuaded anyone to vote for Vanev over Volf. He observes with interest the solemn, almost religious, atmosphere that surrounds the process of queueing and voting. When it is over, Comrade Volf announces that Comrade Dankova will lead a small team of counters and will then announce the results.

The crowd shuffles to the back of the room to give the counters some space. An excited, expectant atmosphere develops as the counting process progresses.

Finally, Comrade Dankova turns to address the room. "Comrades, I am pleased to say that we have a clear result for every position in the new People's Party. As was the tradition in the former Workers' Party, I will announce the results only, not the counts. Silence, please." There is a shuffling and settling in the crowd. Dankova consults her paper and then begins. "Please remember, comrades, to keep your applause and other noise to a minimum. I hereby declare that the leader of the People's Party will be Comrade Volf. Comrade Volf is our new leader."

Rapturous applause sounds around the room as well as sighs of relief. Members of the former Workers' Party knock their tankards and pat each other on the back. Orlov looks over at Vanev, who is clapping and appears unsurprised.

Dankova continues. "And now, deputy leader. I hereby declare that the deputy leader of the People's Party is Comrade Vanev. Comrade Vanev is our deputy leader."

More applause and backslapping, but this time it comes mostly from the members of the former People's Front. Dankova continues to read out the names of the elected officials who will chair the subcommittees on membership, events, and so on. They are Workers' Party members whose names Orlov does not recognize. Until she comes to policy, and announces Comrade Sandor. Enthusiastic applause sounds out from People's Front comrades.

Orlov is under the impression that the evening has ended and is trying to remember where he left his overcoat when Comrade Dankova says, "And finally, security. Please simmer down comrades, and listen to the result of the ballot for the chair of the subcommittee on security." A curious smile crosses her face. "The head of security for the People's Party will be Comrade Orlov. Comrade Orlov is our head of security."

PART FOUR

An Account

of the

National Day

Disaster

CHAPTER TWENTY-ONE

In which our hero receives a challenging new task

The very next morning after the formation of the People's Party, Citizen Orlov opens his curtains wide and sees what appears to be the arrival of spring—a little less snow on the mountains and a few green shoots on the trees.

He looks out at the view with mixed emotions. On the one hand, he can report to Agent Zelle that he is not only a member of the security subcommittee but its chairman. On the other hand, he is now deeply embedded in a movement he does not believe in, on false pretenses. The deceit makes him exhilarated and nauseated in equal measure. He ties the curtains back so there can be no doubt he needs to speak to Zelle.

At the market, standing at the fish stall and awaiting the first customers of the day, Citizens Orlov and Vanev congratulate each other on their election to significant positions in the new party. Orlov uses this as an excuse to ask a question that has been concerning him.

"Is it true, comrade," says Orlov, "that critics accused both the old parties of having secret military wings?"

Vanev looks affronted. "Where did you hear such language?" he asks.

Orlov had not anticipated this question and so must think quickly. "It came up in conversation last evening, during the caucus."

"We never use such language," says Vanev. Orlov says nothing and Vanev continues. "We have a subcommittee on security, nothing more."

"And what, as chair of the subcommittee, am I responsible for?"

"Well," says Vanev, "there's the security of members at events and marches and so on. That is a large part of the role. And background checks on new members."

"Background checks?" says Orlov.

"Yes," says Vanev. "Both parties have had problems in the past with imposters."

Orlov is about to ask about this when a customer appears. He sells two carp, wraps them, and then waits for the woman to walk away before turning back to Vanev. "What do you mean by imposters?"

Vanev lights a cigarette, offers one to Orlov, and continues in a matter-of-fact voice. "Sometimes it's a journalist, sometimes a government agent. They join to glean information on us. It's not common, but when it happens, we have to stamp it out immediately."

Orlov experiences a sinking feeling deep in his gut. He takes a long drag on his cigarette in order to buy himself some time. "Did that happen at the People's Front?"

"Oh, yes," says Vanev. "We've had a couple of journalists over the years. Both from *The Sentinel*. We had to expel them."

"I see," says Orlov. "So, no harm done, in the end."

Vanev laughs. "Lucky for them they did not choose the Workers' Party. Comrade Volf takes no prisoners. Only two years ago they had a new member who was determined to join the security subcommittee. But there was something fishy about his story. They never proved anything, but Volf told me he was convinced the man was undercover. A month later, some climbers found his frozen corpse halfway up Mount Zhotrykaw."

Orlov feels as though a shower of frigid Zhotrykaw snow is sliding down his back and into his trousers. He coughs and tries to gather himself. "I see. So, then, I will need to be very careful about the possibility of imposters."

"Oh, yes," says Vanev. "If you have any concerns at all, you must report the suspicious member to Comrade Volf immediately. He will decide their fate."

"Yes, I see," says Orlov. "I will be sure to do so." He wants to change the subject. "And what about, shall we say, the more offensive role of the security subcommittee?"

Vanev looks around to ensure no one is near and waves his hand as though to erase the question. "My strong advice, comrade, is that you should not raise that issue. That is one of many issues I need to discuss with Comrade Volf. You must do nothing except on his orders. Is that clear?"

"Very clear," says Orlov.

They are interrupted by the arrival of a curious little man in a formal suit and heavy spectacles. He shifts awkwardly from foot to foot while scanning the merchandise. He nods to acknowledge the two fishmongers before speaking.

"Good morning, citizens," says the man. His voice is high and tremulous. "I'm looking for a fish."

Vanev wipes his hands ostentatiously down his filthy, stained overalls. "In that case, you have come to the right place, citizen," he says proudly. "We are the only fish stall in the Grand Plaza."

"So I hear," says the man. "So I hear."

The two fishmongers expect the man to make an order, but instead he continues to inspect their wares while mumbling to himself, "Carp. Haddock. Yes, very good. Bream, yes, excellent. Can't go wrong with bream, I always say."

Orlov and Vanev look at each other, and exchange an unspoken agreement, based on years of experience, that this is the type of customer best left to his own devices. They both smile benevolently at no one in particular, waiting for this strange little man to conclude his ritual.

Another customer arrives and asks Vanev for two haddock. The moment this happens, the demeanor of the bespectacled man changes in an instant.

He steps toward Orlov and says, "Carp. Right now. Just one. Make it quick."

Orlov is taken aback but tries not to show it. "Of course, sir," he says and wraps a carp as quickly as he can.

As Orlov hands over the carp, the man grasps him firmly by the wrist. He speaks to Orlov urgently in a whisper, glancing to his left quickly to make sure Vanev is still engaged with the other customer. "One can no longer see the peak of Mount Zhotrykaw from here. Would you not agree, citizen?"

Orlov is confused. He glances at Vanev and back at the man, replying in a whisper. "I do not follow your meaning, citizen."

The man's grip grows firmer. "Sometimes it is necessary for plans to change," he says, "in response to problems that arise."

Orlov stares into the man's bespectacled eyes in search of a clue. A number of possibilities flash quickly through his mind. For a second, he wonders if Zelle has surpassed herself in terms of disguises, but quickly dismisses this idea; this is definitely a man, more wiry and muscular than Zelle.

Perhaps he is Zelle's messenger, sent to make a change to the arrangements. For all Orlov knows, however, he could be from the Workers' Party, or somewhere else. Unsure what to say, Orlov says nothing.

The man leans in to Orlov's ear. "Take the tram. Clockwise. At dusk." He tucks the wrapped fish into his overcoat and scuttles away.

OVER AN EARLY dinner of cabbage soup, Orlov wonders what exactly is meant by the word *dusk*. He wonders if dusk is when the sun begins to go down, or when it has finished going down, or something in between. To be on the safe side, as soon as there is any sign of the light fading in the early evening, he wraps himself in his overcoat and walks to the tram stop.

As per the instructions, Orlov joins the first clockwise tram and takes a seat. It is a two-car tram with perhaps a half dozen people in each car.

Glancing to the front, Orlov notices that the driver appears to be an unusually young man, in a pristine, blue uniform that looks as good as new. There is no law against young men becoming tram drivers, of course, but in Orlov's experience the drivers are almost always gnarled old men who have been working the same tram lines for years.

As the tram trundles slowly through the outskirts of the capital, Orlov wonders what is supposed to happen next. Is he expected to do something? Will Zelle contact him in some way? What if the strange, bespectacled man was an imposter of some sort? Working for whom? All this secrecy is terribly confusing.

At the next stop, the tram is joined by a uniformed ticket inspector who works his way slowly around both cars, punching holes in tickets. He arrives at Orlov last.

"Good evening, sir," says the inspector, glancing out of the window and then back at Orlov. "If you could follow me, please."

Orlov is taken aback. "There's nothing wrong with my ticket," he says. "I bought it only today."

The inspector ignores this, apparently distracted by something through the window. He holds out a hand and begins to pull Orlov up out of his seat. "Very good, sir. Quickly, please."

Orlov stands and allows the inspector to maneuver him to the closed door of the tram. To Orlov's horror, the inspector opens the door, even though they are between stations and the tram is moving at its top speed. Orlov turns around to the inspector. "What are you doing? This is dangerous."

The inspector lays a heavy hand on Orlov's shoulder. "Not at all, sir. Everything's under control."

In his peripheral vision, Orlov spots an anticlockwise tram about to pass them at speed.

A second later, the inspector shoves Orlov with both hands.

Orlov screams, falls forward, lands on the floor of the anticlockwise tram, and rolls in the dust of a car that needs cleaning. He stands up, nursing a sore shoulder and knocking dust from his overcoat.

He is now traveling at speed back toward the city in a one-car tram whose only other passenger is Agent Zelle. She is sitting on one of the wooden benches with a serene smile on her face.

"Citizen," she says, "how good of you to join me." She gestures to the opposite bench. "Please, take a seat."

Orlov is still knocking dust from his overcoat. "Is all this strictly necessary? I could have been killed."

Zelle shrugs. "There was no danger of that. Your government needs you to stay very much alive."

Orlov looks around the car. "What happens if someone else gets on?"

Zelle smiles. "This tram doesn't stop."

Orlov nods toward the driver in the cabin. "What about him?"

"Don't worry," says Zelle. "He's one of ours."

Orlov slumps into the bench opposite. "All this because of Comrade Weisz emerging in a drunken state from Hotel Melikov?"

"The Grand Plaza is too risky," says Zelle. "We need to be more creative." Orlov is about to ask what this means, but he is interrupted by Zelle clapping her hands in anticipation. "So, comrade, you finally have something interesting for me?"

"Very interesting," says Orlov.

"About time," says Zelle.

"The People's Party was born last night. You are looking at its head of security."

Zelle's eyebrows rise sharply. "Really, citizen?"

"I swear to you it is true."

"I am most impressed, citizen," says Zelle. "How did you achieve this?"

"Let's just say that my reputation regarding the unfortunate business in Kufzig traveled further than I had realized."

"I see, I see," says Zelle. She appears to be pondering something and Orlov is reluctant to interrupt her. Eventually, she says, "I believe we are ready for the next step in our operation."

"You want me to bring you information from the security subcommittee?"

Zelle smiles. "I do, indeed, but I have something much more ambitious in mind."

Orlov does not like the sound of this. "Yes?"

"In just a few weeks it will be National Day," says Zelle. "As usual, the king will appear in front of the Palace to inspect the military parade. Security will be tight; nerves will be frayed. That would, I believe, be the perfect occasion for the military wing of the new People's Party to announce its arrival by planting an explosive device under the podium from which His Majesty delivers his speech."

Orlov grips the handrail and begins to stand up. "Citizen, you cannot be serious," he hisses.

"Do I appear to you to be making a joke?" says Zelle.

"But that is madness," says Orlov, slumping back onto his bench. "Anyone involved in that plot is certain to stand in front of a firing squad."

"I did not say the bomb has to explode," says Zelle. "It need not even be armed. It simply needs to be a plausible device, sufficient to be taken seriously by the police, and planted by members of the People's Party." She looks at Orlov in anticipation of his response.

"Citizen," says Orlov, exasperated, "I have not yet been the head of security for even one day. If I try to rush them into something so ambitious, so reckless, I fear that my cover will be blown and everything you want to achieve will be ruined. I implore you: let me establish myself in the role for a short time, let me gain their trust, and then we can begin with a less risky operation, something more likely to succeed."

Agent Zelle gives him a steely glare. "You seem to be under the misapprehension that this is a negotiation. It is not. I recommend you begin planning the operation forthwith."

Orlov runs both hands through what remains of his hair. "Citizen, please. I do not believe it is possible to execute this plan without exposing myself. Is that what you want?"

Agent Zelle scowls. "I suggest, citizen, that you think a little less about your own safety and a little more about the safety of your mother."

<hr />

AT EXACTLY THREE o'clock in the morning, Orlov sits upright in his bed.

All he can think about is Zelle's knowledge of the security bars he fitted on the doors of his mother's house. Now she has mentioned his mother again, and as a result he cannot sleep. He gets up, puts the coffee pot on the stove, and paces while waiting for it to steam. He drinks coffee and paces until five o'clock, then opens his curtains and walks to the railway station, standing alone on a cold platform, much too early for the first train.

It is still early when Orlov leaves the train in Havlinik and, fighting against a lack of sleep, marches with all his might through the town and up the hill to his mother's house. He is disappointed to see that the front door is unlocked and the security bar is not in place. He needs to impress upon his mother the importance of securing the house before she goes to bed. Otherwise, everything appears normal downstairs, and Orlov is not surprised that his mother is not yet out of bed, given the early hour. He tiptoes upstairs, so as not to wake her, and is disturbed to see some of her ornaments—decorative replicas of the mountains surrounding Havlinik—strewn across the landing. He cannot understand why she did not pick up the ornaments before going to bed. Until he puts his head inside her bedroom, which has been turned upside down. A chair is overturned; bedclothes are strewn across the floor. More importantly, his mother is gone.

CHAPTER TWENTY-TWO

In which our hero announces a daring operation

Citizen Orlov spends some time searching his mother's house for clues as to what has happened. He finds everything undisturbed apart from the messy bedroom, the ornaments, and the unsecured front door. He tidies everything up and then goes out into the back garden for a cigarette. He is breathing hard and forces himself to take slower, deeper breaths. He considers asking the neighbors if they saw or heard anything, he considers reporting her missing to the local police, he considers telling the priest.

He worries, however, that any of these actions could potentially set off a chain reaction of behind-the-scenes government activity that would be out of his control and could make matters worse rather than better. Before taking action, he needs to be sure what is happening. Since he left his curtains open, he will have the opportunity to ask Agent Zelle to explain herself. Having said that, he has no idea where or when they will meet.

Perhaps the mumbling, bespectacled man will return to the fish stall with new instructions.

Orlov takes the next train back to the capital and arrives at the market by late morning. Once again he is forced to apologize to Citizen Vanev for being late for work and must invent a plausible reason.

"My apologies, citizen," says Orlov, panting heavily, as he exchanges his overcoat for his apron. "An emergency visit to Havlinik. My mother is unwell, I'm afraid."

Vanev nodes sagely. "Nothing serious, I hope."

"I hope not, citizen. It is difficult to say."

"Are you sure you can take on the responsibilities of the security subcommittee, in addition to working and caring for your mother?" asks Vanev.

Orlov needs to put an end to this line of thinking. If he loses his position in the People's Party, there is no telling what Zelle might do. "I am certain of it, citizen. Do not fear. Just an occasional visit to check on my mother is all that is required."

"Good, good," says Vanev. "Do not forget our first meeting with Comrade Volf this evening."

⋅→—⋅—→⋅

AT EIGHT O'CLOCK precisely, Orlov carries his ale into the back room of Tavern Kreminic to find Comrade Volf, Comrade Vanev, and the other chairmen of subcommittees gathering around the table. Orlov has spent the whole day feeling exhausted and worrying about this mother; he wishes he were in a better physical and mental state for his first meeting of the People's Party ruling committee. He determines to get through it as best he can, before meeting Zelle later.

Comrade Volf opens the meeting by congratulating everyone on the formation of the party and on their new positions. He distributes papers to each subcommittee chairman listing the members who have volunteered to join their teams. Orlov skims his paper and finds no sign of Comrade Weisz, although Comrade Nemeth is on the list. The others are all former Workers' Party names he does not recognize.

"We shall go around the table in order and discuss priorities for each of you," says Volf. The tone of his voice suggests he will be telling, not asking, what their priorities are.

Orlov sips his ale and struggles to stay awake during long exchanges about a fundraising drive, announcements of the formation of the new party in *The Sentinel*, and plans for Comrade Volf to deliver his first speech as leader.

Finally, they come on to security, and Orlov sits up straighter in his chair.

"Comrade Orlov, welcome," says Volf. "I am told you are the employee of Comrade Vanev in his fish business."

"Yes, sir," says Orlov, falteringly.

"Please, call me comrade," says Volf.

"Yes, comrade," says Orlov, embarrassed.

"Very well, security," says Volf. "My gravest concern at this moment is imposters. The launch of our new party will cause a good deal of interest, not only in the press but also in the government and the royal family. I am counting on you, Comrade Orlov, to stamp out any and all attempts to infiltrate our party. Get your team together immediately and let us have a robust process of checking the bona fides of all new members. If you have the slightest doubts—any doubts at all—then new members must be rejected. Is that clear?"

"Very clear, comrade," says Orlov.

He believes the discussion on security is over, but Volf scans his papers and continues. "I see you have some volunteers with good experience of these matters during their time in the Workers' Party. Please make good use of them." He glances down at the paper again and smiles. "You also have our most experienced explosives expert, but that is not the sort of bang we need to launch our new party."

Polite laughter ripples around the table. Orlov sees an opportunity. He is torn about whether to speak.

Volf has presented him with a perfect opportunity to raise the issue that is on his mind. On the other hand, raising it now, in his first contribution to his first committee meeting, could make him appear out of touch with Volf's agenda and might raise suspicions about his motives.

Whether it is lack of sleep, or ale, or concerns about his mother, Orlov decides to speak.

"I was thinking, comrade, that the other sort of bang might be exactly what we need to let the government know we are serious. After all, National Day is approaching, and that would be the perfect time—"

Volf interrupts by waving both his hands. He glances at the door and back at Orlov. "Comrade, comrade, no, no, no. That is not what we need at this moment. We need to establish the party as a serious entity, and we shall do so peacefully. Any direct action by your committee will occur only if absolutely necessary and after careful deliberation. Is that clear?"

"Very clear, comrade," says Orlov.

As soon as the meeting breaks up, Orlov, concerned that he has overstepped the mark, slips away while the others talk informally. He returns his tankard to the bar and is surprised to be stopped by the barmaid.

"Are you by any chance Citizen Orlov?" she says.

"I am."

"A fellow was here just now." She looks around the bar. "I think he must have left. He said you're to go to the cathedral right away. Don't delay, he said."

Orlov frowns. "That's all?"

"No," says the barmaid, "there was something else. You should wear good shoes."

Orlov looks down at his heavy boots. "I'm wearing the shoes that I'm wearing," he says.

The barmaid shrugs. "Oh, and don't use the main doors."

Citizen Orlov marches as quickly as he is able out of Tavern Kreminic, across the Grand Plaza, and around the corner to the cathedral. He has only ever used the main entrance before. As he skirts along the street that runs along the side of the cathedral, he wonders what Zelle has in store this time. He can see lamps burning inside. At the rear of the building, he finds two small wooden doors. The first is locked. The second door opens into a darkened corridor, very cool thanks to walls of heavy stone. Orlov closes the door behind him and stops to catch his breath. He is leaning against the door, breathing heavily and wondering where to go, when a flustered man in long white robes appears from nowhere and takes him firmly by the arm.

"Thank goodness, citizen," he says, propelling Orlov along the corridor. "You're late. This way."

"Where are we going?" says Orlov.

The man ignores the question and marches them into a small, dimly lit anteroom full of robes hanging in fitted closets. He pulls out a white robe much like his own and turns to Orlov.

"Quickly, coat and jacket, please."

Orlov hands his overcoat and jacket to the man, who expertly splays out the robe and drops it over his head. He smooths it out and stands back to admire his work.

"That will have to be sufficient," says the man. Orlov attempts to ask a question but is interrupted by the man handing him a huge candle in an ornate golden holder. He pushes Orlov through another door. "Just follow her," he says, pointing.

Orlov emerges from the dim anteroom into a bright space filled with candles. There is the heavy scent of incense in the air and the hush of anticipation. He is in the sanctuary of the cathedral. Two priests are officiating at the altar. Just behind them stands Agent

Zelle; she looks positively angelic with her hair down and dressed in a long, white robe, holding a candle just like Orlov's. She turns to him and, hiding her free hand behind the candle, gestures furtively that he should hurry to join her.

Orlov strides across the huge sanctuary in a manner that is intended to be both hurried and reverent. He is not sure this is entirely successful. Only when he arrives at Zelle's side does it become clear that the cathedral is full of people, most of whom were initially hidden from his view by clouds of incense.

He gazes past the priests and the altar at a hundred candlelit faces staring back at him. He feels distinctly out of place, even more so when he looks down to see his filthy, heavy boots under the pristine white robe.

Zelle keeps her attention on the priests in front of her but whispers to Orlov out of the side of her mouth. "You're late."

Orlov also faces forward and whispers sideways. "What the hell are we doing here?"

"Inappropriate language, in the circumstances," says Zelle.

"Sorry," whispers Orlov. "You're not seriously proposing that we talk here?"

"Not yet," she replies. "Follow my lead. And be quiet, until I say so."

Orlov watches the backs of the two priests, who are doing something at the altar while speaking loudly in Latin. Without notice, Zelle suddenly steps forward, rests her candle on a stand, and nods to Orlov to indicate that he should do likewise. Immediately once he has done so, the two priests swivel around, handing a huge goblet of wine to Zelle, while Orlov receives a large basket of wafers. He stays close to Zelle as she parades behind the two priests to the front of the sanctuary.

The congregation has begun to proceed down to the communion rail in long lines. Since the two priests are also carrying wine and wafers, it seems to Orlov that he and Zelle are carrying the spares, although one imagines they are perhaps known formally by a more genteel name.

Congregants begin to receive the elements, kneeling in front of the two priests, and then processing slowly back to their places. Once this pattern has established itself, Zelle turns to Orlov.

"So, you wanted to speak to me?" she whispers.

"Where is my mother?" hisses Orlov.

Zelle frowns. "Citizen, please, lower your voice."

"Answer the question."

Zelle returns her gaze to the priest in front of her before whispering her reply. "I can assure you that your mother is safe and well. She will remain that way for as long as you cooperate."

"Citizen," hisses Orlov, affronted, "have I not cooperated so far?"

"Only yesterday you refused to carry out the operation I requested. I had no choice but to take action to make you change your mind."

Orlov sighs. "I suggested it to Comrade Volf this very evening," whispers Orlov. "He said there were to be no offensive operations without his express permission."

They are interrupted by the priest on Orlov's side, the one administering the wafers, who turns and glares at them. They both look down at their shoes.

A few moments later, the choir begins to sing an anthem, and Zelle looks up at Orlov again, perhaps sensing it is safe to resume whispering.

"Were you planning for Comrade Volf to plant the device personally?" says Zelle.

Orlov does not follow. "Of course not. But the order must come from him."

"Well, then," says Zelle, "simply gather your security team and tell them you have received the order."

THE NEXT AFTERNOON, after closing up the market stall, Orlov bids farewell to Vanev and, instead of walking home, he strolls down to the Palace and makes some circuits of the cloisters among the tourists. Then he strolls down the Palace steps and back up again several times. By six o'clock, as per his instructions, the seven members of the security subcommittee have joined him at the top of the steps.

Orlov smiles and does his best to look like a tour guide. "Thank you for gathering, comrades," he says. "I appreciate your patience. Tavern Kreminic is heavily booked at the moment, but in any case I believe the matters we need to discuss are best covered out here, away from listening ears. Are there any complaints about that approach?" Observing a unanimous shaking of heads, Orlov continues. "Firstly, we have a clear instruction from the leader that rooting out imposters must be a priority. I believe some of you are experienced in this regard."

Comrades Dinev and Smid identify themselves and agree to take on the vetting process.

Orlov continues. "The second issue I need to raise this evening is a little more sensitive. It must be discussed with no one outside this group for any reason. Is that clear?"

"Very clear, comrade," rings around the group.

Orlov pauses for a few moments as a group of tourists passes them on the steps. "I understand someone in the group has explosives experience."

Comrade Rozum identifies himself. He is young, muscular, and stares at Orlov with an intense glare. "Yes, comrade. I recently left the army. I can assist with anything you need regarding explosives."

Orlov shakes his hand and continues. "It is a pleasure to meet you, comrade. I will need assistance from you and others. As you know, a significant event will take place on these very steps in the near future. All I need say at this stage is that we will be making our presence felt at that event in a forceful way. I will call on you as necessary to play your part. For security reasons, we will not discuss this matter in the group again, and it must not be raised with others, even other comrades."

There are serious expressions and solemn nodding. But Citizen Nemeth looks skeptical. "Has this matter been cleared by the leadership?"

Orlov raises his hand. "I can assure you, citizen, that I have discussed this matter with the leadership, up to and including Comrade Volf. But now, for the security of us all, it must be discussed with no one except me. Follow my instructions and I promise you we will blow a hole in this corrupt government."

CHAPTER TWENTY-THREE

In which our hero hears unexpected news

T he second committee meeting of the new People's Party is largely uneventful, until the end. Citizen Orlov, having said as little as possible and nothing controversial, is downing his ale and preparing to follow the others out into the bar when he is detained by an announcement.

"Comrades Vanev and Orlov," says Volf quietly, "please remain for a further discussion." The two colleagues return to their seats. They are joined by Comrade Dankova, the bespectacled counter of votes, not a member of the committee, who arrives from the bar. She takes a seat next to Volf, and he continues, in a solemn manner. "I believe you have met Comrade Dankova. She has only today brought me some serious news. In order to explain the origin of this news, I must bring the two of you into my confidence. I must share with you information I had hoped would be known by no one except Comrade Dankova and myself. Before we begin, I must have your absolute commitment that this information will be shared with no one not currently sitting at this table."

"You have my word, comrade," says Vanev.

"And mine," says Orlov.

"Very well," says Volf. "Comrade Dankova here is not only an excellent administrator and an active member of the Workers' Party and now the People's Party, but she is also a trained typist. For many years she worked in the typing pool at the Krupnik glassworks, which was always a strong supporter of the party. If you were to ask any of the comrades, they will tell you that she is still a member of staff at Krupnik's, but that is not the case. In fact, at my suggestion late last year, Comrade Dankova took a position in the typing pool at the Ministry of Security. As you would imagine, they have a stringent security process, but there is no law against working at Krupnik's, and she has done an excellent job at establishing herself at the ministry. From time to time, the comrade brings me valuable information, and today is one of those days." He opens his hand to invite Comrade Dankova to speak.

"Thank you, comrade," says Dankova. She smiles at Orlov and Vanev before continuing. "Most of my time is spent in the typing pool, where I type reports and letters for the senior officials. Very occasionally I am also asked to minute meetings. This morning I was asked to minute a meeting in which some middle-ranking officers were briefing their seniors on the activities of their *assets*, that is, ordinary citizens who bring them information secretly. The assets all have code names, and of course those of us in the typing pool are not aware of their true identities. But today the conversation rested for a while on an asset whose code name is Lazy Bishop. Now, the organization where Lazy Bishop is active was also not mentioned by name, but the officer said at one point that Lazy Bishop had been a member of the *old party* and was now, by virtue of a merger, a member of the *new party*." She stops speaking and looks across at Volf.

"Thank you, comrade," says Volf, before turning to Vanev and Orlov. "Comrades, this is extremely serious. Unless you are aware of two other political parties which have recently merged to form a new party, then it appears we have a mole. And this mole is not just a journalist or other troublemaker; this mole is an asset providing information to the Ministry of Security."

Vanev glances at Orlov, who does his best to project an appropriate expression of solemn concern, but his mind is racing with possibilities. Is he Lazy Bishop? Is there another government mole in the party? Has Dankova been in a meeting with Agent Zelle? Does Zelle have any idea that the party has its own mole in the ministry? He is suddenly conscious that anything he says or does could expose him. This realization causes goosebumps to break out across his neck and shoulders.

He clears his throat and sits up straighter in his chair.

Vanev speaks first. "This is a very serious situation, comrades. Do we know if this mole is a recent arrival or a long-term member of one of the parties?"

"We have no idea," says Volf. He looks at Orlov. "What is your view, comrade?"

Now all three comrades are staring at Orlov. His immediate thought is that, so long as he controls the search for the mole, he will be able to ensure it remains unsuccessful. "The only way to be sure is a thorough search, comrade," says Orlov, earnestly. "I will convene my subcommittee immediately, and together we will begin a process to root out this mole as a matter of urgency."

Volf, still staring at Orlov, clasps his hands together in front of his chest. He seems to be pondering something. It is unclear to Orlov whether his suggestion has been well received or not. Eventually, Volf says, "Very well, comrade, very well." For a moment, Orlov believes that is the end of the matter, but Volf continues. "With just one amendment. I will ask Comrade Dankova to join you in the search. I am sure you will find her very helpful, and very thorough."

Comrade Dankova nods in agreement while smiling at Orlov.

Orlov wants to refuse help, but dare not. "I am sure I will, comrade," he says.

"Very well," says Volf, "you will begin immediately."

<hr/>

ON THE OCCASION of Orlov's next meeting with Agent Zelle, he returns home from the market to find an envelope has been pushed under the front door of his apartment. The front of the envelope reads *Lupine Festival!* The note inside reads as follows:

> *This is a beautiful time of year to visit the historic town*
> *of Kufzig. The Lupine Festival is in full swing.*
> *If you travel there by train this evening and stroll along*
> *Feldgasse, you are certain to meet an old friend.*

Orlov turns the note over. The back of the note reads: *Burn this.*

Orlov sighs and checks his pocket watch. It is still early enough to take the train to Kufzig, but he is tired and wonders why Zelle feels the need to make their meetings quite so elaborate. What's more, he would be delighted never to set foot in Kufzig again for the rest of his life. On the other hand, he is desperate to speak to Zelle again, given the seriousness of the new information he has acquired. He finds a matchbook, sets fire to the note, flushes the ashes away in the lavatory, and enjoys a simple dinner of cold sausage before leaving for the railway station.

On the train to Kufzig, Orlov alternates between dozing and gazing through the window at billowing steam. He is undecided on how he will make use of the new information in his possession. He rehearses in his head an opening speech in which he offers to tell Zelle the identity of the mole in exchange for the return of his mother. Another version of the speech reveals everything on the spot, including Dankova's identity, to demonstrate his value as an asset. Yet another version reveals only the party's search for the government mole, without explaining how they know they have a mole problem, although Zelle is bound to ask. It occurs to Orlov that the security business is complicated and sometimes taxing on the brain. He cannot imagine why anyone would want to do this sort of thing for a living. It must be exhausting.

Orlov emerges from Kufzig railway station through a cloud of steam and takes the now familiar walk down the hill into the town. As promised, Feldgasse presents a festive mood and lupines everywhere. Orlov sees lupines for sale outside most of the businesses, whether they usually sell flowers or not, paintings of lupines for sale on the streets, and jugglers and musicians galore. As he strolls through the festival, however, Orlov is not in a festive mood. He is racked with uncertainty about how much information to reveal to Agent Zelle.

As he passes Pension Residenz on his left, Orlov cannot resist a brief glance up to the top floor. The balcony of room six appears to be repaired and as good as new. He looks for signs of the explosion that killed Agent Kosek but finds none.

In the event, Orlov is not given the opportunity to make an opening speech of any kind. Zelle appears suddenly from under the awning of a flower merchant, grabs him by the arm, kisses him on the cheek like a long-lost cousin, and marches him swiftly along Feldgasse, her arm in his. Under her other arm she carries a newspaper. Outwardly speaking she might be projecting a pleasant demeanor, but in the firmness of her grip and the speed of her walking, Orlov senses she is focused on business just as much as usual.

"We need to talk," he says, as she propels him along the street in the direction of the fountain.

"Not yet," she says. "Too many people. I have the perfect spot in mind."

She marches him along the full length of Feldgasse all the way to the square, where she stops and perches on the wall of the fountain. The very spot where Orlov was sitting when she shot him.

"Does this spot ring any bells, citizen?" she asks, indicating that he should sit beside her.

Orlov sits. "Yes. The happiest of memories," he says.

Looking back along Feldgasse to Pension Residenz, Orlov finds that the memory of the last time he sat in this spot forces itself into his mind in a sudden, unpleasant manner. He remembers waiting in the dark, the surprising warm sensation in his arm, his attempt to walk away, and hitting his head on the cobbles.

He remembers the smell of the hospital ward where he woke up the next day, the nurse who followed him to the bathroom, and the ache in his head and arm as he walked, heavily bandaged, back into the town.

All of this makes him feel decidedly vulnerable. He is now even less sure about whether and how to use his new information.

Zelle opens up her copy of *The Sentinel* and thrusts it toward Orlov.

"Look at this," she says, pointing to a headline reading, "Bishop Condemns Plans for Lewd Cabaret."

"I'm not sure I understand," says Orlov.

Zelle retrieves the newspaper and reads from the article. "'Bishop Karol issued a statement condemning plans by Hotel Melikov to host what he described as a lewd cabaret. It is believed the top of the bill will be infamous exotic dancer Mata Hari, whose semi-naked act has been banned in a number of European countries. The bishop said it was especially offensive that the show was planned to take place on the eve of National Day, when thousands of citizens would gather in the capital to mark the birth of our nation and hope to see a glimpse of His Majesty, the King.'" She looks at Orlov. "See?"

"Not exactly," says Orlov.

"I am making life easier for you," says Zelle. "I am creating a distraction, on the evening before National Day. Hundreds of people will gather in the Grand Plaza and at the hotel. There will be police and journalists. I promise you, there will be chaos. And in the midst of that chaos, you and your security team will slip down to the Palace and do what is necessary to make National Day go with a bang."

"What if they set up everything at the Palace the next morning?" asks Orlov.

"You are forgetting that I work for the government," says Zelle, "and I hear things. I can assure you that all the arrangements will be made the previous day, including decorations, security barriers, and the king's podium. And I feel sure that when the young men of the palace guard have worked hard on those arrangements all day, they will feel the need to let off a little steam in the evening, so to speak."

Orlov sees an opportunity to deliver his news in a manner far removed from the various speeches he had rehearsed. He takes back *The Sentinel* and points to the grainy photograph of Bishop Karol. "Would you say he is a *lazy bishop*?" he asks.

"What did you say?" asks Zelle, her eyes suddenly wide.

"I am simply wondering," says Orlov, pleased to have the upper hand for once, "if you would describe Bishop Karol as a lazy bishop, or if you would prefer to save that description for someone else?"

Momentarily, Zelle grabs the lapels of Orlov's jacket with both hands. Then she glances at the crowds of lupine festival patrons milling nearby and relents, pretending to straighten his jacket before adopting a fake smile. "Where did you hear that phrase?"

Orlov tries to remain calm. Zelle is now so close to him that her fragrance fills his nostrils. "Your perfume is very pleasant," says Orlov. "Is it a new one?"

Zelle continues to glare directly into his eyes, her fake smile still a fixture. "Citizen, I am warning you. If you want to see your mother again, you will tell me where you heard that phrase."

Orlov is pleasantly surprised that Zelle is so angry and is reluctant to play his cards too early. He wants to see how much he can get in exchange. "I will be pleased to answer that question, citizen, when you bring me proof that my mother is safe and well. After all, your threats are worthless if my mother is already at the bottom of a ravine on Mount Zhotrykaw."

Zelle continues to grip his collar. "I have already told you, citizen, that your mother is safe and well."

"Very well," says Orlov. "Bring some proof, and I will be pleased to answer your question."

"Citizen," hisses Zelle, "you are a long way out of your depth in this swimming pool. These are matters of national security. I need to know where you heard that phrase. Have you been speaking to someone else at the ministry?"

Orlov takes her copy of *The Sentinel*, tucks it under his arm, and stands up. He adopts his own fake smile and turns to walk away. "I am afraid that I'm currently unable to answer your questions, citizen, on account of being very upset about the disappearance of my mother."

CHAPTER TWENTY-FOUR

In which our hero makes a plan

Citizen Orlov slips into Tavern Kreminic late one evening and joins Comrade Rozum, who is already nursing a tankard of ale in a dark corner away from the bar and the fireplace. The sheer size of Rozum's hands and muscular arms make his tankard look like a miniature.

"Good evening, comrade," says Orlov and then looks around nervously, unsure whether one is supposed to use that term in public.

"Do not fear, comrade," says Rozum. "The tavern is safe ground."

"Yes, of course," says Orlov. He takes a sip of his ale. He finds Rozum's intense glare to be disconcerting but continues despite it. "Thank you for meeting me. I have some troubling news, but I also have a proposal that I believe will keep our plans on track."

"Very well," says Rozum.

Orlov continues, now in an urgent whisper. "We have some evidence of a government mole in the party. Comrades Volf and Vanev have asked me to investigate urgently. As of last week, everyone else on the security subcommittee is dedicated to that task."

"So, the operation is off?" says Rozum.

"No," says Orlov, "the operation is on, but it must be carried out by you and me only. No one else can be involved."

"We need three, at least," says Rozum, "preferably four."

"Why?"

"Well, there's the lead technician, that's normally me," says Rozum. "I normally would have an assistant, plus a surveillance officer—to monitor the location and decide on timings and such—plus there's a team leader who makes the decision, decides to proceed or not."

Orlov considers this. "I understand, comrade, but the news about a possible mole has shaken things up. I'm afraid you are the technician, and I am everything else."

Rozum looks concerned and takes a swig of his ale. "And this is cleared by the leadership?"

"Yes, comrade," says Orlov, "I have strict instructions."

"It is not ideal," says Rozum. "It is dangerous, but possible. What do you propose?"

Orlov checks that no one is nearby before continuing. "As you know, the Palace generally erects a podium at the top of steps, for the king and a few dignitaries. He will inspect the parade from there before making his speech. I am told on good authority that the podium will be erected on the previous day. That evening, there will be a show at Hotel Melikov that is expected to create a good deal of interest."

"So I hear," says Rozum.

"Late that night, during the show, you and I will meet under the cover of darkness and plant the device underneath the podium."

"So, you want a timer?" asks Rozum.

"Yes," says Orlov, "the parade always begins at noon, and the king will speak when it is over, perhaps an hour later. The timer should be set to coincide with his speech."

"And how much damage do we want to cause?"

"Oh, we do not want the device to explode," says Orlov.

Rozum looks nonplussed. "We don't?"

"No, no," says Orlov. "We want a real device, capable of explosion, with a ticking timer, but not armed."

"Not armed, you say?"

"Yes," says Orlov. "Is it possible to construct it such that all the parts are in place, but one critical wire, perhaps, is not attached?"

Rozum frowns. "Possible, yes. But, comrade, what is the point of that?"

"Do you trust me?" asks Orlov.

"Ask me after the operation," says Rozum, without hesitation.

"Fair enough, comrade," says Orlov. "The purpose—whether you trust me or not—is that I will ensure the device is discovered by the authorities, thus disrupting National Day and sending a message to the government, without the need for bloodshed."

Rozum ruminates on this for a while. "And how, comrade, will you ensure the device is discovered?"

"That is the part on which you need to trust me," says Orlov, picking up his tankard to take a swig.

Orlov looks down and notices—for the first time—that his beer mat has a rather fetching picture of the Mount Zhotrykaw funicular railway.

Although Tavern Kreminic is known for its decorative beer mats, Orlov has never seen this one before. Rozum is saying something, but Orlov does not hear it because of what happens next. He happens to flip the beer mat over, to see what is on the other side, and finds the following:

Citizen! Take the funicular. Tonight.
Go all the way to the top.
Don't delay.

Orlov slams the beer mat down again and plants his tankard firmly on top of it. He was already expecting to see Zelle this evening, and indeed this is the first time she has summoned him, the curtains in the window above the butcher's shop on Grunplatz having been open when he walked to the market.

But the manner of this message is surprising, to say the least. And it suggests the tavern is not quite the safe ground the comrades think it is. Orlov glances quickly around the bar, to see if he can spot anyone he recognizes.

"Citizen?" says Rozum.

"I'm sorry," says Orlov. "What were you saying?"

Before Rozum can repeat his comment, they are interrupted by someone approaching from the bar. Orlov looks up to see Comrade Dankova.

"Good evening, comrades," says Dankova, standing next to the table with a tankard of ale in her hand. "I am sorry to disturb you."

"Not at all," says Orlov. He forces a smile, but his mind is on his beer mat. He grips his tankard firmly with both hands and presses it down hard.

"If I may be permitted to speak frankly in front of Comrade Rozum," says Dankova, "your investigation must be much more robust. Comrade Volf wants an answer urgently. You will be short-lived in this position unless you produce a result very soon."

Orlov had not considered the possibility that Volf might remove him from his position. He needs to remain in his post at least until National Day, otherwise the entire plan falls apart. Comrade Rozum might not be the sharpest of comrades, but even he will not take orders from the former chairman of the security subcommittee.

"What would you propose, comrade?" asks Orlov.

Dankova smiles. "If Comrade Rozum will forgive me, I would propose that I join you to discuss how we might expedite the process."

Rozum excuses himself and Dankova takes his chair. She sets her tankard down and produces a sheet of paper from her pocket, which she unfolds and attempts to smooth out on the table. Orlov scans it. It is a list of names and dates. He notices his own name at the bottom of the list.

"What is this?" asks Orlov, nervously.

"This is a list of the last ten people to join either the Workers' Party or the People's Front," says Dankova. "My apologies that your name is on the list, but of course we must be thorough."

"Of course," agrees Orlov.

Since the paper is rather crumpled, Dankova is having difficulty making it lie flat on the table. She secures one end of it with her beer mat. Then she says, "May I?" and reaches for Orlov's beer mat. Instinctively, he grabs the mat to prevent her from seeing it. She is taken aback.

Orlov apologizes and moves his beer mat onto the other end of the paper—with the picture facing up—being careful to keep a finger on top of it.

Dankova continues. "Since you are on the list, Comrade Volf decided that he and I should conduct the interviews."

Orlov does not like the sound of this, particularly since the date against his name is the eve of National Day. "An excellent suggestion, comrade," he says.

Orlov is about to continue but is interrupted by Dankova leaning over and pulling his beer mat out from under his finger. She holds it up so that she is looking at the picture and the message is facing toward Orlov. "What a lovely painting of the funicular railway," she says. "I've never seen that one before."

Orlov holds his breath. For a moment he thinks she is about to turn over the beer mat. He leans into the table and—as politely as he can—uses a finger and thumb to grip the beer mat at its corner. "Yes, delightful," he says.

Dankova is still admiring the picture and does not immediately relinquish it. Orlov is unsure what to do. For a few seconds, both of them are gripping the same beer mat in an equally firm manner. Seeking urgently to break the impasse, Orlov lifts his tankard with his other hand to reveal a little pool of moisture on the table. "May I?" he says.

"Of course," says Dankova, smiling, and finally lets go.

Orlov quickly sets the beer mat down and plants his tankard firmly back on top of it. He attempts to hide a heavy exhale. "Regarding the interviews," he says, "if I might propose a minor amendment. I would prefer to be interviewed later, if possible. On the eve of National Day, I am due to attend an event at Hotel Melikov."

Comrade Dankova raises her eyebrows. "Comrade, I do not think our leader will be impressed if I tell him you have refused to be interviewed because of your plans to attend a burlesque cabaret." She stands, folds her paper, and walks away.

Orlov slips the beer mat into his pocket and leaves the tavern, looking around again to see if he is being watched. He takes a tram and then a bus to the funicular station. En route, he wonders what Zelle has in store for him. Perhaps she will bring news of the release of his mother, owing to the excellent progress he is making. Or, at least, she might offer a release date at some point in the near future, contingent upon the successful completion of his mission. That would seem reasonable and perhaps the very least she could do.

Of course, it's not impossible that Zelle has finally lost patience with him and plans to drop him this very evening into one of Zhotrykaw's deep ravines, where—legend has it—the government has deposited many of its more troublesome citizens in recent years. He closes his eyes for a few moments and ponders this very real possibility.

Why would Zelle do it tonight when it is open to her to force Orlov to carry out his mission and, if she chose to do so, dispose of him afterward? That seems more likely. In any case, he has his mother to think about.

The Mount Zhotrykaw Funicular Railway Station sits at the foot of the southern face of the mountain which, although dizzyingly steep, is nevertheless benign and pleasant as compared with the dark, angular eastern face into which Prison Zhotrykaw is hewn. Orlov has not taken the funicular up the mountain since his childhood days, on account of his aversion to heights, but he is reasonably sure that it does not open after dark. When his bus reaches the end of the line—a bus stop just below the railway station, the dark mountain towering above—Orlov is the only remaining passenger.

The bus driver eyes Orlov with some concern. "Are you quite sure you want to be all the way out here on your own at this time of night, citizen?"

"Please don't worry about me, citizen," says Orlov, "I'm on a mission."

He steps down from the bus into a dark and deserted station. It is quite an eerie sight. There is no one at the ticket desk and no one checking tickets on the platform, where Orlov finds a single car waiting for him. He steps on board and takes a seat.

The uniformed driver in the cabin speaks without turning to look at him, while simultaneously throwing a lever that causes the car to creak into life. "She told me you might be late, but this takes the biscuit."

Orlov does not see how it's possible to be late to a meeting with no starting time, but he decides not to pursue this. He looks up at the dark, somber mountain as the car climbs slowly up the slope. Before they have climbed even halfway, swirling snowflakes begin to splatter against the windows. The temperature plummets, and Orlov pulls his overcoat around himself more tightly.

The improperly named Summit Station is far below the actual summit but is sufficiently high and exposed to be the coldest and windiest place Orlov has ever experienced. When the car finally grinds to a halt, he wraps his overcoat around himself and dashes through the snow across the little platform into the meager station building. Agent Zelle is standing at the window, looking down onto the distant lights of the city. A blazing fireplace and two armchairs stand in the corner.

Orlov joins Zelle at the window. She offers him a hip flask, from which he gladly takes a prolonged swig.

"Let us take a seat, citizen," says Zelle.

Orlov slumps into an armchair. "Your meeting locations are becoming ever more exotic," he says.

"Perhaps I am planning to throw you off the mountain," says Zelle.

Orlov leans forward to warm his hands by the fire. "I was thinking the same."

Zelle leans across and hands him a large envelope. "Here you are, citizen. Just as you requested."

Orlov takes the envelope, opens it, and slowly pulls out a large, grainy photograph. In the partial light of the flickering fire, it is difficult to make sense of what he is seeing. It takes him a little while to realize he is looking at a photograph of his mother, sitting in an armchair and reading a newspaper. Since his mother and the armchair fill the photograph, there is no way to tell where she is.

"This proves nothing," says Orlov. "Where is she? And when was this taken?"

"That is classified information," says Zelle. "You asked me to prove that she is safe and well. My word should have been sufficient. But now you also have this photograph."

"Still, it proves nothing," says Orlov.

Zelle, apparently agitated, snatches the photograph from him. "Citizen, you are not thinking straight," she says. "I need you to cooperate with me. I have promised to return your mother safe and well, and that promise is the only leverage I have over you. Were I to allow harm to come to your mother, you would have no reason to cooperate. And so, I have every reason to protect her."

Orlov considers this. He does not like the feeling that Zelle is attempting to outsmart him, but it makes some sense. "Very well," he says. "May I keep the photograph?"

"Of course," says Zelle, handing it back.

"I do not trust you," says Orlov, "but I can see that you have an incentive to keep your word."

Orlov is taken aback when Zelle speaks to him in an imploring tone. In the short time he has known her, this is the first time he can recall her speaking in a such a manner. "Citizen, I need your help. Once you have done your part on National Day, I will see to it personally that your mother is returned to you safe and well. More than that, you will be richly rewarded."

Orlov does not like the idea of being rewarded by Zelle. Since he does not trust her, he has no confidence that any reward she has in mind would be genuinely to his advantage. He decides to ignore this reference and move on. "And now you want to know where I heard the term *lazy bishop*?"

"I do," says Zelle, leaning in a little closer to the fire.

"Here is what I know," says Orlov. "I am not the only mole. The party has its own person inside the ministry, who is now aware that a ministry asset with the code name Lazy Bishop is an imposter in the party. That information has made its way to Comrade Volf, who plans to interview the newest members personally. My interview is scheduled for the eve of National Day. According to Comrade Vanev, the last imposter in the Workers' Party was found frozen stiff in a ravine on the other side of this very mountain."

Agent Zelle listens with an earnest expression. "Citizen, I understand. But you do not need to keep your position in the party for much longer. Only until National Day, in fact, and then you have my word this situation will be resolved. My ability to assure that resolution will be improved if you reveal the name of the informant."

"Yes, I see," says Orlov. "But you must promise me that you will do nothing drastic. Aside from Comrade Volf himself, only Citizen Vanev and I know about the informant. If anything were to happen to her now, Volf will have his mole narrowed down to only two candidates."

"Her?" says Zelle.

"I did not hear your promise."

"Citizen, you have my word," says Zelle. "For the very reason you suggest, I do not want to expose the informant at the moment. However, if I know who she is, I will be able to separate her from any further sensitive information. And that will protect your position."

Orlov considers this. It seems to make sense. "The woman in question is in your typing pool," he says. "Her name is Dankova."

CHAPTER TWENTY-FIVE

In which our hero attends an interview

On the eve of National Day, the numbers of people in the capital are swelling even by the middle of the morning. Along with the other market traders, Citizens Orlov and Vanev work hard to serve their regular customers as crowds of visitors and tourists begin to fill the Grand Plaza. By the middle of the afternoon, as the market traders are packing away their wares, restaurants and street cafés are overflowing with lively patrons in festive mood. A busker with an accordion sets up in the middle of the square and quickly attracts an admiring crowd to listen to his medley of patriotic tunes. The patrons of a nearby street café sing along lustily with songs about victory, strength, and independence.

Once the stall is closed up for the day, Citizen Orlov lights a cigarette and takes a leisurely stroll through the crowds and onto the bridge that leads into the government sector. As expected, he finds Comrade Rozum in the middle of the bridge, and the two shake hands and pretend to be surprised to have bumped into each other. Orlov offers Rozum a cigarette, and together they stand for a while, apparently enjoying the view on a fine spring day, but actually keeping a careful eye on activities at the Palace. The palace guard is out in force, hanging flags from the cloisters and constructing the podium from which the king will deliver his remarks. Orlov is pleased to see that the arrangements appear to be much as they are every year.

He waits for a lull in foot traffic across the bridge before he says, "Is everything in place for this evening, comrade?"

Rozum nods and takes a long drag on his cigarette. "Just as you ordered. It is a complete product in every way. And large enough to make a considerable statement. Only one small connection remains undone. To anyone who discovers it, assuming they have some expertise, it will appear I have made a simple error."

"Very good, comrade," says Orlov. "Very good indeed. Meet me in the Grand Plaza as planned. We will wait until the festivities are at their height before making our move. Please note, however, that I have a meeting with Comrade Volf this evening. I will come to the plaza as soon as the meeting is over."

"I imagine our leader will be looking for your reassurance that everything is in place for tomorrow's festivities," says Rozum.

"Precisely," says Orlov. "That is exactly what he wants to hear."

They stand in silence for several minutes, finishing their cigarettes.

⊷━∘━⊶

AT PRECISELY NINE o'clock in the evening, Orlov arrives at Tavern Kreminic and orders a tankard of ale. His shoulders are heavy with nerves about the ordeal to come. He has heard nothing from Dankova about the other interviews; no doubt she is keeping him in the dark deliberately, so that he is not able to benefit from hearing about the nature of the questions. He takes a deep breath and carries his ale slowly into the back room. He is expecting to find only Comrades

Volf and Dankova, so is surprised to discover that Comrades Nemeth and Weisz are also in the room, not at the table but hovering by the fireplace. As soon as Orlov takes his place at the table, Nemeth moves to cover the back door that opens onto the street and Weisz moves to cover the internal door to the bar. Startled, Orlov looks around at them, and then back at Volf and Dankova at the end of the table.

Volf speaks quietly and calmly. "No need to be alarmed, comrade. I simply asked the two comrades to ensure that our meeting is not disturbed."

"I see. Very well," says Orlov, despite feeling otherwise.

Volf launches into a formal introduction that sounds well practiced. "As you know, comrade, we have a serious problem. We have an imposter in our ranks whom we believe is sharing information about the People's Party with agents at the center of this corrupt government's security operation. It goes without saying that this is not a welcome development, so soon after the creation of our new party. We are therefore asking questions of all those who recently joined the two older parties."

"Do you have evidence that the mole is a recent recruit?" asks Orlov.

Volf raises a hand, apparently agitated at having been interrupted. "No, comrade, we do not. But my view is that recent recruits are a greater risk. Do you have evidence to suggest otherwise?"

"I do not, comrade," says Orlov.

"Very well," says Volf. "Comrade Dankova and I have some questions for you. Please be concise and honest in your replies."

"I will," says Orlov.

Volf turns to Dankova, who begins. "Please tell us when and why you decided to join the People's Front."

Orlov sighs. "Well, it was after the incident in Kufzig. Do I need to explain what happened?"

Volf waves this away. "We are familiar with it, comrade."

"Very well," says Orlov. "After the incident in Kufzig, I realized that the government cannot be trusted. I could no longer sit on the sidelines and watch their corruption. Although I had never been a political person previously, I knew the time had come for me to take action, to become involved in something positive. So, I asked Comrade Vanev about the People's Front, and he was pleased to welcome me into the party."

Volf frowns. "But what were you doing in Kufzig, comrade, if your interest in joining the People's Front did not arise until after the incident?"

Orlov had anticipated this question, and he has an answer prepared. "I was there as a guest of Comrade Vanev. He had often asked me about joining the party, so it was only natural that I should join them at a protest before making a commitment to become a member."

Volf looks at Dankova, who hands him a folded copy of *The Sentinel*. He unfolds it and reads from an article on the front page, sliding his finger slowly until he reaches the relevant line. "*In his statement in open court, Citizen Orlov insisted he was not a member of the People's Front and had been acting on instructions from unidentified 'government agents.'*" Both Volf and Dankova look up at Orlov, saying nothing.

Orlov is momentarily flabbergasted. He has never seen this newspaper article of his court appearance; indeed, he had no idea that his words in court had ever been reported in any detail. "Well, as I say, comrades, it is true to say that I was not a member of the party at the time of Kufzig, nor was I a member at the time of my court appearance. I was there as a guest of Comrade Vanev, and while there I was tricked by someone who I believed was working as part of the king's security detail but, as it turned out, was plotting his assassination. As soon as that became clear, I did my best to disrupt the operation. Unfortunately, that resulted in the death of one of the agents. What else could I do? What would *you* have done?"

Volf ignores the question and folds the newspaper slowly, keeping his eyes on Orlov as he does so. "So, you admit that, at the time of the Kufzig incident, you were acting on the instructions of government agents?"

"Until I realized their intentions were corrupt, yes, for a short time," says Orlov.

"Very well," says Volf, clasping his hands slowly. "How then, comrade, can we be sure that you are not in fact acting on government instructions at the moment? How can we be sure that you did not join the People's Front because you were told to do so by those same agents? How can we be sure that you are not the asset known as Lazy Bishop?"

Orlov feels his face flushing and focuses on remaining calm. "Comrade, please consider that I killed one of those agents and denounced the others in open court. Does that sound to you like an application for a job with the government?"

"I am not interested in what your intentions were regarding Kufzig," says Volf. "I am interested in where your loyalties lie now, today."

Comrade Dankova interjects. "Comrade, who do you work for?"

"I work for Comrade Vanev, in his fish business."

"And have you ever worked for or been paid by anyone else?" says Dankova.

"Aside from national service, no," says Orlov.

Dankova continues. "Here is the problem, comrade. We have interviewed the other nine most recent arrivals in either party. You are the tenth. No one else in that list has any connections with the government, they have never been in trouble with the law, they have done nothing suspicious at all that we could uncover. All of them are ordinary, working people who care about the future of our nation. And then, when we look at your record a little more closely, the hero of Kufzig has all sorts of unexplained connections with shady figures in the government. By your own admission, you were taking instructions from them at one point. You claim to have switched sides, but how do we know that is genuine? For all we know, your actions since your release from prison—even your statements in court—could have been on the instruction of the Ministry of Security."

Orlov does not know what to say. Volf waves his arm, and suddenly the atmosphere changes.

"I've heard enough," says Volf, looking at Nemeth and Weisz.

Orlov hears movement behind him and swivels in his chair. Nemeth and Weisz are already bearing down on him. He struggles, but they grab an arm each and drag him backward, knocking his chair over.

"Comrades," Orlov says, but gets no further words out before Weisz pins him to the floor and kneels on his chest. Nemeth wraps a gag around his head and ties it. They roll him over and tie his hands.

They drag him across the floor toward the back door, which Volf opens. They are hit by a blast of cold night air. Under cover of darkness in the quiet side street, Nemeth opens the back of a brewery truck and Weisz bundles Orlov into the dark, cramped space between wooden barrels. The door is locked behind him. By the time Orlov has struggled to move himself into a sitting position, the truck starts up and drives away.

Citizen Orlov is cold and frightened. With his hands tied behind his back, he lurches violently every time the truck hits a bump, hitting his head against a beer barrel. His thoughts go to Citizen Vanev's story about the Workers' Party imposter whose frozen body was found at the bottom of a ravine on Mount Zhotrykaw.

He focuses on the twists and turns of the truck, trying his best to estimate where they are going, but it is unclear. He believes they are heading west out of the capital, but more than that he cannot tell. He also thinks about the two rendezvous he had planned for this evening: with Rozum, to give the go-ahead for the device to be put in place, and with Zelle, to give confirmation that the deed has been done. He wonders what Rozum will do now. Probably nothing. Worse still, he wonders what his failure will mean for the fate of his mother. He pulls hard against the rope tying his hands, but makes no progress.

After an uncomfortable ride of an hour or more, the truck slows, turns, and then stops. Once the engine is turned off, Orlov can hear muffled voices in the cabin. He hears the doors of the truck closing as the conversation continues outside.

Orlov braces himself for the inevitable moment when the rear doors burst open and he will learn his fate. He moves back into the barrels, as far as possible from the doors. They fling open to reveal Weisz standing behind the truck with a manic glint in his eye. Saying nothing, he reaches into the truck and pulls Orlov by his ankles. Nemeth arrives to assist him. Together they drag Orlov out of the truck, where he falls onto a rough path. A blast of frigid air greets him.

Orlov closes his eyes as he falls and hits his head on gravel. Opening his eyes again, his worst fears are realized: they are somewhere on Mount Zhotrykaw, on a path Orlov does not recognize. The scene is lit by a full moon. He sees snow on the ground above them and ominously craggy outcrops of black rock protruding from sheer walls of scree. A sharp gust of wind blows snow into Orlov's face.

"Take his legs," says Weisz to Nemeth, and suddenly Orlov is hoisted into the air.

Orlov panics. He tries to shout through his gag. "Comrades, please. You are making a mistake."

There is no response from Weisz or Nemeth. The wind whips snow against them so loudly that Orlov is unsure whether he has been heard. He tries to shout again as they carry him away from the truck toward the mountainside; again, there is no reaction.

Orlov attempts to turn and kick, but the two men are gripping him as though their lives depend on it.

A few short moments later, Weisz and Nemeth drop Orlov roughly onto a rock, immediately pressing down on him with their full weight, to prevent him from moving.

"Please," says Orlov through his gag. He turns his head so that he can see beyond the rock on which he is currently pinned. Immediately in front of him is an ominous ravine of sharp, angular rock; it is so deep that the bottom is lost in darkness.

One of Orlov's captors picks up a small rock and throws it into the hole. The rock disappears into the darkness without a sound.

Citizen Orlov closes his eyes and—for the first time in his life—attempts a prayer. He prays quickly and earnestly, apologizing for not believing in the recipient of his prayer until this moment, and pointing out that he finds himself in something of an emergency situation. He mentions that, if the Almighty allows him to fall a thousand feet to his death in the next few moments, he will have no opportunity to rectify the singular lack of devotion which—he must admit—has characterized his life until this point. Therefore, it seems reasonable to conclude that a miracle right at this moment would be to the benefit of both parties.

Orlov's prayer is cut short when Weisz and Nemeth suddenly shift their positions, gripping him by the shoulders and calves.

"Now!" shouts Weisz.

"No!" shouts Orlov.

CHAPTER TWENTY-SIX

In which our hero finds himself in mortal danger once again

itizen Orlov closes his eyes and prepares for the worst.
At the very moment he expects Weisz and Nemeth to push, he hears the sound of another vehicle.

A voice in the distance calls, "No! Stop!"

"Do it now!" shouts Weisz.

"Wait!" shouts Nemeth. He pulls Orlov's legs toward him slightly, away from the precipice.

Now the third voice is nearer. It is Citizen Vanev. "You're making a mistake," he calls, heavily out of breath.

Weisz sounds angry. "I'll do it myself," he says, and begins to push Orlov by the shoulders over the edge.

"Stop!" shouts Vanev. Another pair of hands grips Orlov roughly around the middle.

Orlov's upper body is hanging over the precipice as he stares down into the abyss. He closes his eyes and attempts to roll toward safer ground.

A fight breaks out between the three other men.

Still bound and gagged, Orlov is pushed and pulled in all directions. Shouts and curses fill the freezing air.

Without warning, Orlov finds himself rolling down the slope toward the truck. Coming to a stop, he looks up in time to see Citizen Weisz laid out by a ferocious right hook from Citizen Vanev.

Looking down the path beneath them, Orlov sees a familiar vehicle: the Vodnik and Sons fish delivery van. He is wondering how on earth such a feeble vehicle could possibly have traversed the mountain path when Vanev appears above him, sweating and panting heavily.

Vanev removes the binds and gag. "Quickly," he says. He helps Orlov up and steers him toward the fish van. The engine is still running. Orlov staggers into the passenger seat as Vanev pulls away. Orlov looks back in time to see Nemeth kneeling over a prostrate Weisz.

"How did you?" says Orlov, as the van shudders slowly over the rough ground. He does not complete his question, because he is unsure what to ask.

Vanev speaks urgently, his eyes still on the mountain path. "As soon as I heard about it, I rushed to the tavern, but you were already gone. This is the only vehicle I could get my hands on. Citizen Vodnik was not at home; he will have to forgive me." He looks across at Orlov. "I assured Volf he was making a mistake. I promised him the mole could not be you." He stares at Orlov, as if to acknowledge the possibility that his assurances could have been mistaken.

"Citizen, I am indebted to you," says Orlov. Even for a veteran fishmonger, the stench of the Vodnik and Sons delivery van is overwhelming. Orlov pushes opens the passenger window. Despite nearly losing his life just moments earlier, he laughs. "My goodness. Does Vodnik never clean this vehicle?"

This seems to lighten the somber mood. Vanev laughs, too, and opens his own window. "I believe he prefers an authentic atmosphere."

For the next hour, Vanev works hard to steer the fish delivery van down the winding mountain path.

As they crawl into the city and approach the house of Citizen Vodnik, Orlov checks his pocket watch; it is almost midnight. Orlov hopes that Zelle's cabaret show is still underway and that Rozum is still waiting for him.

Vanev steers the van into the yard next to the house of Citizen Vodnik. Orlov jumps out but turns to address Vanev before he leaves. "Please do not ask me to explain, but the ministry is planning to take action against the party. Get away for a while, if you can. Leave the city. Take care of yourself."

Orlov rushes to the Grand Plaza, where the festive atmosphere still abounds. Loud music emanates from Hotel Melikov, and a huge crowd is gathered outside, as well as a significant police presence. Orlov picks his way through the crowds and finds Comrade Rozum sitting on a bench at the far side of the square, a large suitcase on the cobbles next to his feet.

"Comrade, I was about to abandon the operation," says Rozum.

Orlov is suddenly conscious of his bedraggled appearance. He straightens his suit and hair. "My apologies, comrade," he says. "I was detained on party business much longer than expected."

"Is there any change in our orders?" asks Rozum.

"There is not, comrade. We are to proceed," says Orlov. Looking around at Hotel Melikov, he continues. "I dare say the cabaret is at its height about now. Are you ready?"

Rozum picks up his suitcase and together they stroll calmly onto the bridge, looking for all the world like a couple of tourists anticipating the festivities of National Day. At the apex of the bridge, Rozum sets his suitcase down and they light cigarettes, spending several minutes in silence, looking out across the Palace and the government sector. It is a cold, clear night, and the Palace is illuminated only by the full moon and flickering lamps along the cloisters.

The good news is that there is no one on the steps of the Palace. The bad news is that two soldiers are making slow circuits of the cloisters, marching in the typically exaggerated style of the palace guard.

After they have watched these soldiers make a complete circuit, Rozum whispers, "Next time, start counting as soon as they disappear from view."

Orlov does so. When the soldiers reappear again, he turns to Rozum and says, "One hundred and eighteen."

Rozum nods. "Almost two minutes. The next time, we go. You keep the count."

Orlov nods. They both breathe deeply and watch as the soldiers once again pass along the visible part of the cloisters. The second they round the corner again, Rozum says, "Now."

The two comrades dash off the bridge and up the steps. Orlov is immediately conscious that Rozum is much younger and faster.

Orlov keeps the count going in his head as Rozum reaches underneath the temporary wooden podium to check the extent of the space available. He then opens his suitcase and lifts out a heavy contraption, which appears to Orlov to be larger and more professional than the rough bundle of dynamite he discovered at Pension Residenz in Kufzig. This bomb has a wooden frame and neat cables for the wires. The dynamite is largely hidden by tape, and on top there is a solid metal timer, such as one might find in the kitchen of a professional chef.

Orlov whispers as he counts. "Fifty-one, fifty-two."

Rozum nods to acknowledge the count and leans down to set the timer. He slides the bomb carefully underneath the podium. Then he gets down flat on his stomach and leans under the podium so that he can push the device back until it is level with the lectern up above.

Rozum shuffles out from under the podium as Orlov whispers, "Eighty-four, eighty-five."

As soon as Rozum is standing again, he closes the suitcase and they march back to the bridge. Once they are back in their original place, Rozum sets down the suitcase, lights two cigarettes, and hands one to Orlov.

Orlov nods in thanks and whispers, "One hundred and eleven, one hundred and twelve."

The two men take long drags of their cigarettes. Orlov can feel his heart pumping as the two soldiers emerge into the visible portion of the cloisters once again.

"Thank you, comrade," says Orlov.

"Thank you," says Rozum. He picks up his suitcase and walks away calmly across the government sector.

Orlov returns to the Grand Plaza, where there is now an even larger crowd. It appears the show is over at Hotel Melikov, and a boisterous audience is spilling out. Orlov swims against the tide by dodging through the crowd until he arrives in the lobby of the hotel and continues into the ballroom. The band is still playing, and people are dispersing slowly. The air is heavy with sweat and cigar smoke. Orlov heads to the stage and around the side to the stage door, where he is stopped by a burly bouncer in a tuxedo.

"No entry beyond this point, sir," he says.

"I work for Mata Hari," says Orlov. "She is expecting me."

The guard looks skeptical initially, but then opens the door. Orlov slips around the back of the stage to find Zelle, dressed in a robe and smoking a cigarette in an elegant holder while holding forth in front of a gaggle of several reporters, all men, eagerly taking notes. He hangs back, unnoticed, and listens as she talks with great flair about the meaning of the dances she learned years earlier while living in Java.

Orlov notices something different about Zelle in these circumstances—a twinkle in her eye and a mischief in her voice which never appear when she is focused on ministry business. At one point, while a journalist is asking a question, Zelle looks around, sees Orlov, and nods to acknowledge him.

Finally, Zelle says, "Well, gentlemen, it's late and a lady needs to get changed. That's enough for tonight."

The journalists disperse slowly, and Orlov edges nearer. He leans in to kiss her on the cheek and says, loudly, "Congratulations, a wonderful show."

Zelle answers in a similarly ostentatious stage whisper. "Why, thank you, darling."

Before he pulls out of the kiss, Orlov puts his lips right next to her ear and whispers, "Everything is in place."

CHAPTER TWENTY-SEVEN

In which our hero witnesses a historic event

As befits the occasion, National Day is the brightest, most springlike day of the year so far. The early morning sun glistens off the snowcapped peak of Mount Zhotrykaw. Citizen Orlov opens his curtains wide and ties them back. He wants to meet Zelle as soon as possible, after the operation is over, to confirm the safe return of his mother. He is feeling shaken and vulnerable, given his unscheduled appointment with one of Mount Zhotrykaw's infamous ravines, but Zelle was clear that his undercover membership of the People's Party needed to continue only until National Day, and now the big day has arrived.

Even though the market is closed for the holiday, Orlov takes his usual morning constitutional across the river and through the government sector. Given the early hour, there are just a few tourists on the streets, but numerous members of the palace guard making preparations for the festivities. As he passes the Palace, Orlov is careful not to slow down, but he glances over to the royal podium to see if he can spot anything underneath.

He is pleased to see that nothing but dark shadows are visible.

At a few minutes before noon, Orlov makes his way through the crowds and onto the bridge. Huge, lively crowds fill the streets of the government sector, held back behind safety barriers. The throng spills out across the bridge and all the way up the hill toward the Grand Plaza. In the distance, the familiar strains of the palace guard band ring out, announcing that the parade will soon begin. Orlov jostles into a position at the side of the bridge, from where he will have a limited view of the parade but an excellent view of the royal podium. From the chatter all around him, he concludes that most of his near neighbors are tourists from provincial towns, excited at the opportunity to see His Majesty in person, if only from a distance.

At precisely twelve noon, the marching band of the palace guard draws level with the Palace and the royal party arrives in the cloisters, including the Crown Prince, his wife and young children and his mother, the queen. Finally, several generals proceed onto the podium with the king, all of them in their military finery, replete with countless medals. The king waves to the crowd and the parade begins. The tourists jostling with Orlov on the bridge are beside themselves with excitement. For the next hour, the triumphant sounds of the marching band ring out across the city as military companies from far and wide march past the Palace, saluting the king and his generals.

Despite the festivities, Orlov feels tense. He leans on the wall of the bridge and smokes one cigarette after another, wondering what Zelle has planned regarding the discovery of the device. Will the festivities be interrupted and the royal family cleared out of the way dramatically as the police sweep in to enforce a security cordon and defuse the unexploded bomb? Or will the ministry allow the ceremony to finish and then announce the security threat afterward, once the crowds are at a safe distance? The former would be more dramatic, certainly, but perhaps more difficult to achieve. Orlov is grateful he does not have to organize what happens next. He simply wants it all to be over soon, so that he can leave the party.

Orlov consults his pocket watch; it is a little after one o'clock. The drums of the military band finally die down and the king moves to the podium, flanked by generals. The sun reflects off His Majesty's shock of white hair and his military medals. Despite the newfangled loudspeaker into which the king is speaking, his voice is thin, metallic, and almost indecipherable from the bridge. The enthusiastic tourists standing nearby exhort each other to keep the noise down so that the king can be heard, but it makes no difference.

Orlov is looking down at the river, dropping the butt of his last cigarette into the clear, fast-flowing water, when he sees a bright flash of yellow light in his peripheral vision. Instinctively, he crouches down. He looks up just in time to hear the percussive boom of an explosion. Even at this distance, the sound of the blast forces its way painfully into his eardrums. Many of his compatriots on the bridge also crouch down in shock.

The royal podium is engulfed in a cloud of smoke. The crowd scatters away from the Palace in a messy, frantic wave of humanity. Screams of panic ring out from all directions.

Everyone on the bridge stands again slowly to watch the cloud of smoke plume up and out, until soon it is obscuring their view of the Palace entirely. Orlov peers through the smoke to the cloisters, where members of the royal family are being rushed to safety by the palace guard.

Within a few seconds of the blast, the wave of panic reaches the bridge, as people surge away from the Palace. Orlov is pushed along by the wave, off the bridge, across the tram tracks, and up the hill toward the Grand Plaza. Shaken and breathing heavily, he continues walking through the square toward home, leaving behind crowds of stunned tourists looking for temporary shelter in bars and hotel lobbies.

Orlov's mind is racing with possibilities. His first thought is that Comrade Rozum has made a horrible mistake. Even an explosives expert with military experience could make an error of judgment, presumably. But how could a bomb detonate with incomplete wiring? Orlov realizes that he missed an opportunity to ask Rozum to show him the workings of the device, including the crucial missing connection. They had had very little time, however, and this did not seem a priority, given all the events of the previous evening. Another possibility is that Rozum armed the bomb deliberately, despite clear instructions not to do so.

But what would be his motive? He seems to be a calm and professional sort who often asks about where the orders are coming from. He does not give the impression of someone prepared to act in such a reckless manner.

As Orlov puts distance between himself and the Grand Plaza, the cries and chaos grow fainter. Just before he reaches home, a horrible third option registers in Orlov's brain. Is it possible that the ministry armed the device after it had been planted by Rozum? Just like in Kufzig, were Zelle and Molnar once more twisting an operation intended to frame the party and turning it instead into an assassination attempt? Orlov realizes that he has no idea whether the king is alive or dead. He arrives home, locks himself in, and watches from his window, from where he can just make out a thick cloud of smoke dispersing above the government sector.

Orlov stays at his window for the whole evening, moving away only to prepare a simple dinner of sausage and cabbage, which he eats listlessly back at the window. In all his years in this city, he has never known an atmosphere like this. It is almost as if the very buildings and cobbles are in shock. The constant drone of sirens is interrupted only occasionally by gunshots or fierce orders shouted by the police or the palace guard. No doubt they are searching any suspicious citizens and perhaps making arrests, perhaps worse.

Orlov has lost his appetite for Zelle's games. All day, he has been expecting a message to appear from nowhere instructing him to report to a nonsensical location chosen for no reason other than Zelle's titillation, but no such invitation arrives. Perhaps, in the circumstances, Zelle has also lost her appetite for this nonsense.

Just before midnight, Orlov wraps his heavy overcoat around himself and makes his way carefully to the Grand Plaza, being sure to stay in the shadows. Unusually, there are still crowds of people gathered, including in front of Hotel Melikov.

However, the festive atmosphere has been replaced with a sense of shock. People talk quietly in huddles, looking around suspiciously for anything untoward.

Agent Zelle appears from the shadows, grabs Orlov by the arm, and marches him out of the square toward Grunplatz. "Too many people," she whispers. "This way."

Once they are in the quiet side street, Orlov says, "What the hell is going on? We agreed a dummy device. Not armed. We agreed that."

Zelle looks ahead, not slowing their brisk walk as she replies. "That is *my* question to *you.*"

Orlov stops, turns, and grabs her by the shoulders. But he delays speaking until a young couple has hurried past them in the direction of the square. "I can assure you, citizen, that my technician is very experienced. He said a crucial connection was left undone. The only way the device could explode would be if it had been interfered with by someone else."

Zelle does not take the bait. "Or if he had made an error," she says.

"I do not even know if the king is alive or dead," says Orlov.

"Neither do I," says Zelle quickly, but Orlov sees something in her eyes that makes him doubt this is true. She is more than ruthless enough to hide the truth from him for as long as it serves her purposes to do so.

They reach the end of Grunplatz, and Zelle, still clinging to Orlov's arm, steers them around and back in the direction of the square.

"Whatever happened," says Orlov, "I have delivered my side of the bargain. It's time for me to be relieved of my duties and for my mother to be returned home, as you promised."

"All in good time," says Zelle. "Your mother continues to be safe and well. She will be returned to you in due course. But first, I have one more task for you."

"I do not trust you," says Orlov.

"I understand," says Zelle. "Nevertheless, your mother is well. I need you to be present on the steps of the Palace tomorrow at noon."

"For what purpose?" asks Orlov.

"I am not at liberty to say," says Zelle. "However, I can assure you it will be to your benefit."

Orlov does not like the sound of this. "Are the steps of the Palace not the scene of a crime?"

"Yes, for now," says Zelle. "But I can assure you that by noon tomorrow they will be pristine and the scene of an event just as historic as what happened today."

"So, you know the fate of His Majesty?" says Orlov.

Zelle releases his arm and prepares to leave him on the corner. "Be there at noon tomorrow, citizen. Do not miss it."

CHAPTER TWENTY-EIGHT

In which our hero hears surprising news

Much like on National Day, Citizen Orlov walks to the government sector just before noon, but the circumstances are very different, not only because today is cool and gray. The crowds have disappeared, and the streets are almost empty. The few people out on the streets watch each other nervously. It is an uncomfortable, fraught atmosphere, the likes of which Orlov has never before experienced in the capital. There is a heavy police and military presence in the government sector.

As he reaches the bridge, Orlov sees that the steps of the Palace are being scrubbed clean by members of the palace guard, and whatever was left of the royal podium has been removed. A crowd is gathering at the bottom of the steps, prevented from moving any nearer to the Palace by a line of police officers.

Unsure what to make of this, Orlov walks slowly and joins the crowd. He stands next to a man with a notebook who he takes to be a journalist.

"What's happening?" says Orlov.

"The Crown Prince," says the man. "We are expecting a statement at noon."

The soldiers finish scrubbing the steps and the police move back, allowing the crowd to walk up about halfway. A buzz of anticipation sweeps through the crowd when several government officials appear at the top of the steps, followed by the Crown Prince. Today, he is dressed in a formal suit rather than the military uniform he wore on National Day.

Orlov has never before seen the prince at close quarters; he is barely middle-aged—younger than Orlov himself—but nevertheless distinguished by prematurely gray hair. He looks haggard, like a man who has had no sleep.

The Crown Prince looks out across the assembled crowd and begins speaking, without introduction. He sounds tired but stoical. "Thank you for gathering, citizens. Yesterday was a tragic day for our nation. We do not yet know the perpetrators or their motives, but be assured that justice will be done."

Only now, Orlov realizes that Agent Zelle and Citizen Molnar are among the gaggle of officials flanking the prince. Zelle is dressed formally in a dark suit and is wearing heavy makeup. Orlov attempts to catch her eye, but she does not acknowledge him.

The Crown Prince continues. "His Majesty was severely injured in the blast, as was General Jaros. Both were treated at the royal military hospital but passed away as a result of their injuries. General Simek sadly died at the scene."

Orlov is shocked at the news but, as he looks about the crowd, it seems that this information was already widely known, since there is little reaction from the journalists, aside from frantic scribbling in notebooks.

"Please note that I will be making no statements today about plans for my coronation," says the Crown Prince. "My first priority is the security of our nation. For that reason, my immediate focus will be on identifying the terrorists who committed this terrible act and restoring order to the capital."

Orlov looks up at Zelle again. This time she spots him and nods very slightly to acknowledge his presence, while maintaining an intense focus on the monarch.

"In order to ensure we make the strongest possible response to this act of aggression, and because we have sadly lost two of our most experienced generals, I am today making some immediate changes to my government."

A number of the journalists glance at each other. It is strange to hear the Crown Prince refer to *my government*. For the whole of Orlov's life, the only person who has ever used that phrase was the king.

The prince continues. "With immediate effect, the new Minister of Justice will be General Vitek. General Vitek is the new Minister of Justice. His deputy at the Ministry of Justice is Citizen Salko, the new Deputy Minister of Justice." The prince pauses briefly, and the journalists scribble down the names. There is a brief exchange of whispers between them before he continues. "The new Minister of Intelligence will be Citizen Molnar. Citizen Molnar is the new Minister of Intelligence." Orlov glances up at Molnar, who smiles at Zelle. "His deputy is Citizen Boch. Citizen Boch is the new Deputy Minister of Intelligence." Again, there is a pause while the journalists capture the names and exchange comments. So far, Molnar's is the only name familiar to Orlov. The prince continues. "Finally for today, the Ministry of Security. The new Minister of Security is Citizen Zelle. Citizen Zelle is the new Minister of Security. Her deputy at Security will be Citizen Orlov. The new Deputy Minister of Security is Citizen Orlov."

PART FIVE

The Aftermath

of the

National Day

Disaster

CHAPTER TWENTY-NINE

In which our hero sits behind a desk

Citizen Orlov takes his early morning constitutional in a state of some confusion, dressed in his one and only formal suit. For the sake of completeness, he leaves his curtains closed and, while walking along Grunplatz, finds that Agent Zelle—now Minister Zelle—has done likewise. However, it seems likely that this form of communication has run its course, given that he and Zelle are now supposed to be colleagues at the ministry. He makes a mental note to check this with Zelle. Walking along Grunplatz to the Grand Plaza, he determines also to pin her down on exactly where his mother has been and when she will be returned home. How could he be a deputy minister in the same government that kidnapped his mother? On top of all that, he has no idea what a deputy minister does; he has never even had a desk job.

Orlov arrives at the market a little later than normal. There is no sign of Citizen Vanev. The greengrocer confirms he has not seen Vanev since yesterday. Has Vanev heeded Orlov's advice to disappear for a while, or has he fallen foul of whatever action the ministry is taking against the People's Party? He wonders if the Deputy Minister of Security has the power to dismiss charges against an alleged criminal.

Arriving in the grand lobby of the Ministry of Security, where he was turned away only a short while ago, Citizen Orlov is treated like a celebrity. He is wondering whether he should visit the security desk when he is approached by a distinguished, gray-haired woman in formal attire. She is tall and wiry, with intense eyes that seem to look right into Orlov's brain.

"Deputy Minister, welcome," she says and offers her hand. "I am Citizen Bartova, your private secretary."

Orlov shakes her hand. "I have a secretary?" he says.

"Private secretary," says Bartova. "You also have a typist and a valet, of course. I will introduce you to them in due course."

Orlov is unsure what a valet is, but prefers not to admit this. Bartova leads him through the lobby and past the security guards, who stand to attention as they pass. He follows her up a sweeping, curved staircase and past a grand wooden door.

"This is the minister's office," says Bartova, without slowing.

She leads him to the other side of the staircase and through a similar wooden door. Inside is the grandest suite of offices Orlov has ever seen. There is wooden wainscotting, formal wallpaper, and ornate, golden wall lamps.

"This is your office," says Bartova. "Please make yourself comfortable, and I will ask the staff to introduce themselves."

Orlov walks to his window, from where he sees a splendid view down onto the street and across the government sector. His desk is a grand, wooden affair with a leather writing pad and a lamp that matches those on the walls. He sinks tentatively into the green leather chair and wonders what is going on. How did he get here, and what does it mean? Presumably, it is Zelle's doing; but why? He does not imagine enjoying a job at this desk in such elaborate surroundings. Even the thought of doing the job of deputy minister feels like someone else's life, not to mention the sense of guilt regarding what has happened to his mother and what may have happened to Citizen Vanev.

Bartova returns with a timid young woman and a wizened old man. The latter wears something akin to a butler's uniform. They curtsy and bow, respectively, with great reverence. Orlov stands up.

"This is Citizen Henrik, your valet, and Citizen Voros, your typist."

Orlov emerges from behind the desk to shake their hands. "A pleasure to meet you," he says.

The two newcomers quickly retreat again into an outer office, but Bartova remains.

"Where would you like to begin?" she asks.

"May I speak to Agent Zelle?" says Orlov.

"Minister Zelle," says Bartova. "Of course. Let me check her schedule. Perhaps we can fit you in this afternoon, if that is acceptable."

Orlov is unsure why he would have to wait half a day to speak to Zelle, and equally unsure what he would do in the meantime. Before he can answer, however, they are interrupted by a knock at the door. Zelle walks in.

"Ah, here he is. Welcome, Deputy Minister," she says.

Bartova excuses herself and Zelle takes a seat in one of the visitor chairs, also of green leather.

Orlov waits for Bartova to close the door before speaking. "Citizen, what is going on here?"

"Minister, please," says Zelle. "We are no longer mere citizens, Deputy Minister."

"Minister, then," says Orlov. "How can I possibly be a deputy minister in the government given what the government is doing to my mother?"

Zelle looks horrified. "I can assure you, Deputy Minister, that your mother is safe and well and enjoying life in her rather attractive cottage in the lovely town of Havlinik."

Orlov has no idea whether he can believe this. "If that is true, citizen, then I must leave at once to see her."

"Minister," says Zelle.

"Minister," repeats Orlov.

"Very well, I understand," says Zelle. "You must visit her in due course. But we have other matters to discuss."

"Yes," says Orlov. "For one, what am I doing here?"

"I am simply keeping my word," says Zelle. "I promised you would be rewarded for your assistance. The Crown Prince—soon to be our new king—needed to make some changes to his government, and here we both are." She walks over to the window to admire the view. "A little better than standing out in that cold market, would you not agree?"

"I happen to like the fish business," says Orlov.

"Yes, but think about all the good we can do here, together. Here, you can make a difference."

Orlov is unsure what to make of this. "Did you arm the device?" he says.

Zelle glances at the door and sits back in the visitor chair. "Deputy Minister, please. That sort of talk is not appropriate here."

"This is the Ministry of Security, is it not?"

Zelle stands again and paces around the room. "Let us change the subject. What are your other priorities, Deputy Minister, besides visiting your mother?"

"I'd like to know the latest regarding the People's Party. In particular, have they arrested Citizen Vanev?"

"Well, that is a good question," says Zelle. "I believe there have been a number of arrests regarding the incident on National Day, but I do not have all the names at the front of my mind."

"I do not believe you, Minister," says Orlov.

Zelle sits down again and gives him a steely glare. "Very well. I believe Citizens Volf and Vanev have been arrested and are both now awaiting trial in Prison Zhotrykaw. Citizen Dankova has also been arrested and charged with the illegal dissemination of state secrets. We do not have any information on who built and planted the device, but I dare say you might be able to assist in that regard."

"Vanev has done nothing," says Orlov.

"Very well, then," says Zelle, "If the deputy minister feels the charges against Citizen Vanev are unjustified, he need only provide the minister with the identity of the bomber, and we have a reasonable exchange."

<hr />

TOWARD THE END of the afternoon, Orlov steps onto the railway platform at Havlinik and takes the familiar walk to his mother's house. He tries the door and is encouraged to find it has been secured. He knocks hard and waits. He has an agonizing wait of at least a minute during which he fears Zelle has been untruthful yet again. His mother appears, opens the door and seems surprised to see him.

"I wasn't expecting you," she says.

Uncharacteristically, Orlov engulfs his mother in a long hug. "I was worried about you. Where have you been?"

"Oh, that's a long story," she says. "I'll make us some tea."

They sit by the fireplace with tea and Madam Orlov tells a story about staying in a *safe house* by a lake, where the food was not at all bad and there were always polite staff on hand for her every need. She was allowed to walk around the garden every day and sometimes she walked down to the lake, but only with a member of staff, never on her own. The staff were not permitted to tell her exactly where they were, but she assumed it was one of the southern lakes because the weather was warmer. In the end, she had grown to enjoy the lifestyle, particularly having people on hand to do her shopping and make the food, but it was a little strange not to be able to go anywhere.

When the story has finished, Orlov says, "Did they say why you needed a safe house? Safe from what?"

His mother considers this. "They said it was a secret. They were not allowed to tell me the problem exactly, but it would be safer for me to be away from home for a while."

"What about the mess upstairs?" says Orlov. "Did they hurt you?"

"Well, you said I should not talk to any strangers so, when they first arrived, I refused to cooperate. They said it was an emergency and carried me out to their car. At first I was frightened, but when I saw the house and the lake, I thought it was rather pleasant."

Orlov stays for dinner but excuses himself from staying the night. He must get back for work in the morning. He considers telling his mother about his new position but decides against it for now. It would be difficult to explain, not least because he himself is unsure what exactly is going on. Sitting on a quiet train out of Havlinik, he considers at first that the best course of action—now that his mother has returned—would be to resign his new position and suggest to Zelle that she finds someone more qualified for the role of deputy minister. As the journey goes on, however, he realizes this would be a mistake. There is no need to resign immediately and, were he to do so, any power bestowed on him by the position would, of course, be lost. He needs to prove Zelle and Molnar assassinated the king and ensure Vanev is released. Both would be difficult to achieve as a mere fishmonger. It would be better to be the Deputy Minister of Security, at least for a while.

CHAPTER THIRTY

In which our hero makes a prison visit

Deputy Minister Orlov arrives at his office early the next morning to find a large box piled with papers in the middle of his desk. Even before he has removed his overcoat, Citizen Bartova appears.

"Good morning, Deputy Minister. Most of these papers are purely for your information. I've marked the papers that you need to sign or where we need a decision on something. I recommend going through them before ten o'clock, when you have a meeting with the minister."

Before Orlov can respond, Citizen Henrik arrives with a silver tray. "Coffee, sir?"

Orlov takes a coffee and asks Bartova to close the door after Henrik has left. "Citizen," he says, "I have a confession to make."

"Yes, Deputy Minister."

He indicates the box of papers. "I do not really understand the nature of the role. What I mean to say is, I have no idea what the Deputy Minister of Security does."

Bartova seems unperturbed.

"Yes, sir. No one does, at first, but they always pick it up, in time."
She heads to the door. "I'll be right here, if you need anything."

Orlov begins to work through the papers. They include reports
of secret operations and detailed descriptions of security threats at
home and abroad that he finds difficult to follow. Each one has a box
for Orlov to tick when he has read it. He can see that, in most cases,
the papers have already been read by various officials and are des-
tined to go to Minister Zelle once he has finished with them. There
are arrest warrants to sign and requests for new operations to be au-
thorized.

He does his best to tick and sign in the right places, but the
whole exercise fills him with a sense of inadequacy. He still has no
idea if he is able to do the job, nor indeed why Zelle has chosen him.
He wonders whether he will see anything on the People's Party or
the assassination of the king.

One does not need to be an expert in national security to guess
that this issue must be the top priority currently at the Ministry of
Security. And yet there is nothing in the box about the king, or the
bomb, or about Zelle's operation to frame the People's Party. He
reaches the end of the box and calls Bartova back in.

"Citizen, I see nothing here regarding the incident on National
Day or the arrests," he says.

"May I speak frankly, Deputy Minister?" says Bartova.

"Please."

"I was told by the minister's office that you were, until your appointment, the asset code-named Lazy Bishop." Orlov looks alarmed
and Bartova continues. "Do not worry; this is a safe area."

"I was," says Orlov.

"I'm afraid there is a strict policy on this. You are not allowed to
see papers on any operations you previously worked on as an exter-
nal asset. Never. There are no exceptions."

Orlov is deflated but tries to hide it.

If he cannot get his hands on any papers regarding the operation, it will be much more difficult to prove what Zelle and Molnar were up to. "Naturally," he says. "Quite right."

"One other thing," says Bartova. "The photographer will be here this afternoon, for your portrait."

"Portrait?"

"Yes. We hang a large photograph of both ministers in the lobby, and we send copies to the newspapers."

Orlov spends the rest of the morning in a long, confusing meeting in Zelle's office, attended by a gaggle of senior officials whose names he heard but cannot remember. He watches on with admiration as Zelle steers the meeting through a series of decisions. On several occasions, she jousts verbally with the officials—all of them men of a certain age—and invariably emerges victorious.

High on the agenda is a discussion about whether the ministry should advise the Crown Prince to outlaw political parties. Orlov can scarcely believe his ears. Even the stories he has heard from Citizen Vanev have not prepared him for what is being discussed.

Introducing the issue, Zelle says, "You all know my preference is to leave the moderate parties alone and to deal with extreme parties through," she hesitates, "other means."

One of the officials speaks up, apparently agitated. "But Minister, with respect, we cannot frame every troublesome party as terrorists. New parties establish themselves all the time. The public will simply not believe that all or most of them are run by terrorists."

"Then we must be more creative in our solutions," says Zelle. "What about tax fraud? Bank fraud? I'm quite sure we have other means available to close down the worst offenders."

Another official speaks up in support of his colleagues. "Minister, these types of solutions are certainly possible, but they take a significant amount of time and resources. Think of all the papers that must be generated just to create a common or garden fraud case. I believe the Crown Prince will be open to the argument that his government needs a fresh start, free from the interference of political parties, or labor unions."

Orlov is still trying to understand what he is hearing when, to his horror, Zelle turns to him. "Deputy Minister, you have some experience with political extremists," she says. "Where do you stand on this issue?"

Orlov gazes around the table. A dozen or more pairs of eyes are resting on him, but all he can think about is Citizen Vanev languishing in Zhotrykaw for no reason. He addresses the two rather pompous officials who challenged Zelle's proposal. "Are you seriously suggesting that we should ban political parties from existing? All of them? And labor unions? What are you afraid of? Is the Crown Prince so incapable of governing fairly that he must wipe out all his critics before he has even started?"

There is uncomfortable silence and shuffling around the table. The officials look at Zelle, who looks at Orlov with a steely glare. Finally, Zelle breaks the silence. "We will return to this issue later, after I have had a chance to explain the ministry's thinking to the deputy minister."

The rest of the meeting is mostly interminable discussions about operations and budgets, which leave Orlov cold. His interest is piqued by one item, however, in which Zelle requests a report from an eccentric, bowtie-clad officer whom she describes as the Chief Scientist. He talks at length about a contraption known as a Telegraphone, now being used in several operations to capture the voices of persons of interest in such a way that can be played back later, both in the ministry and potentially in court.

There is a good deal of interest around the table, and Zelle encourages them to make more use of this technique. It seems to Orlov, however, that some of the operations described involve listening in on ordinary people who have done nothing. He waits for the Chief Scientist to justify the various operations currently under way, but no reasons are offered.

Zelle is about to move on to the next agenda item when Orlov decides to ask a question.

"I'm sorry, before we move on," he says, "I assume the people with recording devices planted in their homes are terrorists or criminals of some sort?"

A pregnant pause around the table is broken by the Chief Scientist. He speaks without conviction. "In some cases, Deputy Minister, yes. In other cases, they are ordinary citizens who, shall we say, are of interest to the ministry, for one reason or another."

"Could you give me an example of those reasons?" says Orlov. "Just to aid my understanding."

"Well," says the Chief Scientist slowly, apparently playing for time, "for example, let's say an ordinary citizen—someone who had never before been a cause for concern—suddenly joins a political party. In those circumstances, it might be useful to have a recording of their conversations with, say, the party recruiter who visited them. Just to gauge their reasons for joining, you understand. By way of an example."

Zelle is about to move on again, but Orlov interrupts her by replying to the Chief Scientist. "I see, thank you. So, let's take my mother, for example. She is an ordinary, patriotic citizen, now a widow, who has never been involved in politics." He glances at Zelle and then returns his gaze to the Chief Scientist. "Let's say, for the sake of our discussion, that my elderly mother decided to join the new People's Party." A murmur of amusement ripples around the table. Orlov ignores it. "If I understand you correctly, you are saying that, even though my mother has spent her whole life as a model citizen, the ministry might, in these circumstances, begin to record her private conversations."

The Chief Scientist raises a finger. "With respect, Deputy Minister, in those circumstances, such conversations would no longer be private. Those conversations could be of legitimate interest to the ministry, if they concerned her membership of a political party on our blacklist."

Orlov raises his eyebrows. "I see, thank you. Perhaps you could name for me all those political parties that do *not* appear on this blacklist."

The Chief Scientist appears nonplussed. "Well, Deputy Minister, with great respect . . ."

Minister Zelle interrupts, fixing Orlov with a steely glare. "That's enough, thank you. Once again, I suggest we return to this topic once I have had an opportunity to brief the new deputy minister on these issues and bring him up to speed with the ministry's thinking."

Orlov offers a polite smile in return and replies in a deliberately unconvincing monotone. "Thank you, Minister. I am quite sure that your briefing will aid my understanding of these complex matters."

Zelle continues to glare at him. "I have no doubt your understanding will be enhanced," she says.

As soon as the meeting is over, Orlov spends an uncomfortable hour with Zelle and a photographer, having their portraits taken. He returns to his office and summons Bartova.

"Citizen," says Orlov. "I need your absolute discretion."

"Of course, Deputy Minister."

"I will be working on something top secret for a while. With the minister's blessing, of course. It cannot be discussed with anyone outside this office."

"Naturally," says Bartova.

Orlov continues. "I need your assistance to identify two experts from the ministry to assist me."

"Of course," says Bartova. "Which areas of expertise do you require?"

"I will need someone technical, preferably someone who under-stands how to use the new Telegraphone. And I need a lawyer, some-one who understands the prosecution of criminal cases."

Bartova considers this. "The technical issue is no problem; we have some excellent technicians right here in the ministry. For a criminal lawyer, I would probably need to bring someone in from the Ministry of Justice."

"Can it be done discreetly?"

"Of course."

"Very well," says Orlov. "Please clear my afternoon schedule for a personal appointment."

IN THE MIDDLE of the afternoon, Orlov steps off a bus and into the visitor waiting room at Prison Zhotrykaw. He is concerned that he might be recognized following his brief stay as a prisoner and—worse still—that he might be recognized as the new deputy minister of security. He wears the collar of his overcoat up around his face and a fedora that once belonged to his father. He gives his name to the officer and asks to see Prisoner Vanev.

An hour later, Orlov enters the same waiting room where he once waited for Citizen Uzelac, a meeting he prefers to forget. He sees Citizen Vanev and approaches the table. Vanev looks haggard, but nevertheless rises to shake his hand.

They sit.

Orlov speaks first. "First of all, citizen, let me say how sorry I am that you are here again."

"I dare say you are not as sorry as I am," says Vanev, forlornly.

"Did you not attempt to get away from the capital?"

"I did," says Vanev. "I was en route to my brother's house when they arrested me."

Orlov checks that no guards are nearby. "I promise, citizen, I will get you out of here."

"I heard you have a role in the government," says Vanev.

"For now. For as long as it is useful."

"Be careful that you do not become one of them," says Vanev.

"I assure you that will never happen," says Orlov.

"Why, then, did you get yourself mixed up in the National Day affair?"

"They had my mother," whispers Orlov. "They kidnapped her and forced me to cooperate. There is nothing these people will not do. But I assure you, citizen, I will finish them."

Vanev slumps in his chair and sighs. "Your zealot friends finally got their way."

"Yes," says Orlov. "Zelle now runs Security and Molnar runs Intelligence. What I cannot understand is why Zelle wants me as her deputy."

Vanev considers this. "May I speak frankly?"

"Please."

Vanev continues. "She first involved you in the Kufzig business because she thought you would be easy to manipulate, did she not?"

Orlov shrugs. He does not like this logic, but he cannot deny it. "Perhaps so."

"And by the sound of it, she has also been manipulating you into doing her dirty work with regard to what happened on National Day."

"That is true."

Vanev continues. "I hate to say this, citizen, but there is a pattern here. I dare say she wants you as her deputy for the same reason. Perhaps a career agent with years of experience would make it much more difficult to get away with whatever schemes she and Molnar are planning next."

Orlov considers this.

The more he thinks about Zelle's scheming, the more his blood boils. "As usual, citizen, you are full of wisdom."

Vanev looks around the shabby waiting room. "Much good it does me in here."

"I promise you, citizen, that you will be out of here soon," says Orlov, "and your place will be taken by zealots."

CHAPTER THIRTY-ONE

In which our hero renews some acquaintances

Early next morning, Deputy Minister Orlov is at his desk when Citizen Bartova steps into his office.

"Good morning, Deputy Minister," she says. "When you are ready, I have your two experts here."

Orlov stands. "Please send them in."

Bartova leaves, returns moments later, and ushers into Orlov's office two familiar figures.

Orlov can scarcely believe his eyes. Standing before him, each extending a hand in greeting, are Citizen Petrovich the handyman and Citizen Uzelac the lawyer.

There is a long pause while the three men stare at each other.

Uzelac speaks first. "When they announced the new deputy minister was Citizen Orlov . . ."

Orlov completes his sentence. "You assumed it must be a different Orlov."

"Yes, citizen," says Uzelac.

Bartova glares at him.

"Deputy Minister," he corrects.

Petrovich coughs. "A most curious turn of events."

"I was as surprised as anyone at my appointment," says Orlov. He shakes their hands and invites them to sit down. "Have you gentlemen met each other before today?" They shake their heads and Orlov continues. "I, however, have met you both before, in rather different circumstances."

"Yes, Deputy Minister," they both say, almost in unison.

"Let me make a suggestion," says Orlov. "Let us put past incidents behind us. Yesterday has gone and today is what it is."

"Quite right, Deputy Minister," says Uzelac, eagerly.

"Of course, Deputy Minister," says Petrovich.

Orlov continues. "Citizens, I will speak frankly. We have no time to waste. I am looking into a very sensitive situation. I need your assistance, but that assistance must remain between us and only us. Is that clear?"

"Very clear, Deputy Minister," they say together.

Orlov turns to Uzelac. "Firstly, a matter of the law. Are you familiar, citizen, with a newfangled recording device known as a Telegraphone?"

"I am," says Uzelac.

"Good," says Orlov. "Can you tell me, if someone admitted to committing a crime and was recorded saying so on such a device, would that evidence be allowed in a court?"

"A confession," clarifies Uzelac.

"Yes, a confession," says Orlov.

"It would," says Uzelac. "The question is whether the sound is clear—such that the voice could be identified—and whether the confession clearly relates to the crime in question. If so, then a court would most probably take such a recording into account."

"Very good," says Orlov, turning to Petrovich. "And, for your part, citizen, do you have experience operating such a device—a

Telegraphone—and perhaps installing one secretly, such that the targets would not be aware they were being recorded?"

"I do not, Deputy Minister," says Petrovich. Orlov's heart sinks, but Petrovich continues. "However, I am familiar with the devices, and I believe a microphone could be hidden easily, with a good length of cable, such that the Telegraphone itself could be stored out of sight."

"Excellent," says Orlov. "Please acquire a device from ministry stock and send confirmation via Citizen Bartova. Then, await further instructions."

The two men stand. "One question, Deputy Minister," says Petrovich. "What is the name of the operation? I will need it for the requisition."

"I see," says Orlov. "We shall call it Operation Lazy Bishop. If anyone has a question, you must direct them to me personally. No one else."

<hr />

IN THE LATE afternoon, Orlov walks home via the Grand Plaza. The market has already closed, but he is hit with a sense of nostalgia when he sees the fish stall standing lifeless and unmanned. There is something reassuring and satisfying about the simple life of the fishmonger. The same cannot be said for the strange, Machiavellian ways of government. Orlov determines to return to the fish business, just as soon as justice has been done.

He slips into Hotel Melikov and asks to speak to the manager. She is a forthright woman with a ruddy complexion and sufficient beads to sink a ship.

"I am planning an important business dinner," says Orlov. "For myself and two guests. We will need absolute privacy and a lot of wine."

The manager grins, as though delighted at the challenge. "Of course, citizen," she says. "Follow me." She leads him through the restaurant and into a private room with a single table. "Our Royal Room is ideal for such occasions. It is very private, as you can see, and you will have your own dedicated staff for the evening."

Orlov makes a circuit of the room. "I believe this is ideal," he says. "My office will be in touch to arrange the date."

⊷━━⊶

THE NEXT MORNING, Orlov summons Bartova into his office.

"Citizen," he says, "I have been thinking how grateful I am to Minister Zelle for this opportunity to serve our great nation. I would like to host a dinner for her and Minister Molnar. I think the Hotel Melikov would be ideal. A table for three in the Royal Room, as soon as the two ministers are available."

"Excellent, Deputy Minister," says Bartova. "Anything else?"

"Yes. As soon as the date is set, please ask Citizen Petrovich to step in."

By the end of the afternoon, Petrovich is back in Orlov's office with the door closed.

"Citizen," says Orlov. "The date and venue are set. I will meet the two persons of interest at Hotel Melikov, in the Royal Room, on the seventeenth. The microphone must be well hidden. The Telegraphone must be completely out of sight, as must you yourself."

Petrovich seems unperturbed by this challenge. "Certainly, Deputy Minister. I will conduct reconnaissance in advance. Everything will be ready."

He is about to leave and indeed has his hand on the doorknob before Orlov speaks again.

"One more thing, citizen," says Orlov.

"Yes, Deputy Minister?"

"I hope we can avoid the sort of terrible mix-up that caused such confusion in Kufzig."

Petrovich looks genuinely nonplussed. "Mix-up?" he says.

"Never mind," says Orlov.

CHAPTER THIRTY-TWO

In which our hero hosts a dinner

The seventeenth is a promising spring day on which one might even go without an overcoat. The early evening sun lends an orange hue to the snowcapped peak of Mount Zhotrykaw. Deputy Minister Orlov arrives very early at Hotel Melikov and goes straight to the Royal Room. He exchanges pleasantries with a waiter who is setting the table.

As soon as the waiter leaves, Orlov looks underneath the table and finds a microphone, well hidden. He is pleased to see that the cable seems to disappear, and he is not able to tell where it goes. Walking a circuit around the outside of the Royal Room, he finds Citizen Petrovich hidden in a janitor's closet off a service corridor next to the kitchen. The Telegraphone—a heavy wooden box with two metal spools—is perched on a shelf in front of him.

Petrovich jumps. "Deputy Minister, good evening. You startled me. My apologies."

"Everything is in place?" says Orlov.

"Yes, Deputy Minister. I have made a test. It is working well."

Orlov looks around at waiters marching to and from the kitchen. "And the hotel does not object to this sort of intrusion?"

Petrovich smiles. "On the contrary. They were most cooperative, once I explained that I represented the Deputy Minister of Security."

"Very good," says Orlov. "You and I must not see each other again this evening. Please bring the recording to my office early tomorrow. Hand it to Citizen Bartova, no one else."

Orlov returns to the Royal Room, his heart pounding. He stops to straighten his tie in the ornate mirror that hangs above a drinks cabinet. It appears on this occasion that Citizen Petrovich has acquitted himself well.

Now the pressure is on Orlov to steer the conversation in an incriminating direction.

Minister Molnar arrives first, dressed immaculately as always in a three-piece suit with a watch chain. He is the roundest person Orlov has ever seen, and just as ebullient as he was the first day Orlov stepped into the ministry in search of Agent Kosek, having just taken a phone call from Citizen Petrovich who—unbeknownst to Molnar—is now hidden just yards away, recording his every word.

The waiter returns with aperitifs. As per Orlov's instructions, he is very generous with his measures.

Molnar grabs Orlov's hand in both of his and shakes it enthusiastically. "Deputy Minister, my thanks for this kind invitation. And what an excellent choice of venue. I have been watching your rise with interest. Minister Zelle speaks ever so highly of you. But I am sure you are aware of that already."

Minister Zelle arrives soon after, having changed into a stunning evening gown and pearls. She takes an aperitif and kisses both men on both cheeks before making a circuit of the Royal Room with an admiring gaze.

"What a splendid venue," she says. "In all my visits to Hotel Melikov, I have never before been invited into the Royal Room."

As she rounds the far end of the table in front of the drinks cabinet—which sits against the wall behind which Citizen Petrovich is hiding with his Telegraphone—Zelle trips. She staggers forward, holding her glass out in front to minimize the spillage. Nevertheless, much of her aperitif sloshes onto the elaborate carpet. Using her other hand to steady herself, she finally comes to rest against the wall, and quickly turns to see what she had tripped over.

His heart missing a beat, Orlov rushes around the table. Before Zelle can investigate, he kneels down and feigns straightening the carpet. He can clearly feel a cable underneath and does his best to make it lie flat.

Orlov mumbles under his breath. "These expensive carpets are always the lumpiest." He jumps up to prevent Zelle from taking a closer look. "I'm sorry to say that you have lost most of your drink, Minister," he says. "Let us rectify that at once."

The waiter replaces Zelle's aperitif. She looks down at the carpet and says, "You gentlemen should be grateful that you are not required to navigate the world in high heels." Molnar and Orlov laugh heartily. They enjoy another round of aperitifs, during which the conversation turns to the day's ministry business. Zelle enquires after Molnar's deputy, Citizen Boch.

"He is a good man, but he has much to learn," says Molnar.

Zelle smiles at Orlov. "I am sure we all have much to learn."

"What is Citizen Boch's background?" asks Orlov.

"He is a former asset, much like yourself," says Molnar. "We took the decision to promote some new talent, in both our ministries."

"And yet you could have found candidates with much greater experience from within the ranks of your officers," says Orlov, wondering if this will provoke a reaction.

Molnar looks at Zelle before saying, "That is true. But they tend to have such rigid ideas. In giving yourself and Citizen Boch an opportunity to rise to the top, we are promoting new ideas, fresh thinking."

It seems to Orlov that Citizen Vanev's analysis of the situation is correct once again. "And perhaps it also allows you to ensure that your deputies are, how shall we say, thinking along the same lines as yourselves," he says.

Zelle intervenes. "I am quite sure you are capable of thinking for yourself, Deputy Minister."

"I certainly hope so," says Orlov, indicating that they should take a seat at the table.

The waiter returns with wine, followed by cabbage soup. The conversation moves on to an overseas operation which is causing Molnar some concerns.

Orlov feigns interest and occasionally chimes in to empathize, but his focus is on topping up the wine glasses of the two ministers. Before the soup course is finished, he has sent back the empty first bottle and poured much of the second bottle into the ministers' wine glasses, while sipping slowly himself.

By the time the main course of sausage goulash arrives, they are on to their third bottle of wine and both ministers are speaking freely, and a little more loudly.

Molnar notices that Orlov's glass is mostly full. "Deputy Minister, you really must keep up with us in terms of wine consumption."

Orlov takes a token sip. "Yet another area in which I have much to learn from your experience, Minister," he says, causing both ministers to laugh.

The waiter returns with an enquiry. "Digestifs?"

Orlov jumps in quickly. "Certainly. Vodka for everyone."

While the waiter is pouring the vodka, Orlov makes his move. "I must commend you, colleagues, on your cunning with regard to National Day." Both ministers are busy accepting glasses of vodka; neither speaks, so Orlov continues. "I was absolutely convincing when I told the party technician that the device must be complete in all respects but one. Not because I am a great actor, you understand, but because I believed that was all you intended. It never occurred to me the device would subsequently be armed by the ministry."

Zelle looks at him, hesitantly, while sipping her vodka. Molnar speaks first, his speech slightly slurred. "You give us too much credit. We have excellent officers who devise these things."

Zelle looks at the door and back at Molnar. "Minister, I am not sure this is the place."

Molnar waves away her complaint. "Minister, we are among friends. In any case, as I have said before, our deputies will need to be brought into our confidence on many issues, in due course."

"Yes, in due course," says Zelle.

Orlov senses that Zelle is wavering. "Speaking personally, I am delighted to be on the team, and I would certainly prefer to be in your confidence. I dare say that Deputy Minister Boch feels likewise. After all, how can we support you in achieving your aims, if we are in the dark?"

Molnar replies to Orlov, while looking at Zelle. "I tend to agree. What do you say, Minister?"

Zelle takes a long sip of vodka. "Whatever is said here must go no further than the three of us and Deputy Minister Boch."

"Naturally," says Orlov, sensing that the conversation has reached a tipping point.

The two ministers look at each other, apparently undecided on who will tell the story. Zelle opens her hand to Molnar. "Please," she says.

"Very well," says Molnar, but he pauses when the waiter returns to refill the vodka glasses. He allows the waiter to leave before continuing in a stage whisper. "We discussed your instructions many times, between the two of us. I have to say Minister Zelle was more confident than I was about what you might be able to achieve. She said we could ask you to deliver an armed device and you would find a way. My concern was that the party would balk at the idea."

Orlov realizes he has been holding his breath as Molnar speaks. Things are moving in the right direction, but he believes that Molnar has not yet said enough, and tries to encourage him. "In fact, they did. And it was Agent Zelle," he nods reverentially, "pardon me, Minister Zelle, who suggested I should proceed regardless."

"But only with an incomplete device," says Zelle.

"Yes," continues Molnar. "I won out in the end with a more conservative plan. My contention was that, for a successful police operation and court case, it was necessary only that the device was built and planted by the party. If the party's technician left a single wire unconnected, our technician could connect it."

"Which reminds me that I have not yet provided you with the name of the party's technician," says Orlov, "but perhaps this is not the place."

"No, this is not the place," says Zelle, glancing briefly at the door.

The sweat on Orlov's palms is causing his vodka glass to slip. He believes he might now have enough, but wants one further piece of information. "I must say, the plan was most cunning. I am wondering if you had made the Crown Prince aware of it."

Molnar spits a mouthful of vodka onto the table and mops it up apologetically with his napkin.

Zelle raises a hand. "Please, Deputy Minister, do not bring the Palace into this. We would never discuss such matters with His Majesty. The poor soul has no clue what goes on in the real world."

Molnar, now slurring badly, uses his vodka glass to point at Orlov. "The man claims to be ambitious, but he loved his father. He would never have contemplated anything like this. He would have sat on the sidelines for decades, if necessary, becoming increasingly frustrated. You can thank your lucky stars that the minister and I"—now he waves his glass toward Zelle—"had the foresight to bring his misery to an end."

CHAPTER THIRTY-THREE

In which our hero demands an audience at the Palace

Citizen Bartova walks into Deputy Minister Orlov's office in the early morning carrying a small, metal drum.

"Citizen Petrovich delivered this," she says. "He said it's urgent."

Orlov looks up. "It is. I need a meeting with the Crown Prince, today."

Bartova looks at him, dumbfounded. "Forgive me, Deputy Minister. That is not the standard protocol."

"What is the standard protocol?"

Bartova shuffles nervously. "The minister has a monthly meeting with the Crown Prince. The deputy minister does not attend."

Orlov waits to hear more, but it becomes apparent that Bartova has finished speaking. "That is the extent of communication between the Palace and the ministry?" he says. "What if something urgent arises?"

"There are other channels," says Bartova. "For example, I often speak to my opposite number, the private secretary to the Crown Prince."

"Is he discreet? Trustworthy?"

"Oh, most certainly," says Bartova.

"Very well," says Orlov. "Please believe me when I say this is a matter of utmost importance and urgency. I need you to deliver this drum to your opposite number, personally. No one else must be involved. Go there immediately. Tell him it is sent by me, and it is for the Crown Prince's ears only. If he needs a listening device, Citizen Petrovich can provide one. In fact, please ask Petrovich to deliver a device to the Palace in any case. That will save some time. Is everything clear?"

"Very clear, Deputy Minister," says Bartova. "Is there anything else?"

"Yes. Regarding what you call the standard protocol. Unless I am very much mistaken, on hearing the contents of this drum, the Crown Prince will summon me to the Palace for a meeting. If so, do not delay. Tell me immediately, and I will be there at his earliest convenience."

AS USUAL SINCE he began his strange new job, Orlov goes home with a briefcase full of papers he is supposed to read by the following day. He spreads the papers out on his dining table, fully intending to read them, but tonight his heart is not in it. Although it is late, almost eleven o'clock, he opens the curtains for the view of the city and the mountains beyond. He puts the teakettle on the stove and stands at the window wondering what will happen next. It has been an exhausting few days. Not for the first time, he longs for the days when he could leave work behind at three o'clock in the afternoon, once the market stall was closed. More than that, the fish business is rather more straightforward in terms of the issues one has to address. He had never, in all his years as a fishmonger, found it necessary to record anyone secretly. Nor had he paced his apartment late at night wondering how his message to the monarch would be received.

Orlov pours his tea and moves a chair under the window. Normally, the city is quiet and peaceful at this time. But tonight, he can hear police sirens in the distance. Not one, but several. He attempts to follow the sounds, but he can see nothing out of the ordinary.

A little after eleven o'clock, Orlov admits to himself that he is not going to read the papers until tomorrow. He is packing them back into the briefcase when the doorbell rings. Although he had just checked the time minutes earlier, instinctively he pulls out his pocket watch to check again. It is six minutes after eleven. He opens the door to find Citizen Bartova with a sheepish expression and a heavy overcoat.

"Deputy Minister, I am so sorry to trouble you at home."

"Not at all," says Orlov. "What is it?"

"A message from my colleague at the Palace. The Crown Prince requests your presence at seven in the morning. You said to let you know immediately."

"I did, thank you," says Orlov. "Is there anything else?"

"I recommend arriving early," says Bartova. "My colleague will meet you and explain the protocol."

"Very well," says Orlov. "Thank you for coming here so late in the day."

Bartova excuses herself and Orlov returns to his tea at the window. He digs out the shoe polish and shines his best dress shoes. He can add being summoned to the Palace to the list of things that do not routinely happen to a fishmonger.

CHAPTER THIRTY-FOUR

In which our hero visits the Palace

The sun is already reflecting from the snowcapped peak of Mount Zhotrykaw when Deputy Minister Orlov climbs the steps of the Palace. He has never before been beyond the cloisters. He stops just short of the gate to straighten his tie. As soon as he walks through the gate, a tall, distinguished man in a dark suit appears from nowhere and offers his hand.

"Deputy Minister, good morning," he says, in clipped tones. "I am Citizen Galin, the private secretary."

"Good morning," says Orlov, suddenly self-conscious about whether his attire is sufficiently formal for this setting.

"Thank you for attending at such short notice."

"It is my pleasure," says Orlov. He stops dead to admire the grand courtyard they have entered. "I have never been inside the Palace before. What a splendid building."

Galin smiles. "Indeed. We are most fortunate to work here. This way, please." He leads the way into an elegant anteroom and invites Orlov to take a seat in one of the grand leather chairs. "Before we go in, a few words of protocol. When you first meet His Majesty, bow slightly, from the neck. Not a deep bow, you understand. Please shake his hand and greet him with *Your Royal Highness*. After that, you may refer to him as *Your Majesty*. And please remember to bow again, as you leave the room. Is everything clear?"

"Very clear," says Orlov.

Galin stands and leads him to an ornate double door. "I will introduce you," he says.

Orlov feels his starched collar pinching his sweaty neck. He is gripped by the twin pressures of a first meeting with the monarch and the sensitivity of the matters at hand. He takes a deep breath and hopes for the best. The room is a surprisingly functional office space with easy chairs in the center, positioned around an impressive Persian rug. The Crown Prince, dressed in a business suit, rises from behind his desk.

"Let us sit in the comfortable chairs," he says and strides across the room to meet Orlov.

Galin says, "May I present Deputy Minister Orlov."

The Crown Prince offers his hand.

Trying hard to remember the instructions, Orlov bows his head, shakes the prince's hand, and says, "Your Royal Highness," all at the same time.

Orlov has seen the Crown Prince many times before, but never closer than at the press conference on the steps of the Palace, the day after National Day. Up close, he is smaller and more wiry than expected. His deeply furrowed brow suggests a lifetime of worry.

They sit and a valet appears instantly. "Let's have some coffee," says the Crown Prince to the valet, before turning to Orlov. "A pleasure to meet you, Deputy Minister Orlov."

"The pleasure is mine, Your Majesty," says Orlov.

"I wish we could have met in happier circumstances, but here we are," says the Crown Prince. He allows the valet to pour the coffee before continuing. "I am most grateful to you for providing the recording, which I heard late yesterday. As you can imagine, it came as a significant shock for me personally. By way of a progress report, I have suspended both Minister Zelle and Minister Molnar from their duties. Both are being held by the police pending an investigation into a possible conspiracy to assassinate His Majesty, the King. As you can imagine, I will be paying close personal attention to those developments. For now, however, I want to focus on the smooth running of the government. Yesterday's events leave us with something of a gap in two of our crucial ministries. My first question is whether you would be prepared to take on the role of acting minister, at least until the investigation is complete."

Orlov is in the process of picking up his coffee cup and quickly returns it to the saucer. His mind turns to the market stall, and his hope that he might one day return to it. He dare not raise this, however, and so he says, "It would be an honor, Your Majesty."

"Excellent," says the Crown Prince. "Your service to your country is much appreciated. My second question concerns the People's Party. I am told we are currently holding three of their number in Zhotrykaw pending trial. I need your professional opinion. Given what we suspect regarding Zelle and Molnar's schemes, do these charges against the People's Party hold any water whatsoever?"

Orlov feels a pressure behind his eyes, which he attributes to the unique experience of being asked by the monarch for his opinion on a matter of national security.

"May I speak frankly, Your Majesty?"

"I would prefer it," says the Crown Prince.

"In my view, any charges against members of the People's Party regarding the explosion and conspiracy against the king are false. As you have heard in the recording, the party was merely being used by the two ministers. In fact, I have personal knowledge that the party leader, Citizen Volf, wanted no violence of any kind regarding National Day, and the deputy leader, Citizen Vanev, was not involved in any way. I hope all those charges will be dropped." Orlov notices that Galin is taking notes of these details.

The Crown Prince glances at Galin. "Very good. We will certainly take that into account. Is there anything else I need to know?"

Orlov exhales heavily to steady his nerves. He takes a sip of coffee to buy some time. He has the extraordinary opportunity of a private audience with the next monarch. Perhaps this will be the only such opportunity in a lifetime. He does not want the opportunity to go to waste.

"There is another matter, your majesty, if I may," says Orlov, rubbing his hands together to prevent them from sweating.

The Crown Prince opens his hand to invite Orlov to continue. "Please."

"Officials at the ministry are considering advising you to outlaw all political parties and perhaps also labor unions," says Orlov.

The Crown Prince interrupts. "I am aware of it."

"May I offer an opinion?" says Orlov.

"I hope so," says the Crown Prince. "After all, you are my acting minister of security."

"Thank you," says Orlov. "From what I have seen, there is no need to ban political parties or labor unions. I believe most of them are patriotic citizens simply trying to make our great nation a better place to live and work. How will it look if you begin your reign by banning these patriots from making a contribution? I believe it will make you look weak." The Crown Prince raises his eyebrows a little and Orlov feels the need to soften the end of his comments. "If you don't mind me saying so, Your Majesty."

The Crown Prince sips his coffee, keeping his eyes firmly fixed on Orlov. "I appreciate your candor," he says. "You should be aware that some of your fellow ministers see things a little differently. I will certainly take your views into account. Anything else?"

"I believe that is all, Your Majesty," says Orlov.

They stand. Orlov follows Galin's lead in making another bow before heading to the door. The Crown Prince returns to his desk. He speaks again just before Orlov leaves the room.

"Minister Orlov, one more thing."

"Yes, Your Majesty."

"This business could drag on for some time. You should appoint a deputy minister. Do you have anyone in mind?"

Orlov is caught off guard. He has been the acting minister for a matter of minutes and had not even considered this. "Well, Your Majesty," he says, "there are many talented officers in the ministry. I am sure many of them would be up to the task."

The Crown Prince shakes his head. "Let me offer some advice."

"Of course, Your Majesty."

"All those experienced officers in the ministry will still be at your disposal in any case. Leave them be. Your deputy minister should be someone you can trust. Someone you can rely on when you can rely on no one else. Do you have someone like that?"

"I do, Your Majesty," says Orlov. He considers explaining that the person he has in mind is the very same Citizen Vanev he just asked to be released from Zhotrykaw, but thinks better of it.

"Very well," says the Crown Prince, "then he is your deputy minister."

<hr />

THE MINISTRY OF Security is in something of a panic. Officials huddle in corridors, whispering. When Minister Orlov reaches his outer office, he finds several officials gathered in a huddle with Bartova. The visitors excuse themselves quickly.

"We need to talk, citizen," says Orlov to Bartova. She follows him into the inner office and closes the door. Orlov continues. "I take it everyone has heard what happened to the minister?"

"I believe it is now well known," says Bartova.

"The Crown Prince has asked me to be acting minister, for an unknown period, starting now."

"Congratulations, Minister," says Bartova.

Orlov smiles wanly. He is unsure whether congratulations are in order. "What happens now?"

"Well," says Bartova, her eyes darting as she thinks quickly of all the implications. "Firstly, we must move you into the minister's office across the hall. Secondly, I am sad to say that I will have to leave you, since the minister's office has its own staff in place."

Orlov ponders this. "What is to stop me from taking you along?"

Apparently, Bartova had not considered this. "Well, I suppose that would be possible, if that is your decision."

"It is," says Orlov. "I will move into the minister's office, if you insist, but only if you, Voros, and Henrik accompany me across the hallway. The other team can take care of the new deputy minister, can they not?"

"They could," agrees Bartova. "Do you have anyone in mind?"

"I do," says Orlov, "but he is currently indisposed. I need to rely on your discretion once more. Do you have a good contact at the Ministry of Justice?"

"Of course," says Bartova.

"As you know, three members of the People's Party are currently being held at Zhotrykaw. Given recent developments, I believe there is a good chance they will soon be released. You will no doubt be aware of the deputy leader, one Citizen Vanev."

"I am, indeed."

"Please keep an eye on the situation. If Citizen Vanev is released, ask them to deliver him straight here. Tell him the Minister of Security wants to speak to him."

CHAPTER THIRTY-FIVE

In which our hero makes an offer

The next morning is a whirlwind of activity in which Orlov receives a long stream of earnest senior officials who need to brief the new minister urgently on operations, search warrants, arrest warrants, and budget decisions, until his brain aches. It is so busy that the planned move across the hallway into the minister's office is postponed until later in the week. By early afternoon, Orlov has had enough, and is hoping to find a reason to take a break, when Bartova walks into his office in the middle of a meeting about budgets.

"Minister, my apologies," says Bartova. "You asked to be interrupted if Citizen Vanev arrived."

Delighted at the interruption, Orlov turns to the gaggle of officials filling his office. "My apologies, gentlemen. We will need to finish this discussion another time."

Bartova ushers the officials out and returns with Citizen Vanev, who trudges in behind her, looking tired and disheveled. His rough-hewn clothes and unshaven face seem thoroughly out of place in the genteel surroundings of the deputy minister's office. Orlov rises to shake Vanev's hand and then returns to his desk. Much as Orlov himself did on first seeing this splendid office, Vanev makes a circuit to admire the decor and then approaches the window to take in the view.

"For whatever you did, thank you," says Vanev, still looking through the window.

"Please, take a seat," says Orlov.

Vanev slumps into a chair, exhaling heavily but saying nothing. Henrik arrives with coffee. Vanev sinks his coffee in one and holds out his cup for a refill.

As soon as Henrik has left, Vanev says, "Your office is very grand, I must say."

"This is *your* office," says Orlov.

Vanev swigs more coffee while eyeing Orlov suspiciously. "I do not follow you, citizen."

Orlov leans across his desk, suddenly becoming more animated. "Think of what we could achieve together, if you join the ministry as my deputy."

Vanev sets down his coffee cup. "You are joking, of course."

Orlov ignores this remark and continues with breathless enthusiasm. "Look, I know I have often been lukewarm about your warnings, but the reality is worse than you think. They're spying on ordinary citizens for no reason, and they're planning to outlaw political parties and labor unions."

Vanev throws his head back and begins to laugh. He laughs so heartily that his huge frame shakes uncontrollably. He is still laughing when Bartova pokes her head around the door to check that all is well. Orlov waves her away.

Vanev wipes his eyes with a handkerchief before replying. "Citizen, for how many years have we been discussing these things? Why do you suppose we formed the People's Front in the first place? The system is rotten to the core; it needs to be dismantled."

"You were right, citizen, and I was wrong," says Orlov. "I'm sorry about that. But now we have an opportunity to do something about it. From the inside."

Vanev puts away his handkerchief and sips his coffee. "Do you seriously suppose that this system will allow itself to be reformed by a pair of fishmongers?"

Disheartened by Vanev's initial response, Orlov sees an opportunity. "I think it is possible, citizen. Only yesterday, while you were still in Zhotrykaw, I had an audience with the Crown Prince. Just our future monarch and myself."

Vanev sets down his coffee and sits up straighter. "The Crown Prince?"

"Yes. And I gave him advice on political parties."

"What did you say?"

"I told him that banning parties and unions would make him look weak."

"True enough," agrees Vanev. "How did he respond?"

Orlov hesitates. "He said he would take my advice into consideration."

Vanev sits back in his chair as though considering this. "Let me ask you a question," he says. "How many other ministers are there in the government, apart from you?"

"I don't know," says Orlov. "Fifteen, perhaps twenty."

"And do you seriously believe that, as one of fifteen or twenty, you can cure this wretched royal dynasty of its wretchedness?"

"I prefer my chances over those of a fishmonger waving a sign in the street," says Orlov, a little more sharply than he had intended.

Vanev shuffles in his chair but appears undeterred in his argument. "Let me ask you another question, citizen. How do you know the Crown Prince is any more reasonable than his father? For all you know, he was behind what happened on National Day."

"He just had Zelle and Molnar arrested for it," says Orlov.

"Perhaps that simply makes him more ruthless than they are," says Vanev.

Orlov had not considered this.

He is taken aback but tries not to show it. "Look, citizen, all I am saying is this: there are more ways to change things than protesting from the outside. If honest patriots such as ourselves are handed the chance to do some good on the inside, should we not at least consider it? If you and I do not sit behind these grand desks, someone else will."

Vanev swigs the last of his coffee and sighs heavily. "For you, citizen, I will at least consider it. But only because it is you who is asking. If it were anyone else, I would laugh in his face."

"Your consideration is all I can expect," says Orlov.

They stand and shake hands. Orlov calls for Bartova, whose head appears momentarily around the door.

"I would like to escort Citizen Vanev out of the ministry," says Orlov. "Is there a way to exit without the need to walk through security?"

"Yes, I would be pleased to show you," says Bartova.

Orlov picks up his cigarettes from the desk and the two fishmongers follow Bartova down one floor via a darkened rear staircase. She stops at a door at the foot of the stairs.

"This door takes you out to the back of the building," she says, and sets off back up the stairs.

"Thank you," says Orlov. He holds the door for Vanev as they step outside.

Orlov instantly recognizes where he is. This is the dank alley that runs along the rear of both the Ministry of Security and the Ministry of Intelligence. For years, it has been an alternative route on his early morning constitutional, a shortcut, if necessary, in case of bad weather.

"Will you go home?" asks Orlov.

"Too late for the market," says Vanev. "I'll open the stall tomorrow."

"And you will consider my offer?"

"I will," says Vanev, and he sets out wearily along the alley. After a few yards, he pauses and looks back at Orlov. "Be careful, citizen. Do not become one of them," he says, before walking on again.

Minister Orlov is weary from a long day of meetings and has no desire to return to his office quickly. He leans against the door, takes in a long gulp of fresh air, then lights a cigarette and smokes it slowly.

Orlov is on to his second cigarette when a smartly dressed young man walks into the alley from the Palace end, in the direction of the Grand Plaza. He nods politely to acknowledge Orlov as he passes. At that very moment, a telephone begins to ring loudly somewhere nearby. The ringing sound is so loud that Orlov assumes a window must be open somewhere, a potential breach of security.

Some yards after he has passed Orlov, the young man stops and looks into an open window. The telephone is still ringing. He turns back to Orlov. "Do you think I should answer that, citizen?" he calls.

Orlov takes a long drag on his cigarette and shakes his head. "I would advise against it, citizen. Please let it ring. One can never know the trouble these things will cause."

ABOUT THE AUTHOR

Jonathan Payne was born and raised in Lancashire, England. He read social sciences at Keele University before joining the Home Office, where he worked on matters of national security, including immigration, crime, and terrorism. He remained in the British civil service until 2010, serving in London, New York, and Kabul.

After leaving government service, Jonathan moved to the suburbs of Washington, DC, with his wife and two sons. He soon began to write fiction, publishing short stories in magazines including *Turnpike*, *Twist In Time*, and *Fiction Kitchen Berlin*. His short fiction was also featured in audio format at the North London Story Festival.

In 2019, Jonathan earned a Master of Arts degree (with Distinction) in Novel Writing from Middlesex University. *Citizen Orlov* is his first novel.

ACKNOWLEDGMENTS

Thanks to Sue Arroyo and the whole team at CamCat Books for believing in this strange little tale. Your enthusiasm for my novel was the sign it had found the right home.

To my brilliant editor, Elana Gibson: thanks for your creativity and collaboration. The world of *Citizen Orlov* is all the more Orlovian thanks to you.

To fellow writer and occasional travel companion, Dixe Wills: your wisdom and advice on the writing life have been invaluable.

Thanks to Adam Lively and all in the creative writing faculty at Middlesex University, London, especially Paul Cobley, Jonathan Kemp, Sarah Law, and Kate Potts.

I am grateful for the northern Virginia writing community, including past and present members of Reston Writers' Review. Particular thanks to my gallant beta readers: Micah Abresch, Jessica Johnson, Bill Krieger, Jennifer Loizeaux, Gordon McFarland, Stephanie Siebert, and Mark Whittle.

Most of all, thanks to Sonya, Stanley, and Arthur Payne for your encouragement and creativity. The best inspiration for my writing is your art, songwriting, and filmmaking, respectively.

If you like

Jonathan Payne's *Citizen Orlov*,

you will also like

The Wayward Target by Susan Ouellette.

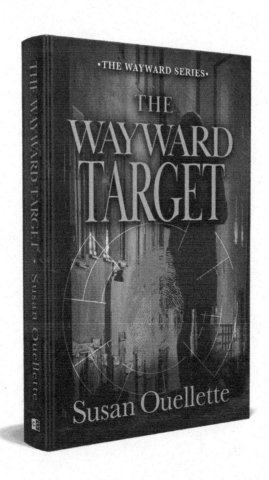

CHAPTER ONE

Tyson's Fitness and Health Club, McLean, Virginia,
Sunday, June 12, 2005

M aggie Jenkins increased the pace on the treadmill, her auburn ponytail swaying like a pendulum with every step. She'd upped her workout regimen over the past several months and the results showed—firm, muscular legs, a trim waist, and well-defined arms. Last fall, Roger had convinced her to join him at the gym. *It'll be good for you,* he'd promised. *Get you out of the house, get your mind off everything.*

Everything. It was his catch-all word for what she'd been through. The terrorist attacks. Zara. All the bloodshed.

An image of hundreds of terrified children flashed in her mind. No! She upped the treadmill speed. The faster she ran, the more her body ached, the easier it was to fight off the memories. The gym had become her therapy, sweat her medication. After several months of intensive exercise, she'd begun to sleep better. The nightmares came less often.

But every now and then, like last night, the images crept into her dreams and she woke in a sweat, stomach churning, pulse pounding.

She knew what had triggered it—the hearing on Capitol Hill about the school siege.

Nearby, a man hopped off a stationary bike, grabbed a remote control from the weight rack, and jacked up the volume on the television hanging on the wall. Maggie shot him a look in the mirror, but he didn't notice, absorbed as he was in the breaking news blaring from the TV.

She snatched her headphones and MP3 player from the treadmill console. Today was her day off. The latest violence and mayhem, whether domestic or international, could wait. Volume cranked, *Refugee*, whose lyrics seemed written for her, filled her ears. The man stood, staring up at the TV. Maggie squinted to read the graphic scrolling across the bottom of the screen.

Terrorist Issues Threat.

Now what? Another bin Laden missive from some cave in Afghanistan? She didn't want to think about work today. In a few weeks, she'd be headed to the beach for a getaway with Roger. After the gym, she planned to go shopping. A new bathing suit, sandals, and a sundress or two were in order. Thoughts of the trip were interrupted by movement in the mirror. Now several people huddled together near the TV. She tugged out an earphone and caught the anchor mid-sentence.

"—*videoed in what British authorities say was his former residence in London.*"

Maggie removed the other earphone. The screen filled with the image of an upholstered chair standing before a vivid, abstract painting hung on an off-white wall. The view darkened for a moment as someone in a blue shirt passed in front of the chair. The person turned and sat, his face level with the camera.

Maggie's fingers punched frantically at the treadmill's off button. She stumbled as the tread came to a sudden stop, sending her flying forward, her face missing the console by millimeters.

"You okay?" a male voice asked.

She scrambled to her feet, her breath heavy, the weight on her chest suddenly unbearable. "Yeah," she said without looking at him.

"*Our brave and glorious martyrs have their reward in paradise. Those responsible for their deaths will be hunted down and executed.*"

Behind the gaggle of people watching Imran Bukayev speak, Maggie's knees went weak. Those responsible? He meant her. She squeezed her eyes shut for a moment before turning her attention back to Bukayev. This video was filmed inside his house, the one she'd broken into in London last year. She'd recognize that garish painting anywhere. And his olive skin and shock of graying black hair were unmistakable.

"*Our work is not done. Your children are not safe. No enemy of Allah is safe. Our valiant soldiers are in place and ready to strike again at my command.*"

Maggie tried to make sense of it. Bukayev wasn't in London anymore. He must've filmed this video after the school attack, but before he'd fled. Now, nearly nine months later, the Brits had no idea where he was. Neither did she, despite her spending the better part of every day at Langley trying to track him down.

"I dare him to try something again," one man said, his voice full of bravado.

Sweat coursed down Maggie's face. She steadied herself with one hand on the treadmill rail. The news anchor was speaking, but she couldn't hear him, not with the ringing in her ears. *Roger!* She had to call Roger. *Deep breath. Calm down.* Her lungs felt full, her heart about to burst.

"Is this yours?" A woman's voice cut through the noise in her head.

Maggie blinked. A petite blonde extended her hand, Maggie's headphones and MP3 player resting on her palm.

She nodded. "Thanks."

"You need some water?"

Maggie shook her head, snatched her phone and water bottle from the treadmill console, and hurried for the locker room. Inside, she slumped onto a wooden bench set across from a row of lockers. After taking a swig of water and counting backward from twenty, she flipped open the phone.

"Roger? Did you see the news? It's Bukayev. I think he's coming for me."